Contents

1

Mr Shelby

LATE in the afternoon of a chilly day in February, two gentlemen were sitting alone over their wine, in a well furnished dining-parlour, in the town of P—, in Kentucky. There were no servants present, and the gentlemen, with chairs closely approaching, seemed to be discussing some subject with great earnestness.

For convenience sake, we have said, hitherto, two *gentlemen*. One of the parties, however, when critically examined, did not seem, strictly speaking, to come under the species. He was a short, thick-set man, with coarse, commonplace features and that swaggering air of pretension which marks a low man who is trying to elbow his way upward in the world. He was much overdressed; his hands, large and coarse, were plentifully bedecked with rings; and he wore a heavy gold watch-chain, with a bundle of seals of portentous size, and a great variety of colours, attached to it. His conversation was in free and easy defiance of grammar.

His companion, Mr Shelby, had the appearance of a gentleman; and the arrangements of the house, and the general air of the housekeeping, indicated easy circumstances. As we before stated, the two were in the midst of an earnest conversation and Mr Shelby was speaking.

"Why, the fact is, Haley, Tom is an uncommon fellow; he is certainly worth that sum anywhere—steady, honest, capable, manages my whole farm like a clock."

"You mean honest, as niggers go," said Haley, helping himself to a glass of brandy.

"No; I mean really, Tom is a good, steady, sensible, pious fellow. He got religion at a camp meeting, four years ago; and I believe he really *did* get it. I've trusted him, since then, with everything I have—money, house, horses—and let him come and go round the country; and I always found him true and square in everything."

"Some folks don't believe there is pious niggers, Shelby," said

Haley, with a candid flourish of his hand, "but I *do*. Yes, I consider religion a valuable thing in a nigger, when it's the genuine article, and no mistake."

"Well, Tom's got the real article, if ever a fellow had," rejoined the other. "Why, last fall, I let him go to Cincinnati alone, to do business for me, and bring home five hundred dollars. "Tom," says I to him, "I trust you, because I think you are a Christian— I know you wouldn't cheat." Tom comes back, sure enough; I knew he would. Some low fellows, they say, said to him, "Tom, why don't you make tracks for Canada?"—"Ah, master trusted me, and I couldn't!" They told me about it, I am sorry to part with Tom, I must say. You ought to let him cover the whole balance of the debt; and you would, Haley, if you had any conscience."

"Well, I've got just as much conscience as any man in business can afford to keep—but this yer, you see, is a leetle too hard on a fellow—a leetle too hard." The trader sighed contemplatively, and poured out some more brandy.

"Well, then, Haley, how will you trade?" said Mr Shelby, after an uneasy interval of silence.

"Well, haven't you a boy or gal that you could throw in with Tom?"

"Hum—none that I could well spare; to tell the truth, it's only hard necessity makes me willing to sell at all. I don't like parting with any of my hands, that's a fact."

Here the door opened, and a small quadroon boy, between four and five years of age, entered the room. There was something in his appearance remarkably beautiful and engaging. His black hair, fine as floss silk, hung in glossy curls about his round, dimpled face, while a pair of large dark eyes, full of fire and softness, looked out from beneath the rich long lashes, as he peered curiously into the apartment. A gay robe of scarlet and yellow plaid, carefully made and neatly fitted, set off to advantage the dark and rich style of his beauty; and a certain comic air of assurance, blended with bashfulness, showed that he had been not unused to being petted and noticed by his master.

"Hullo, Jim Crow!" said Mr Shelby, whistling and snapping a bunch of raisins toward him, "pick that up now!"

The child scampered, with all his little strength, after the prize, while his master laughed.

"Come here, Jim Crow," said he. The child came up, and the

master patted the curly head, and chucked him under the chin. "Now, Jim, show this gentleman how you can dance and sing."

The boy commenced one of those wild, grotesque songs common among the negroes, in a rich, clear voice, accompanying his singing with many evolutions of the hands, feet, and whole body, all in perfect time to the music.

"Hurrah! bravo! what a young un!" said Haley; "that chap's a case, I'll promise. Tell you what," said he, suddenly slapping his hand on Mr Shelby's shoulder, "fling in that chap and I'll settle the business—I will. Come, now, if that an't doing the thing up the rightest!"

At this moment, the door was pushed gently open, and a young quadroon woman, apparently about twenty-five, entered the room.

There needed only a glance from the child to her to identify her as its mother. There was the same rich, full, dark eye with its long lashes; the same ripples of silky black hair. The brown of her complexion gave way on the cheek to a perceptible flush, which deepened as she saw the gaze of the strange man fixed upon her in bold and undisguised admiration. Her dress was of the neatest possible fit, and set off to advantage her finely-moulded shape; a delicately-formed hand and a trim foot and ankle were items of appearance that did not escape the quick eye of the trader, well used to run up at a glance the points of a fine female article.

"Well, Eliza?" said her master, as she stopped and looked hesitatingly at him.

"I was looking for Harry, please, sir"; and the boy bounded toward her.

"Well, take him away, then," said Mr Shelby; and hastily she withdrew, carrying the child on her arm.

"By Jupiter!" said the trader, turning to him in admiration, "there's an article, now! You might make your fortune on that ar gal in Orleans, any day. I've seen over a thousand, in my day, paid down for gals not a bit handsomer. Come, how will you trade about the gal?—what shall I say for her—what'll you take?"

"Mr Haley, she is not to be sold," said Shelby. "My wife would not part with her for her weight in gold."

"Ay, ay! women always say such things, cause they han't no sort of calculation. Just show 'em how many watches, feathers, and trinkets one's weight in gold would buy, and that alters the case, I reckon."

"I tell you, Haley, this must not be spoken of; I say no, and I mean no," said Shelby decidedly.

"Well, you'll let me have the boy, though," said the trader; "you must own I've come down pretty handsomely for him."

"What on earth can you want with the child?"

"Why, I've got a friend that's going into this yer branch of the business—wants to buy up handsome boys to raise for the market. Fancy articles entirely—sell for waiters, and so on, to rich uns, that can pay for handsome uns. It sets off one of yer great places— a real handsome boy to open door, wait, and tend. They fetch a good sum; and this little devil is such a comical, musical concern, he's just the article."

"I would rather not sell him," said Mr Shelby thoughtfully; "the fact is, I'm a humane man, and I hate to take the boy from his mother, sir."

"Oh, you do? La!—yes, something of that ar natur. I understand, perfectly. It is mighty onpleasant getting on with women, sometimes, I al'ays hates these yer screechin', screamin' times. They are *mighty* onpleasant; but, as I manages business, I generally avoids 'em, sir. Now, what if you get the girl off for a day, or a week, or so; then the thing's done quietly—all over before she comes home. Your wife might get her some earrings, or a new gown, or some such truck, to make up with her."

"I'm afraid not."

"Lor bless ye, yes! These critters an't like white folk, you know; they gets over things, only manage right. Now, they say," said Haley, assuming a candid and confidential air, "that this kind o' trade is hardening to the feelings; but I never found it so. Fact it, I never could do things up the way some fellers manage the business. I've seen 'em as would pull a woman's child out of her arms, and set him up to sell and she screechin' like mad all the time; very bad policy—damages the article—makes 'em quite unfit for service sometimes. It's always best to do the humane thing, sir; that's been my experience. I believe I'm reckoned to bring in about the finest droves of niggers that is brought in—at least, I've been told so; if I have once, I reckon I have a hundred times, all in good case—fat and likely; and I lose as few as any man in the business. And I lays it all to my management, sir; and humanity, sir, I may say, is the great pillar of my management."

"And do you find your ways of managing do the business better than others'?" said Mr Shelby.

"Why, yes, sir, I may say so. You see, when I anyways can, I takes a leetle care about the onpleasant parts, like selling young uns and that—get the gals out of the way—out of sight, out of mind, you know—and when it's clean done, and can't be helped, they naturally get used to it. 'Tan't, you know, as if it was white folks, that's brought up in the way of 'spectin' to keep their children and wives, and all that. Niggers, you know, that's fetched up properly, han't no kind of 'spectations of no kind; so all these things comes easier."

"I'm afraid mine are not properly brought up, then," said Mr Shelby.

"S'pose not; you Kentucky folks spile your niggers. You mean well by 'em, but 'tan't no real kindness, arter all. Now, a nigger you see, what's got to be hacked and tumbled round the world, and sold to Tom, and Dick, and the Lord knows who, 'tan't no kindness to be givin' on him notions and expectations, and bringin' on him up too well, for the rough and tumble comes all the harder on him arter."

"Well," said Mr Shelby, "I'll think the matter over, and talk with my wife. Meantime, Haley, if you want the matter carried on in the quiet way you speak of, you'd best not let your business in this neighbourhood be known. It will get out among my boys, and it will not be a particularly quiet business getting away any of my fellows, if they know it, I'll promise you."

"Oh, certainly, by all means, mum! of course. But I'll tell you, I'm in a devil of a hurry, and shall want to know, as soon as possible, what I may depend on," said he, rising and putting on his overcoat.

"Well, call up this evening, between six and seven, and you shall have my answer," said Mr Shelby; and the trader bowed himself out of the apartment.

"I'd like to have been able to kick the fellow down the steps," said he to himself, as he saw the door fairly closed, "with his impudent assurance; but he knows how much he has me at advantage. If anybody had ever said to me that I should sell Tom down South to one of those rascally traders, I should have said, "Is thy servant a dog, that he should do this thing?" And now it must come, for aught I see. And Eliza's child too! I know that I shall have some fuss with my wife about that; and, for that matter, about Tom too. So much for being in debt—heigh-ho! The fellow sees his advantage, and means to push it."

Mr Shelby was a fair average kind of man, good-natured and kindly, and disposed to easy indulgence of those around him, and there had never been a lack of anything which might contribute to the physical comfort of the negroes on his estate. He had, however, speculated largely and quite loosely; had involved himself deeply, and his notes to a large amount had come into the hands of Haley; and this small piece of information is the key to the preceding conversation.

Now, it had so happened that, in approaching the door, Eliza had caught enough of the conversation to know that a trader was making offers to her master for somebody. She would gladly have stopped at the door to listen, as she came out; but her mistress just then calling, she was obliged to hasten away. Still, she thought she heard the trader make an offer for her boy—could she be mistaken? Her heart swelled and throbbed, and she involuntarily strained him so tight that the little fellow looked up in astonishment.

"Eliza, girl, what ails you today?" said her mistress, when Eliza had upset the wash-pitcher, knocked down the workstand, and finally was abstractedly offering her mistress a long nightgown in place of the silk dress she had ordered her to bring from the wardrobe.

Eliza started. "Oh, missis!" she said; then, bursting into tears, she sat down in a chair, and began sobbing.

"Why, Eliza, child! what ails you?" said her mistress.

"Oh, missis," said Eliza, "there's been a trader talking with master in the parlour! I heard him."

"Well, silly child, suppose there was?"

"Oh, missis, *do* you suppose mas'r would sell my Harry?" And the poor creature threw herself into a chair, and sobbed convulsively.

"Sell him! No, you foolish girl! You know your master never deals with those Southern traders, and never means to sell any of his servants, as long as they behave well. Why, you silly child, who do you think would want to buy your Harry? Do you think all the world are set on him as you are, you goosie? Come, cheer up, and hook my dress. There, now, put my back hair up in that pretty braid you learned the other day, and don't go listening at doors any more."

"But, missis, you never would give your consent—to—to—"

"Nonsense, child! to be sure I shouldn't. What do you talk so for? I would as soon have one of my own children sold. But really, Eliza, you are getting altogether too proud of that little fellow. A man can't put his nose into the door, but you think he must be coming to buy him."

Reassured by her mistress's confident tone, Eliza proceeded nimbly and adroitly with her toilet, laughing at her own fears as she proceeded.

Mrs Shelby was a woman of a high class, both intellectually and morally. To that natural magnanimity and generosity of mind which one often marks as characteristic of the women of Kentucky, she added high moral and religious sensibility and principle, carried out with great energy and ability into practical results. Her husband, who made no professions to any particular religious character, nevertheless reverenced and respected the consistency of hers, and stood, perhaps, a little in awe of her opinion.

The heaviest load on his mind, after the conversation with the trader, lay in the foreseen necessity of breaking to his wife the arrangement contemplated, meeting the importunities and opposition which he knew he should have reason to encounter.

Mrs Shelby, being entirely ignorant of her husband's embarrassments, and knowing only the general kindliness of his temper, had been quite sincere in the entire incredulity with which she had met Eliza's suspicions. In fact, she dismissed the matter from her mind, without a second thought; and, being occupied in preparations for an evening visit, it passed out of her thoughts entirely.

Eliza had been brought up by her mistress, from girlhood, as a petted and indulged favourite. She had been married to a bright and talented young mulatto man, a slave on a neighbouring estate, who bore the name of George Harris.

Eliza

THIS young man had been hired out by his master to work in a bagging factory, where his adroitness and ingenuity caused him to be considered the first hand in the place. He had invented a machine for cleaning the hemp.

He was possessed of a handsome person and pleasing manners, and was a general favourite in the factory. Nevertheless, as this young man was in the eye of the law not a man, but a thing, all these superior qualifications were subject to the control of a vulgar, narrow-minded, tyrannical master. This same gentleman, having heard of the fame of George's invention, took a ride over to the factory, to see what this intelligent chattel had been about. He was received with great enthusiasm by the employer, who congratulated him on possessing so valuable a slave.

He was waited upon over the factory, shown the machinery by George, who, in high spirits, talked so fluently, held himself so erect, looked so handsome and manly, that his master began to feel an uneasy consciousness of inferiority. What business had his slave to be marching around the country, inventing machines, and holding up his head among gentlemen? He'd soon put a stop to it. He'd take him back, and put him to hoeing and digging, and "see if he'd step about so smart". Accordingly, the manufacturer and all hands concerned were astounded when he suddenly demanded George's wages, and announced his intention of taking him home.

"But, Mr Harris," remonstrated the manufacturer, "isn't this rather sudden?"

"What if it is?—isn't the man *mine*?"

"We would be willing, sir, to increase the rate of compensation."

"No object at all, sir. I don't need to hire any of my hands out, unless I've a mind to."

"But, sir, he seems peculiarly adapted to this business."

"Dare say he may be: never was much adapted to anything that I set him about, I'll be bound."

"But only think of his inventing this machine," interposed one of the workmen, rather unluckily.

"Oh, yes!—a machine for saving work, is it? He'd invent that, I'll be bound; let a nigger alone for that, any time. They are all labour-saving machines themselves, every one of 'em. No, he shall tramp!"

George had stood like one transfixed, at hearing his doom thus suddenly pronounced by a power that he knew was irresistible. He folded his arms, tightly pressed in his lips, but a whole volcano of bitter feelings burned in his bosom, and sent streams of fire through his veins. He breathed short, and his large dark eyes flashed like live coals; and he might have broken out into some dangerous ebullition, had not the kindly manufacturer touched him on the arm, and said, in a low tone:

"Give way, George; go with him for the present. We'll try to get you, yet."

George was taken home, and put to the meanest drudgery of the farm. He had been able to repress every disrespectful word; but the flashing eye, the gloomy and troubled brow, were part of a natural language that could not be repressed—indubitable signs, which showed too plainly that the man could not become a thing.

It was during the happy period of his employment in the factory that George had seen and married his wife. During that period— being much trusted and favoured by his employer—he had free liberty to come and go at discretion. The marriage was highly approved of by Mrs Shelby, who, with a little womanly complacency in match-making, felt pleased to unite her handsome favourite with one of her own class who seemed in every way suited to her; and so they were married in her mistress's great parlour, and her mistress herself adorned the bride's beautiful hair with orange-blossoms, and threw over it the bridal veil, which certainly could scarce have rested on a fairer head. For a year or two Eliza saw her husband frequently, and there was nothing to interrupt their happiness, except the loss of two infant children, whom she mourned with intense grief.

After the birth of little Harry, however, she had gradually become tranquillized and settled; and every bleeding tie and throbbing nerve, once more entwined with that little life, seemed to become sound and healthful, and Eliza was a happy woman up to the time that her husband was rudely torn from his kind employer, and brought under the iron sway of his legal owner.

The manufacturer, true to his word, visited Mr Harris a week or two after George had been taken away, when, as he hoped, the heat of the occasion had passed away, and tried every possible inducement to lead him to restore him to his former employment.

"You needn't trouble yourself to talk any longer," said the tyrant doggedly. "I know my own business, sir."

"I did not presume to interfere with it, sir. I only thought that you might think it for your interest to let your man to us on the terms proposed."

"It's a free country, sir; the man's *mine*, and I do what I please with him—that's it!"

And so fell George's last hope; nothing before him but a life of toil and drudgery, rendered more bitter by every little smarting vexation and indignity which tyrannical ingenuity could devise.

A very human jurist once said, "The worst use you can put a man to is to hang him." No; there is another use that a man can be put to that is WORSE!

George

MRS Shelby had gone on her visit, and Eliza stood in the verandah, rather dejectedly looking after the retreating carriage, when a hand was laid on her shoulder. She turned, and a bright smile lighted up her fine eyes.

"George, is it you? How you frightened me! I am so glad you's come! Missis is gone to spend the afternoon; so come into my little room, and we'll have the time all to ourselves."

Saying this, she drew him into a neat little apartment opening on the verandah, where she generally sat at her sewing, within call of her mistress.

"How glad I am!—why don't you smile?—and look at Harry—how he grows." The boy stood shyly regarding his father through his curls, holding close to the skirts of his mother's dress. "Isn't he beautiful?" said Eliza, lifting his long curls and kissing him.

"I wish he'd never been born!" said George bitterly. "I wish I'd never been born myself!"

Surprised and frightened, Eliza sat down, leaned her head on her husband's shoulder, and burst into tears.

"There now, Eliza, it's too bad for me to make you feel so, poor girl!" said he fondly; "it's too bad! Oh, how I wish you never had seen me—you might have been happy!"

"George! George! how can you talk so? What dreadful thing has happened, or is going to happen?"

Drawing his child on his knee, George gazed intently on his glorious dark eyes.

"Just like you, Eliza; and you are the handsomest woman I ever saw, and the best one I ever wish to see; but oh, I wish I'd never seen you, nor you me!"

"Oh, George; how can you!"

"Yes, Eliza; it's all misery, misery, misery! My life is bitter as wormwood; the very life is burning out of me. I'm a poor, miserable, forlorn drudge; I shall only drag you down with me, that's all. What's the use of our trying to do anything, trying to know anything, trying to be anything? What's the use of living? I wish I was dead!"

"Oh, now, dear George, that is really wicked! I know how you feel about losing your place in the factory, and you have a hard master; but be patient, and perhaps something—"

"Patient!" said he, interrupting her, "haven't I been patient? Did I say a word when he came and took me away, for no earthly reason, from the place where everybody was kind to me? I'd paid him truly every cent of my earnings—and they all say I worked well."

"Well, it *is* dreadful," said Eliza; "but, after all, he is your master, you know."

"My master! and who made him my master? That's what I think of—what right has he to me? I'm a man as much as he is. I'm a better man than he is. I know more about business than he does; I am a better manager than he is; I can read better than he can; I can write a better hand—and I've learned it all myself, and no thanks to him—I've learned it in spite of him; and now what right has he to make a drayhorse of me—to take me from things I can do, and do better than he can, and put me to work that any horse can do? He tries to do it; he says he'll bring me down and humble me, and he puts me to just the hardest, meanest and dirtiest work, on purpose!"

"Oh, George! George! you frighten me! Why! I never heard you talk so; I'm afraid you'll do something dreadful. I don't wonder at your feelings at all; but oh, do be careful—do, do—for my sake—for Harry's!"

"I have been careful, and I have been patient, but it's growing worse and worse; flesh and blood can't bear it any longer; every chance he can get to insult and torment me, he takes. I thought I could do my work well, and keep on quiet, and have some time to read and learn out of work hours; but the more he sees I can do, the more he loads on. He says that, though I don't say anything, he sees I've got the devil in me, and he means to bring it out; and one of these days it will come out in a way that he won't like, or I'm mistaken! Only yesterday, as I was busy loading stones into a cart, young Mas'r Tom stood there, slashing his whip so near the horse that the creature was frightened. I asked him to stop, as pleasantly as I could—he just kept right on. I begged him again, and then he turned on me, and began striking me. I held his hand, and then he screamed and kicked and ran to his father, and told him that I was fighting him. He came in a rage, and said he'd teach me who was my master; and he tied me to a tree, and cut switches for young master, and told him that he might whip me till he was tired—and he did do it! If I don't make him remember it, some time!" and the brow of the young man grew dark, and his eyes burned with an expression that made his young wife tremble. "Who made this man my master? That's what I want to know!" he said.

"Well," said Eliza mournfully, "I always thought that I must obey my master and mistress, or I couldn't be a Christian."

"There is some sense in it, in your case; they have brought you up like a child, fed you, clothed you, indulged you, and taught you, so that you have a good education; that is some reason why they should claim you. But I have been kicked and cuffed and sworn at, and at the best only let alone; and what do I owe? I've paid for all my keeping a hundred times over. I *won't* bear it. No, I *won't!*" he said, clenching his hand with a fierce frown.

Eliza trembled, and was silent. She had never seen her husband in this mood before; and her gentle system of ethics seemed to bend like a reed in the surges of such passions.

"You know poor little Carlo, that you gave me," added George; "the creature has been about all the comfort that I've had. He has slept with me nights, and followed me around days, and kind o' looked at me as if he understood how I felt. Well, the other day I was just feeding him with a few old scraps I picked up by the kitchen door, and mas'r came along, and said I was feeding him at his expense, and that he couldn't afford to have every nigger keeping his dog, and ordered me to tie a stone to his neck and throw him in the pond."

"Oh, George, you didn't do it!"

"Do it? not I!—but he did. Mas'r and Tom pelted the poor drowning creature with stones. Poor thing! he looked at me so mournful, as if he wondered why I didn't save him. I had to take a flogging because I wouldn't do it myself. I don't care. Mas'r will find out that I'm one that whipping won't tame. My day will come yet, if he don't look out."

"What are you going to do? Oh, George, don't do any-thing wicked! If you only trust in God, and try to do right, He'll deliver you."

"I an't a Christian like you, Eliza; my heart's full of bitterness; I can't trust in God. Why does He let things be so?"

"Oh, George! we must have faith. Mistress says that when all things go wrong with us, we must believe that God is doing the very best."

"That's easy to say for people that are sitting on their sofas and riding in their carriages; but let 'em be where I am. I guess it would come some harder. I wish I could be good; but my heart burns, and can't be reconciled, anyhow. You couldn't in my place—you can't now, if I tell you all I've got to say. You don't know the whole yet."

"What can be coming now?"

"Well, lately mas'r has been saying that he was a fool to let me marry off the place; that he hates Mr Shelby and all his tribe, because they are proud, and hold their heads up above him, and that I've got proud notions from you; and he says he won't let me come here any more, and that I shall take a wife and settle down on his place. At first he only scolded and grumbled these things; but yesterday he told me that I should take Mina for a wife, and settle down in a cabin with her, or he would sell me down river."

"Why—but you were married to me, by the minister, as much as if you'd been a white man!" said Eliza simply.

"Don't you know a slave can't be married? There is no law in this country for that; I can't hold you for my wife if he chooses to part us. That's why I wish I'd never seen you—why I wish I'd never been born. It would have been better for us both—it would have been better for this poor child if he had never been born. All this may happen to him yet!"

"Oh, but master is so kind!"

"Yes; but who knows?—he may die—and then he may be sold to nobody knows who. What pleasure is it that he is handsome, and smart, and bright? I tell you, Eliza, that a sword will pierce through your soul for every good and pleasant thing your child is or has; it will make him worth too much for you to keep!"

The words smote heavily on Eliza's heart. The vision of the trader came before her eyes, and, as if someone had struck her a deadly blow, she turned and gasped for breath. She would have spoken to tell her husband her fears, but checked herself. "No, no—he has enough to bear, poor fellow!" she thought. "No, I won't tell him; besides, it an't true. Missis never deceives us."

"So, Eliza, my girl," said the husband mournfully, "bear up, now; and good-bye, for I'm going."

"Going, George! Going where?"

"To Canada," said he, straightening himself up; "and when I'm there, I'll buy you. That's all the hope that's left us. You have a kind master, that won't refuse to sell you. I'll buy you and the boy—God helping me, I will!"

"Oh, dreadful! if you should be taken?"

"I won't be taken, Eliza; I'll *die* first! I'll be free, or I'll die!"

"You won't kill yourself?"

"No need of that. They will kill me, fast enough!"

"Oh, George, for my sake, do be careful! Don't do anything wicked; don't lay hands on yourself, or anybody else. You are tempted too much—too much; but don't—go you must—but go carefully, prudently; pray God to help you."

"Well, then, Eliza, hear my plan. Mas'r took it into his head to send me right by here with a note to Mr Symmes, that lives a mile past. I believe he expected I should come here to tell you what I have. It would please him if he thought it would aggravate "Shelby's folks", as he calls 'em. I'm going home quite resigned, you understand, as if all was over. I've got some preparations made—and there are those that will help me; and in the course of a week or so, I shall be among the missing, some day. Pray for me, Eliza; perhaps the good Lord will hear *you*."

"Oh, pray yourself, George, and go trusting in Him; then you won't do anything wicked."

"Well, now, *good-bye*," said George, holding Eliza's hands, and gazing into her eyes, without moving. They stood silent; then there were last words, and sobs, and bitter weeping—and the husband and wife were parted.

4

Uncle Tom's Cabin

THE CABIN of Uncle Tom was a small log building close adjoining to "the house", as the negro *par excellence* designates his master's dwelling. In front it had a neat garden-patch, where, every summer, strawberries, raspberries, and a variety of fruits and vegetables flourished under careful tending.

Let us enter the dwelling. The evening meal at the house is over, and Aunt Chloe, who presided over its preparation as head cook, has left to inferior officers in the kitchen the business of clearing away and washing dishes, and come out into her own snug territories, to "get her ole man's supper". A round, black, shining face is hers, so glossy as to suggest the idea that she might have been washed over with white of eggs, like one of her own tea rusks. Her whole plump countenance beams with satisfaction and contentment from under her well-starched checked turban, bearing on it, however, if we must confess it, a little of that tinge of self-consciousness which becomes the first cook of the neighbourhood, as Aunt Chloe was universally held and acknowledged to be.

A cook she certainly was, in the very bone and centre of her soul. Not a chicken or turkey or duck in the barnyard but looked grave when they saw her approaching, and seemed evidently to be reflecting on their latter end; and certain it was that she was always meditating on trussing, stuffing, and roasting, to a degree that was calculated to inspire terror in any reflecting fowl living. Her corn-cake, in all its varieties of hoe-cake, dodgers, muffins, and other species too numerous to mention, was a sublime mystery to all less practised compounders.

Just at present, however, Aunt Chloe is looking into the bakepan; in which congenial operation we shall leave her till we finish our picture of the cottage.

In one corner of it stood a bed, covered neatly with a snowy spread, and by the side of it was a piece of carpeting, of some considerable size. On this piece of carpeting Aunt Chloe took her stand, as being decidedly in the upper walks of life; and it and the bed by which it lay, and the whole corner, in fact, were treated with distinguished consideration, and made, so far as possible, sacred from the marauding inroads and desecrations of little folks. In fact, that corner was the *drawing-room* of the establishment. In the other corner was a bed of much humbler pretensions, and evidently designed for *use*.

On a rough bench in the corner, a couple of woolly-headed boys, with glistening black eyes and fat, shining cheeks, were busy in superintending the first walking operations of the baby which, as is usually the case, consisted in getting up on its feet, balancing a moment, and then tumbling down—each successive failure being violently cheered, as something decidedly clever.

A table, somewhat rheumatic in its limbs, was drawn out in front of the fire, and covered with a cloth, displaying cups and saucers of a decidedly brilliant pattern, with other symptoms of an approaching meal. At this table was seated Uncle Tom, Mr Shelby's best hand, who, as he is to be the hero of our story, we must describe for our readers. He was a large, broad-chested, powerfully-made man, of a full glossy black, and a face whose truly African features were characterized by an expression of grave and steady good sense, united with much kindliness and benevolence. There was something about his whole air self-respecting and dignified, yet united with a confiding and humble simplicity.

He was very busily intent at this moment on a slate lying before him, on which he was carefully and slowly endeavouring to accomplish a copy of some letters, in which operation he was overlooked by young Mas'r George, a smart, bright boy of thirteen, who appeared fully to realize the dignity of his position as instructor.

"Not that way, Uncle Tom—not that way," said he briskly, as Uncle Tom laboriously brought up the tail of his *g* the wrong side out; "that makes a *q*, you see."

"La sakes, now, does it?" said Uncle Tom, looking with a respectful, admiring air, as his young teacher flourishingly scrawled out *q*'s and *g*'s innumerable for his edification; and then, taking the pencil in his big, heavy fingers, he patiently recommenced.

"How easy white folks al'us does things!" said Aunt Chloe, pausing while she was greasing a griddle with a scrap of bacon on her fork, and regarding young Master George with pride. "The way he can write, now! and read, too! and then to come out here evenings and read his lessons to us—it's mighty interestin'!"

"But, Aunt Chloe, I'm getting mighty hungry," said George. "Isn't that cake in the skillet almost done?"

"Mos' done, Mas'r George," said Aunt Chloe, lifting the lid and peeping in—"browning beautiful—a real lovely brown." And she whipped the cover off the bake-kettle, and disclosed to view a neatly baked pound-cake, of which no city confectioner need to have been ashamed. "Now, Mas'r George, you jest take off dem books and set down now with my old man, and I'll take up de sausages, and have de first griddleful of cakes on your plates in less dan no time."

"They wanted me to come to supper in the house," said George; "but I knew what was what too well for that, Aunt Chloe. Now for the cake." And with that, the youngster flourished a large knife over the article in question.

"La bless you, Mas'r George!" said Aunt Chloe with earnestness, catching his arm, "you wouldn't be for cuttin' it wid dat ar great heavy knife! Smash it all down—spile all the pretty rise of it. Here, I've got a thin old knife I keeps sharp a purpose. Dar now, see! comes apart light as a feather! Now, eat away—you won't get anything to beat dat ar."

When Master George had arrived at that pass to which even a boy can come (under uncommon circumstances), when he really could not eat another morsel, George and Tom moved to a comfortable seat in the chimney-corner, while Aunt Chloe, after baking a goodly pile of cakes, took her baby on her lap, and began alternately filling its mouth and her own.

Then Aunt Chloe, set the baby down in Tom's lap, while she busied herself in clearing away supper. The baby employed the intervals in pulling Tom's nose, scratching his face, and burying her fat hands in his woolly hair, which last operation seemed to afford her special content.

"An't she a peart young un?" said Tom, holding her from him to take a full-length view; then, getting up, he set her on his broad shoulder and began capering and dancing with her.

"Well, now, I hopes you're done," said Aunt Chloe at last, "for we's goin' to have the meetin", though what we's to do for cheers, now, *I* declar' I don't know," said Aunt Chloe. As the meeting had been held at Uncle Tom's weekly for an indefinite length of time, without any more "cheers", there seemed some encouragement to hope that a way would be discovered at present.

"Well, cle man," said Aunt Chloe, "you'll have to tote in them ar bar'ls."

Two empty casks were rolled into the cabin, and being secured from rolling, by stones on each side, boards were laid across them, which arrangement, together with the turning down of certain tubs and pails, and the disposing of the rickety chairs, at last completed the preparation.

"Mas'r George is such a beautiful reader, now, I know he'll stay to read for us," said Aunt Chloe; "pears like 'twill be so much more interestin'."

George very readily consented, for your boy is always ready for anything that makes him of importance.

The room was soon filled with a motley assemblage, from the old grey-headed patriarch of eighty, to the young girl and lad of fifteen. A little harmless gossip ensued on various themes, such as where old Aunt Sally got her new red headkerchief, and how "Missis was a-going to give Lizzy that spotted muslin gown, when she'd got her new berage made up"; and how Mas'r Shelby was thinking of buying a new sorrel colt, that was going to prove an addition to the glories of the place. A few of the worshippers belonged to families hard by, who had got permission to attend, and who brought in various choice scraps of information about the sayings and doings at the house and on the place, which circulated as freely as the same sort of small change does in higher circles.

After a while the singing commenced, to the evident delight of all present. Not even all the disadvantages of nasal intonation could prevent the effect of the naturally fine voices in airs at once wild and spirited. The words were sometimes the well-known

and common hymns sung in the churches about, and sometimes
of a wilder, more indefinite character picked up at camp-
meetings.

The chorus of one of them, which ran as follows, was sung
with great energy and unction:

> "Die on the field of battle
> Die on the field of battle,
> Glory in my soul,"

Another special favourite had, oft repeated, the words:

> "Oh, I'm going to glory—won't you come along with me?
> Don't you see the angels beck'ning, and a-calling me
>   away?
> Don't you see the golden city and the everlasting day?"

There were others, which made incessant mention of "Jordan's
banks", and "Canaan's fields", and the "New Jerusalem"; for
the negro mind, impassioned and imaginative, always attaches
itself to hymns and expressions of a vivid and pictorial nature;
and, as they sang, some laughed, and some cried, and some
clapped hands, or shook hands rejoicingly with each other, as if
they had fairly gained the other side of the river.

Mas'r George, by request, read the last chapters of Revelation,
often interrupted by such exclamations as "The *sakes* now!"
"Only hear that!" "Jest think on't!" "Is all that acomin' sure
enough?"

Uncle Tom was a sort of patriarch in religious matters in the
neighbourhood. It was in prayer that he especially excelled.
Nothing could exceed the touching simplicity, the childlike
earnestness of his prayer, enriched with the language of Scripture,
which seemed so entirely to have wrought itself into his being as
to have become a part of himself, and to drop from his lips
unconsciously; in the language of a pious old negro, he "prayed
right up".

*   *   *   *   *   *   *   *

WHILE this scene was passing in the cabin of the man, one quite otherwise passed in the halls of the master.

The trader and Mr Shelby were seated together in the dining-room aforenamed, at a table covered with papers and writing utensils. The latter was busy in counting some bundles of bills, which, as they were counted, he pushed over to the trader, who counted them likewise.

"All fair," said the trader; "and now for signing these yer."

Mr Shelby hastily drew the bills of sale towards him, and signed them, like a man that hurries over some disagreeable business, and then pushed them over with the money. Haley produced from a well-worn valise a parchment, which, after looking over it a moment, he handed to Mr Shelby, who took it with a gesture of suppressed eagerness.

"Wal, now, the thing's *done*!" said the trader, getting up.

"It's *done*!" said Mr Shelby, in a musing tone; and, fetching a long breath he repeated, "*It's done*!"

"Yer don't seem to feel much pleased with it, 'pears to me," said the trader.

"Haley," said Mr Shelby, "I hope you'll remember that you promised, on your honour, you wouldn't sell Tom without knowing what sort of hands he's going into."

"Why, you've just done it, sir," said the trader.

"Circumstances, you well know, *obliged* me," said Shelby haughtily.

"Wal, you know, they may 'blige *me* too," said the trader.

"Howsomever, I'll do the very best I can in gettin' Tom a good berth; as to my treatin' on him bad, you needn't be a grain afeared. If there's anything that I thank the Lord for, it is that I'm never noways cruel."

5

Eliza Overhears

MR AND Mrs Shelby had retired to their apartment for the night. He was lounging in a large easy-chair, looking over some letters that had come in the afternoon mail, and she was standing before her mirror brushing out the complicated braids and curls in which Eliza had arranged her hair; for, noticing her pale cheeks and haggard eyes, she had excused her attendance that night and ordered her to bed. The employment, naturally enough, suggested her conversation with the girl in the morning; and, turning to her husband, she said carelessly:

"By the by, Arthur, who was that low-bred fellow that you lugged in to our dinner-table today?"

"Haley is his name," said Shelby, turning rather uneasily in his chair, and continuing with his eyes fixed on a letter.

"Haley! Who is he? What may be his business here, pray?"

"Well, he's a man that I transacted some business with, last time I was at Natchez," said Mr Shelby.

"And he presumed on it to make himself quite at home and call and dine here, eh?"

"Why, I invited him; I had some accounts with him."

"Is he a negro-trader?" said Mrs Shelby, noticing a certain embarrassment in her husband's manner.

"Why, my dear, what put that into your head?" said Shelby, looking up.

"Nothing—only Eliza came in here after dinner, in a great worry, crying and taking on, and said you were talking with a trader, and that she heard him make an offer for her boy—the ridiculous little goose!"

"She did, hey?" said Mr Shelby, returning to his paper, which he seemed for a few moments quite intent upon, not perceiving that he was holding it bottom upward.

"I told Eliza," said Mrs Shelby, as she continued brushing her hair, "that she was a little fool for her pains, and that you never had anything to do with that sort of persons. Of course, I knew you never meant to sell any of our people—least of all to such a fellow."

"Well, Emily," said her husband, "so I have always felt and said; but the fact is that my business lies so that I cannot get on without. I shall have to sell some of my hands."

"To that creature? Impossible! Mr Shelby, you cannot be serious."

"I am sorry to say that I am," said Mr Shelby. "I've agreed to sell Tom."

"What! our Tom?—that good, faithful creature!—been your faithful servant from a boy! Oh, Mr Shelby!—and you have promised him his freedom, too—you and I have spoken to him a hundred times of it. Well, I can believe anything now—I can believe *now* that you could sell little Harry, poor Eliza's only child!" said Mrs Shelby, in a tone between grief and indignation.

"Well, since you must know all, it is so. I have agreed to sell Tom and Harry both; and I don't know why I am to be rated, as if I were a monster, for doing what every one does every day."

"But why, of all others, choose these?" said Mrs Shelby. "Why sell them, of all on the place, if you must sell at all?"

"Because they will bring the highest sum of any—that's why. I could choose another, if you say so. The fellow made me a high bid on Eliza, if that would suit you any better," said Mr Shelby.

"The wretch!" said Mrs Shelby vehemently.

"Well, I didn't listen to it a moment—out of regard to your feelings, I wouldn't; so give me some credit."

"My dear," said Mrs Shelby, recollecting herself, "forgive me. I have been hasty. I was surprised, and entirely unprepared for this; but surely you will allow me to intercede for these poor creatures. Tom is a noble-hearted, faithful fellow, if he is black. I do believe, Mr Shelby, that if he were put to it, he would lay down his life to you."

"I know it—I dare say; but what's the use of all this? I can't help myself."

"Why not make a pecuniary sacrifice? I'm willing to bear my part of the inconvenience. Oh, Mr Shelby, I have tried—tried most faithfully, as a Christian woman should—to do my duty to these poor, simple, dependent creatures. I have cared for them, instructed them, watched over them, and known all their little cares and joys, for years; and how can I ever hold up my head again among them, if, for the sake of a little paltry gain, we sell such a faithful, excellent, confiding creature as poor Tom, and tear from him in a moment all we have taught him to love and value? I have taught them the duties of the family, of parent and child, and husband and wife; and how can I bear to have this open acknowledgement that we care for no tie, no duty, no relation, however sacred, compared with money? I have talked with Eliza about her boy—her duty to him as a Christian mother, to watch over him, pray for him, and bring him up in a Christian way; and now what can I say, if you tear him away, and sell him, soul and body, to a profane, unprincipled man just to save a little money? I have told her that one soul is worth more than all the money in the world; and how will she believe me when she sees us turn round and sell her child?—sell him, perhaps, to certain ruin of body and soul!"

"I'm sorry you feel so about it, Emily—indeed I am," said Mr Shelby; "and I respect your feelings, too, though I don't pretend to share them to their full extent; but I tell you now, solemnly, it's of no use—I can't help myself. I didn't mean to tell you this, Emily; but in plain words, there is no choice between selling these two and selling everything. Either they must go, or *all* must. Haley has come into possession of a mortgage, which, if I don't clear off with him directly, will take everything before it. I've raked, and scraped, and borrowed, and all but begged—and the price of these two was needed to make up the balance, and I had to give them up. Haley fancied the child; he agreed to settle the matter that way and no other. I was in his power, and *had* to do it. If you feel so to have them sold, would it be any better to have *all* sold?"

Mrs Shelby stood like one stricken, finally, turning to her toilet, she rested her face in her hands, and gave a sort of groan.

"This is God's curse on slavery!—a bitter, bitter, most accursed thing!—a curse to the master and a curse to the slave! I was a fool to think I could make anything good out of such a deadly evil. It is a sin to hold a slave under laws like ours."

"Why, wife, you are getting to be an abolitionist, quite."

"Abolitionist! We don't need them to tell us; you know I never thought that slavery was right—never felt willing to own slaves."

"I am sorry, very sorry, Emily," said Mr Shelby. "I'm sorry this takes hold of you so. The fact is, Emily, the thing's done; the bills of sale are already signed and in Haley's hands; and you must be thankful it is no worse. That man has had it in his power to ruin us all—and now he is fairly off. If you knew the man as I do, you'd think that we had had a narrow escape."

"Is he so hard, then?"

"Why, not a cruel man, exactly, but a man of leather—a man alive to nothing but trade and profit."

"And this wretch owns that good, faithful Tom, and Eliza's child!"

"Well, my dear, the fact is that this goes rather hard with me; it's a thing I hate to think of. Haley wants to drive matters, and take possession tomorrow. I'm going to get out my horse bright and early, and be off. I can't see Tom, that's a fact; and you had better arrange a drive somewhere and carry Eliza off. Let the thing be done when she is out of sight."

"No, no," said Mrs Shelby; "I'll be in no sense accomplice or help in this cruel business. I'll go and see poor old Tom, God help him in his distress! They shall see, at any rate, that their mistress can feel for them. As to Eliza, I dare not think about it. The Lord forgive us! What have we done, that this cruel necessity should come on us?"

There was one listener to this conversation whom Mr and Mrs Shelby little suspected.

Communicating with their apartment was a large closet, opening by a door into the outer passage. When Mrs Shelby had dismissed Eliza for the night, her feverish and excited mind had suggested the idea of this closet; and she had hidden herself there, and with her ear pressed against the crack of the door, had lost not a word of the conversation.

When the voices died into silence, she rose and crept stealthily away. Pale, shivering, with rigid features and compressed lips, she looked an entirely altered being from the soft and timid creature she had been hitherto. She moved cautiously along the entry, paused one moment at her mistress's door and raised her hands in mute appeal to Heaven, and then turned and glided into her own room. It was a quiet, neat apartment, on the same floor with her mistress. There was the pleasant sunny window, where she had often sat singing at her sewing: there, a little case of books, and various little fancy articles, ranged by them, the gifts of Christmas holidays; there was her simple wardrobe in the closet and in the drawers: here was, in short, her home; and, on the whole, a happy one it had been to her. There, on the bed, lay her slumbering boy, his long curls falling negligently around his unconscious face, his rosy mouth half open, his little fat hands thrown out over the bedclothes, and a smile spread like a sunbeam over his whole face.

"Poor boy! poor fellow!" said Eliza; "they have sold you! but your mother will save you yet!"

No tear dropped over that pillow; in such straits as these the heart has no tears to give—it drops only blood, bleeding itself away in silence. She took a piece of paper and a pencil, and wrote hastily:

"Oh, missis! dear missis! don't think me ungrateful—don't think hard of me, anyway—I heard all you and master said tonight. I am going to try to save my boy—you will not blame me! God bless and reward you for all your kindness!"

Hastily folding and directing this, she went to a drawer and made up a little package of clothing for her boy, which she tied with a handkerchief firmly round her waist; and, so fond is a mother's remembrance that, even in the terrors of that hour, she did not forget to put in the little package one or two of his favourite toys, reserving a gaily-painted parrot to amuse him, when she should be called on to awaken him. It was some trouble to arouse the little sleeper; but after some effort he sat up, and was playing with his bird, while his mother was putting on her bonnet and shawl.

"Where are you going, mother?" said he, as she drew near the bed with his little coat and cap.

His mother looked so earnestly into his eyes that he at once divined that something unusual was the matter.

"Hush, Harry!" she said; "mustn't speak loud, or they will hear us. A wicked man was coming to take little Harry away from his mother; but mother won't let him—she's going to put on her little boy's cap and coat, and run off with him, so the ugly man can't catch him."

Saying these words, she had tied and buttoned on the child's simple outfit, and, taking him in her arms, she whispered to him to be very still; and, opening a door in her room which led into the outer verandah, she glided noiselessly out.

It was a sparkling, frosty, starlight night, and the mother wrapped the shawl close round her child, as, perfectly quiet with vague terror, he clung round her neck. A few minutes brought them to the window of Uncle Tom's cottage and Eliza, stopping, tapped lightly on the window-pane.

The prayer-meeting at Uncle Tom's had, in the order of hymn-singing, been protracted to a very late hour; and, as Uncle Tom had indulged himself in a few lengthy solos afterwards, the consequence was that, although it was now between twelve and one o'clock, he and his worthy helpmeet were not yet asleep.

"Good Lord! what's that?" said Aunt Chloe, starting up and hastily drawing the curtain. "My sakes alive, if it an't Lizy! Get on your clothes, old man, quick! I'm gwine to open the door."

The door flew open, and the light of the tallow candle, which Tom had hastily lighted, fell on the haggard face and dark, wild eyes of the fugitive.

"Lord bless you!—I'm skeered to look at ye, Lizy! Are ye tuck sick, or what's come over ye?"

"I'm runnin' away—Uncle Tom and Aunt Chloe—carrying off my child—master sold him!"

"Sold him!" echoed both, lifting up their hands in dismay.

"Yes, sold him!" said Eliza firmly. "I crept into the closet by mistress's door tonight, and I heard master tell missis that he had sold my Harry, and you, Uncle Tom, both, to a trader; and that he was going off this morning on his horse, and that the man was to take possession today."

Tom had stood, during this speech, with his hands raised, and his eyes dilated, like a man in a dream. Slowly and gradually, as its meaning came over him, he collapsed, rather than seated himself, on his old chair, and sunk his head down upon his knees.

"The good Lord have pity on us!" said Aunt Chloe. "Oh, it don't seem as if it was true! What has he done, that mas'r should sell *him*?"

"He hasn't done anything—it isn't for that. Master don't want to sell: and missis—she's always good. I heard her plead and beg for us; but he told her 'twas no use; that he was in this man's debt, and that this man had got the power over him; and that if he didn't pay him off clear, it would end in his having to sell the place and all the people, and move off. Yes, I heard him say there was no choice between selling these two and selling all, the man was driving him so hard. Master said he was sorry; but oh, missis—you ought to have heard her talk! It she an't a Christian and an angel, there never was one. I'm a wicked girl to leave her so, but, then, I can't help it. She said herself, one soul was worth more than the world; and this boy has a soul, and if I let him be carried off, who knows what'll become of it?"

"Well, old man!" said Aunt Chloe, "why don't you go too? Will you wait to be toted down river, where they kill niggers with hard work and starving? I'd a heap rather die than go there, any day! There's time for ye—be off with Lizy—you've got a pass to come and go any time. Come, bustle up, and I'll get your things together."

Tom slowly raised his head, and looked sorrowfully but quietly around, and said:

"No, no—I an't going. Let Eliza go—it's her right! I wouldn't be the one to say no—'tan't in *natur* for her to stay; but you heard what she said! If I must be sold, or all the people on the place, and everything go to rack, why, let me be sold. I s'pose I can b'ar it as well as any on 'em," he added, while something like a sob and a sigh shook his broad, rough chest convulsively. "Mas'r always found me on the spot—he always will. I never have broke trust, nor used my pass noways contrary to my word, and I never will. It's better for me alone to go than to break up the place and sell all. Mas'r an't to blame, Chloe, and he'll take care of you and the poor—"

Here he turned to the rough trundle-bed full of little woolly heads, and broke fairly down. He leaned over the back of the chair, and covered his face with his large hands. Sobs, heavy, hoarse, and loud, shook the chair, and great tears fell through his fingers on the floor.

"And now," said Eliza, as she stood in the door, "I saw husband only this afternoon, and I little knew then what was to come. They have pushed him to the very last standing-place, and he told me, today, that he was going to run away. Do try, if you can, to get word to him. Tell him how I went, and why I went; and tell him I'm going to try and find Canada. You must give my love to him, and tell him, if I never see him again'—she turned away and stood with her back to them for a moment, and then added, in a husky voice—"tell him to be as good as he can, and try and meet me in the kingdom of heaven."

A few last words and tears, a few simple adieus and blessings, and, clasping her wondering and affrighted child in her arms, she glided noiselessly away.

6

Morning

MR AND Mrs Shelby, after their protracted discussion of the night before, did not readily sink to repose, and, in consequence, slept later than usual the ensuing morning.

"I wonder what keeps Eliza," said Mrs Shelby, after giving her bell repeated pulls to no purpose.

Mr Shelby was standing before his dressing-glass sharpening his razor; and just then the door opened, and a coloured boy entered with his shaving-water.

"Andy," said his mistress, "step to Eliza's door, and tell her I have rung for her three times. Poor thing!" she added to herself, with a sigh.

Andy soon returned, with eyes very wide in astonishment.

"Lor, missis! Lizy's drawers is all open, and her things all lying every which way; I believe she's just done clared out!"

The truth flashed upon Mr Shelby and his wife at the same moment. He exclaimed:

"Then she suspected it, and she's off!"

"The Lord be thanked!" said Mrs Shelby. "I trust she is."

"Wife, you talk like a fool! Really, it will be something pretty awkward for me, if she is. Haley saw that I hesitated about selling this child, and he'll think I connived at it, to get him out of the way. It touches my honour!" And Mr Shelby left the room hastily.

There was great running and ejaculating, and opening and shutting of doors, and appearance of faces in all shades of colour in different places, for about a quarter of an hour. One person only, who might have shed some light on the matter, was entirely silent, and that was the head cook, Aunt Chloe. Silently, and with a heavy cloud settled down over her once joyous face, she proceeded making out her breakfast biscuits, as if she heard nothing of the excitement around her.

When, at last, Haley appeared, booted and spurred, he was saluted with bad tidings on every hand.

"I say, now, Shelby, this yer's a most extr'or'nary business!" said Haley, as he abruptly entered the parlour. "It seems that gal's off, with her young un."

"Yes, sir," said Mr Shelby. "I regret to say that the young woman, excited by overhearing, or having reported to her, something of this business, has taken her child in the night, and made off."

"I did expect fair dealing in this matter, I confess," said Haley.

"Well, sir," said Mr Shelby, turning sharply round upon him, "what am I to understand by that remark? If any man calls my honour in question, I have but one answer for him."

The trader cowered at this, and in a somewhat lower tone said that "it was plaguy hard on a fellow, that had made a fair bargain, to be gulled that way."

"Mr Haley," said Mr Shelby, "I shall allow of no insinuations cast upon me, as if I were at all partner to any unfairness in this matter. Moreover, I shall feel bound to give you every assistance, in the use of horses, servants, etc., in the recovery of your property. So, in short, Haley," said he suddenly, dropping from the tone of dignified coolness to his ordinary one of easy frankness, "the best way for you is to keep good-natured and eat some breakfast, and we will then see what is to be done."

*   *   *   *   *   *   *   *   *

NEVER did fall of any prime minister at court occasion wider surges of sensation than the report of Tom's fate among his compeers on the place. It was the topic in every mouth, everywhere; and nothing was done in the house or in the field, but to discuss its probable results. Eliza's flight—an unprecedented event on the place—was also a great accessory in stimulating the general excitement.

Black Sam, as he was commonly called, from his being about three shades blacker than any other son of ebony on the place, was revolving the matter profoundly in all its phases and bearings, with a comprehensiveness of vision and a strict look-out to his own personal well-being that would have done credit to any white patriot in Washington.

"Now, dar, Tom's down—wal, course der's room for some nigger to be up—and why not dis nigger?—dat's the idee. Tom, aridin' round de country—boots blacked—pass in his pocket. Now, why shouldn't Sam?—dat's what I want to know."

"Halloo, Sam—oh, Sam! Mas'r want you to cotch Bill and Jerry," said Andy, cutting short Sam's soliloquy.

"Hi! what's afoot now, young un?"

"Why, you don't know, I s'pose, that Lizy's cut stick, and clared out, with her young un?"

"You teach your granny!" said Sam, with infinite contempt; "knowed it a heap sight sooner than you did; this nigger an't so green, now!"

"Well, anyhow, mas'r wants Bill and Jerry geared right up; and you and I's to go with Mas'r Haley, to look arter her."

"Good, now! dat's de time o' day!" said Sam. "It's Sam da's called for in dese yer times. He's de nigger. See if I don't cotch her, now; mas'r'll see what Sam can do!"

"Ah! but, Sam," said Andy, "you'd better think twice; for missis don't want her cotched, and she'll be in yer wool."

"Hi!" said Sam, opening his eyes. "How you know dat?"

"Heard her say so, my own self, dis blessed mornin', when I bring in mas'r's shaving-water. She sent me to see why Lizy didn't come to dress her; and when I told her she was off, she jest ris up, and ses she, 'The Lord be praised'; and mas'r, he seemed rael mad, and ses he, 'Wife, you talk like a fool'. But Lor! she'll bring him to! I knows well enough how that'll be—it's allers best to stand missis' side the fence, now I tell yer."

Black Sam, upon this, scratched his woolly pate.

"Now, sartin I'd 'a' said that missis would 'a' scoured the 'varsal world after Lizy," added Sam thoughtfully.

"So she would," said Andy; "but can't ye see through a ladder, ye black nigger? Misses don't want dis yer Mas'r Haley to get Lizy's boy; dat's de go."

"Hi!" said Sam, with an indescribable intonation, known only to those who have heard it among the negroes.

"And I'll tell yer more'n all," said Andy; "I 'spect you'd better be making tracks for dem hosses—mighty sudden, too—for I hearn missis 'quirin' arter yer—so you've stood foolin' long enough."

Sam upon this began to bestir himself in real earnest, and after a while appeared, bearing down gloriously toward the house, with Bill and Jerry, in a full canter, and adroitly throwing himself off before they had any idea of stopping, he brought them up alongside of the horse-post like a tornado. Haley's horse, which was a skittish colt, winced, and bounced, and pulled hard at his halter.

"Ho, ho!" said Sam, "skeery, ar ye?" and his black visage lighted up with a curious, mischievous gleam. "I'll fix ye now!" said he.

There was a large beech tree overshadowing the place, and the small, sharp, triangular beechnuts lay scattered thickly on the ground. With one of these in his fingers, Sam approached the colt, stroked and patted, and seemed apparently busy in soothing his agitation. On pretence of adjusting the saddle, he adroitly slipped under it the sharp little nut, in such manner that the least weight brought upon the saddle would annoy the nervous sensibilities of the animal, without leaving any perceptible graze or wound.

"Dar!" he said, rolling his eyes with an approving grin; "me fix 'em!"

At this moment Mrs Shelby appeared on the balcony beckoning to him.

"Why have you been loitering so, Sam? I sent Andy to tell you to hurry."

"Lord bless you, missis!" said Sam, "horses won't be cotched all in a minute; they'd done clared out way down to the south pasture, and the Lord knows whar!"

"Sam, how often must I tell you not to say "Lord bless you", and "The Lord knows", and such things? It's wicked."

"Oh, Lord bless my soul! I done forgot, missis! I won't say nothing of de sort no more."

"Well, Sam, you are to go with Mr Haley, to show him the road, and help him. Be careful of the horses, Sam; you know Jerry was a little lame last week; *don't ride them too fast.*"

Mrs Shelby spoke the last words with a low voice, and strong emphasis.

"Let dis child along for dat!" said Sam, rolling up his eyes with a volume of meaning. "Lord knows! Hi! Didn't say dat!" said he, suddenly catching his breath, with a ludicrous flourish of apprehension, which made his mistress laugh, spite of herself. "Yes, missis, I'll look out for de hosses!"

"Now, Andy," said Sam, returning to his stand under the beech tree, "you see I wouldn't be t'all surprised if dat ar gen'l'man's crittur should gib a fling by and by, when he come to be a gettin' up. You know, Andy, critturs *will* do such things"; and there with Sam poked Andy in the side, in a highly suggestive manner.

"Hi!" said Andy, with an air of instant appreciation.

"Yes, you see, Andy, missis wants to make time—dat ar's clar to der most or'nary 'bserver. I jis make a little for her. Now, you see, get all dese yer hosses loose, caperin' permiscus round dis yer lot and down to de wood dar, and I 'spec mas'r won't be off in a hurry. Yer see, Andy, if any such thing should happen as that Mas'r Haley's horse *should* begin to act contrary, and cut up, you and I jist lets go of ourn' to help him, and *we'll help him*—oh, yes!" And Sam and Andy laid their heads back on their shoulders, and broke into a low, immoderate laugh, snapping their fingers and flourishing their heels with exquisite delight.

At this instant, Haley appeared on the verandah. Somewhat mollified by certain cups of very good coffee, he came out smiling and talking, in tolerably restored humour.

"Well, boys," said Haley, "look alive now; we must lose no time."

"Not a bit of him, mas'r!" said Sam, putting Haley's rein in his hand, and holding his stirrup, while Andy was untying the other two horses.

The instant Haley touched the saddle the mettlesome creature bounded from the earth with a sudden spring that threw his master sprawling, some feet off, on the soft, dry turf. Sam, with frantic ejaculations, made a dive at the reins, but only succeeded in brushing the blazing palm-leaf aforenamed into the horse's eyes, which by no means tended to allay the confusion of his nerves. So, with great vehemence, he overturned Sam, and, giving two or three contemptuous snorts, flourished his heels vigorously in the air, and was soon prancing away toward the lower end of the lawn, followed by Bill and Jerry, whom Andy had not failed to let loose, according to contract, speeding them off with various direful ejaculations. And now ensued a miscellaneous scene of confusion. Sam and Andy ran and shouted—dogs barked here and there—and Mike, Mose, Mandy, Fanny, and all the smaller specimens of the place, both male and female, raced, clapped hands, whooped, and shouted, with outrageous officiousness and untiring zeal.

Haley's horse, which was a white one, and very fleet and spirited, appeared to enter into the spirit of the scene with great gusto; he appeared to take infinite delight in seeing how near he could allow his pursuers to approach him, and then, when within a hand's breadth, whisk off with a start and a snort, like a mischievous beast he was, and career far down into some alley of the wood-lot. Nothing was further from Sam's mind than to have any one of the troop taken until such season as should seem to him most befitting—and the exertions that he made were certainly most heroic. His palm-leaf was to be seen everywhere when there was the least danger that a horse could be caught—there he would bear down full tilt, shouting, "Now for it! cotch him! cotch him!" in a way that would set everything to indiscriminate rout in a moment.

Haley ran up and down, and cursed and swore and stamped miscellaneously. Mr Shelby in vain tried to shout directions from the balcony, and Mrs Shelby from her chamber window laughed and wondered—not without some inkling of what lay at the bottom of all this confusion.

At last, about twelve o'clock, Sam appeared triumphant, mounted on Jerry, with Haley's horse by his side, reeking with sweat, but with flashing eyes and dilated nostrils.

"He's cotched!" he exclaimed triumphantly. "If 't hadn't been for me, they might 'a' bust theirselves, all on 'em; but I cotched him!"

"You!" growled Haley, in no amiable mood. "If it hadn't been for you, this never would have happened."

"Lord bless us, mas'r," said Sam, in a tone of the deepest concern, "and me that has been racin' and chasin' till the sweat jest pours off me!"

"Well, well!" said Haley, "you've lost me near three hours, with

your cursed nonsense. Now let's be off, and have no more
fooling."

"Why, mas'r," said Sam, in a deprecating tone, "I believe you
mean to kill us all clar, horses and all. Here we are all jest ready
to drop down, and the critturs all in a reek of sweat. Why, mas'r
won't think of startin' on now till after dinner. Mas'r's hoss wants
rubben' down; see how he splashed hisself; and Jerry limps too;
don't think missis would be willin' to have us start dis yer way,
nohow. Lord bless you, mas'r, we can ketch up, if we do stop.
Lizy never was no great of a walker."

Mrs Shelby, who, greatly to her amusement, had overheard
this conversation from the verandah, now resolved to do her part.
She came forward, and pressed him to stay to dinner, saying that
the cook should bring it on the table immediately.

Thus, all things considered, Haley, with rather an equivocal
glance, proceeded to the parlour, while Sam, rolling his eyes after
him with unutterable meaning, proceeded with the horses to the
stable-yard.

"Yer see," said Sam, beginning gravely to wash down Haley's
pony, "I'se 'quired what ye may call a habit o' *bobservation*, Andy.
It's a very 'portant habit, Andy, and I 'commend yer to be
cultivatin' it, now yer young. Hist up that hind foot, Andy. Yer
see, Andy, it's *bobservation* makes all de difference in niggers.
Didn't I see which way the wind blew dis yer mornin'? Didn't I
see what missis wanted, though she never let on? Dat ar's
bobservation, Andy. I 'spects it's what you may call a faculty.
Faculties is different in different peoples, but cultivation of 'em
goes a great way."

"I guess if I hadn't helped your bobservation dis mornin', yer
wouldn't have seen your way so smart," said Andy.

"Andy," said Sam, "you's a promisin' child, der an't no manner
o' doubt. I thinks lots of yer, Andy; and I don't feel noways
ashamed to take idees from you. We oughtenter overlook nobody,
Andy, 'cause the smartest on us gets tripped up sometimes. And
so, Andy, let's go up to the house now. I'll be boun' missis'll give
us an uncommon good bite, dis yer time."

7

The Pursuit

IT IS impossible to conceive of a human creature more wholly desolate and forlorn than Eliza, when she turned her footsteps from Uncle Tom's cabin.

Her husband's sufferings and dangers, and the danger of her child, all blended in her mind with a confused and stunning sense of the risk she was running in leaving the only home she had ever known, and cutting loose from the protection of a friend whom she loved and revered. Then there was the parting from every familiar object—the place where she had grown up, the trees under which she had played, the groves where she had walked many an evening in happier days, by the side of her young husband.

But stronger than all was maternal love, wrought into a paroxysm of frenzy by the near approach of a fearful danger. Her boy was old enough to have walked by her side, and, in an indifferent case, she would only have led him by the hand; but now the bare thought of putting him out of her arms made her shudder, and she strained him to her bosom with a convulsive grasp, as she went rapidly forward.

The frosty ground creaked beneath her feet, and she trembled at the sound; every quaking leaf and fluttering shadow sent the blood backward to her heart, and quickened her footsteps; and every flutter of fear seemed to increase the supernatural power that bore her on, while from her pale lips burst forth, in frequent ejaculations, the prayer to a Friend above—"Lord help! Lord, save me!"

The boundaries of the farm, the grove, the wood-lot, passed by her dizzily, as she walked on; and still she went, leaving one familiar object after another, slacking not, pausing not, till reddening daylight found her many a long mile from all traces of any familiar objects upon the open highway.

She had often been, with her mistress, to visit some

connections in the little village of T—, not far from the Ohio River, and knew the road well. To go thither, to escape across the Ohio River, were the first hurried outlines of her plan of escape; beyond that she could only hope in God.

When horses and vehicles began to move along the highway, with that alert perception peculiar to a state of excitement, and which seems to be a sort of inspiration, she became aware that her headlong pace and distracted air might bring on her remark and suspicion. She therefore put the boy on the ground, and, adjusting her dress and bonnet, she walked on at as rapid a pace as she thought consistent with the preservation of appearances. In her little bundle she had provided a store of cakes and apples, which she used as expedients for quickening the speed of the child.

After a while they came to a thick patch of woodland, through which murmured a clear brook. As the child complained of hunger and thirst, she climbed over the fence with him; and, sitting down behind a large rock which concealed them from the road, she gave him a breakfast out of her little package. The boy wondered and grieved that she could not eat; and when, putting his arms round her neck he tried to wedge some of his cake into her mouth, it seemed to her that the rising in her throat would choke her.

"No, no, Harry darling! mother can't eat till you are safe! We must go on—on—till we come to the river!" And she hurried again into the road, and again constrained herself to walk regularly and composedly forward.

She was many miles past any neighbourhood where she was personally known. If she should chance to meet any who knew her, she rejected that the well-known kindness of the family would be of itself a blind to suspicion, as making it an unlikely supposition that she could be a fugitive. As she was also so white as not to be known as of coloured lineage, without a critical survey, and her child was white also, it was much easier for her to pass on unsuspected.

On this presumption she stopped at noon at a neat farmhouse to rest herself and buy some dinner for her child and self; for, as the danger decreased with the distance, the supernatural tension of the nervous system lessened, and she found herself both weary and hungry.

The good woman, kindly and gossiping, seemed rather pleased than otherwise with having somebody come in to talk with; and accepted without examination Eliza's statement that she "was going on a little piece, to spend a week with her friends"—all which she hoped in her heart might prove strictly true.

An hour before sunset she entered the village of T, by the Ohio River, weary and footsore, but still strong in heart, Her first glance was at the river, which lay, like Jordan, between her and the Canaan of liberty on the other side.

It was now early spring, and the river was swollen and turbulent; great cakes of floating ice were swinging heavily to and fro in the turbid waters. Owing to the peculiar form of the shore on the Kentucky side, the land bending far out into the water, the ice had been lodged and detained in great quantities, and the narrow channel which swept round the bend was full of ice, piled one cake over another, forming a temporary barrier to the descending ice, which lodged and formed a great, undulating raft, filling up the whole river and extending almost to the Kentucky shore.

Eliza stood for a moment contemplating this unfavourable aspect of things, which she saw at once must prevent the usual ferry-boat from running, and then turned into a small public house on the bank, to make a few inquiries.

The hostess, who was busy in various fizzing and stewing operations over the fire, preparatory to the evening meal, stopped, with a fork in her hand, as Eliza's sweet and plaintive voice arrested her.

"Isn't there any ferry or boat that takes people over to B—, now?" she said.

"No, indeed!" said the woman; "the boats has stopped running."

Eliza's look of dismay and disappointment struck the woman, and she said inquiringly:

"Maybe you're wanting to get over?—anybody sick? Ye seem mighty anxious!"

"I've got a child that's very dangerous," said Eliza. "I never heard of it till last night, and I've walked quite a piece today, in hopes to get to the ferry."

"Well, now, that's onlucky," said the woman, whose motherly sympathies were much aroused; "but there's a man a piece down here, that's going over with some truck this evening, if he durs' to; he'll be in here to supper tonight, so you'd better set down and wait. That's a sweet little fellow," added the woman, offering him a cake.

But the child, wholly exhausted, cried with weariness.

"Poor fellow! he isn't used to walking, and I have hurried him on so," said Eliza.

"Well, take him into this room," said the woman, opening into a small bedroom, where stood a comfortable bed. Eliza laid the weary boy upon it, and held his hand in hers till he was fast asleep. For her there was no rest. As a fire in her bones, the thought of the pursuer urged her on; and she gazed with longing eyes on the sullen, surging waters that lay between her and liberty.

Here we must take our leave of her for the present, to follow the course of her pursuers.

*   *   *   *   *   *   *   *   *

THOUGH Mrs Shelby had promised that the dinner should be hurried on the table, yet it was soon seen that it required more than one to make a bargain. So, although the order was fairly given out in Haley's hearing, and carried to Aunt Chloe by at least half a dozen juvenile messengers, that dignitary only gave certain very gruff snorts and tosses of her head, and went on with every operation in an unusually leisurely and circumstantial manner.

For some singular reason an impression seemed to reign among the servants generally that missis would not be particularly disobliged by delay; and it was wonderful what a number of counter-accidents occurred constantly to retard the course of things. One luckless wight contrived to upset the gravy; and then gravy had to be got up *de novo*, with due care and formality, Aunt Chloe watching and stirring with dogged precision, answering shortly, to all suggestions of haste, that she "warn't agoing to have raw gravy on the table, to help nobody's catchings". One tumbled down with the water, and had to go to the spring for more; and another precipitated the butter into the path of events; and there was from time to time giggling news brought into the kitchen that "Mas'r Haley was mighty oneasy, and that he couldn't sit in his cheer noways, but was walkin' and stalkin' to the winders and through the porch".

"Sarves him right!" said Aunt Chloe indignantly. "He's broke a many, many, many hearts—I tell ye all," she said, stopping with a fork uplifted in her hands, "it's like what Mas'r George reads in Revelations—souls a-callin' under the altar! and a-callin' on the Lord for vengeance on sich! and by and by the Lord He'll hear 'em—so He will!"

"Sich'll be burnt up forever, and no mistake; won't ther?" said Andy.

"Chil'en!" said a voice that made them all start. It was Uncle Tom who had come in, and stood listening to the conversation at the door.

"Chil'en!" he said, "I'm a-feared you don't know what ye're sayin'. Forever is a *dre'ful* word, chil'en; it's awful to think on't. You oughtenter wish that ar to any human crittur."

"We wouldn't to anybody but the soul-drivers," said Andy; "nobody can help wishing it to them, they's so awful wicked."

"Don't natur herself kinder cry out on 'em?" said Aunt Chloe. "Don't dey tear der suckin' baby right off his mother's breast, and sell him, and der little chil'en as is crying and holding on by her clothes—don't dey pull 'em off and sells 'em? Don't dey tear wife and husband apart?" said Aunt Chloe, beginning to cry, "when it's jest takin' the very life on 'em?—and all the while does they feel one bit—don't dey drink and smoke, and take it oncommon easy! Lor, if the devil don't get them, what's he good for?" And Aunt Chloe covered her face with her checked apron, and began to sob in good earnest.

"Pray for them that 'spitefully use you, the good book says," said Tom.

"Pray for 'em!" said Aunt Chloe; "Lor, it's too tough! I can't pray for 'em."

"It's natur, Chloe, and natur's strong," said Tom, "but the

Lord's grace is stronger; besides, you oughter think what an awful state a poor crittur's soul's in that'll do them ar things; you oughter thank God that you an't *like him*, Chloe. I'm sure I'd rather be sold, ten thousand times over, than to have all that ar poor crittur's got to answer for."

"I'm glad mas'r didn't go off this morning, as he looked to," continued Tom; "that ar hurt me more than sellin', it did. Mebbe it might have been natural for him, but 'twould have come desp't hard on me, as has known him from a baby; but I've seen mas'r, and I begin to feel sort o' reconciled to the Lord's will now. Mas'r couldn't help hisself; he did right: but I'm feared things will be kinder goin' to rack, when I'm gone. Mas'r can't be 'spected to be a-prying' round everywhar, as I've done, akeepin' up all the ends. The boys all means well, but they's powerful car'less. That ar troubles me."

The bell here rang, and Tom was summoned to the parlour.

"Tom," said his master kindly, "I want you to notice that I give this gentleman bonds to forfeit a thousand dollars if you are not on the spot when he wants you. He's going today to look after his other business, and you can have the day to yourself. Go anywhere you like, boy."

"Thank you, mas'r," said Tom.

"And mind yerself," said the trader, "and don't come it over yer master with any o' yer nigger tricks; for I'll take every cent out of him, if you an't thar. If he'd hear to me he wouldn't trust any on ye—slippery as eels!"

"Mas'r," said Tom—and he stood very straight—"I was jist eight years ole when ole missis put you into my arms, and you wasn't a year old. "That," says she, "Tom, that's to be your young mas'r; take good care on him," says she. And now I just ask you, mas'r, have I broke word to you, or gone contrary to you, 'specially since I was a Christian?"

Mr Shelby was fairly overcome, and the tears rose to his eyes.

"My good boy," said he, "the Lord knows you say but the truth; and if I was able to help it, all the world shouldn't buy you."

"And sure as I am a Christian woman," said Mrs Shelby, "you shall be redeemed as soon as I can anyway bring together the means. Sir," she said to Haley, "take good account of whom you sell him to, and let me know."

"Lor, yes, for that matter," said the trader, "I may bring him up in a year, not much the wuss for wear, and trade him back."

"I'll trade with you then, and make it for your advantage," said Mrs Shelby.

"Of course," said the trader, "all's equal with me."

At two o'clock Sam and Andy brought the horses up to the posts, apparently greatly refreshed and invigorated by the scamper of the morning.

"I shall take the straight road to the river," said Haley decidedly, after they had come to the boundaries of the estate. "I know the way of all of 'em—they makes tracks for the underground."

"Sartin," said Sam, "dat's the idee. Mas'r Haley hits de thing right in de middle. Now, dere's two roads to de river—de dirt road and der pike—which mas'r mean to take?"

Andy looked up innocently at Sam, surprised at hearing this new geographical fact, but instantly confirmed what he said by a vehement reiteration.

"Cause," said Sam, "I'd rather be 'clined to 'magine that Lizy'd take de dirt road, bein' it's de least travelled."

"If yer warn't both on yer such cussed liars, now!" Haley said contemplatively as he pondered a moment.

"Course," said Sam, "mas'r can do as he'd ruther; go de straight road if mas'r thinks best—it's all one to us. Now, when I study 'pon it, I think the straight road de best, *deridedly*."

"She would naturally go a lonesome way," said Haley, thinking aloud and not minding Sam's remark.

"Dar an't no sayin'," said Sam; "gals is pecul'ar; they never does nothin' ye thinks they will; mose gen'lly the contrar. Gals is nat'lly made contrary; and so, if you thinks they've gone one road, it is sartin you'd better go t'other, and they you'll be sure to find 'em. Now, my private 'pinion is, Lizy took der dirt road; so I think we'd better take de straight one."

This profound generic view of the female sex did not seem to dispose Haley particularly to the straight road; and he announced decidedly that he should go the other, and asked Sam when they should come to it.

"A little piece ahead," said Sam, giving a wink to Andy with the eye which was on Andy's side of the head; and he added gravely, "but I've studded on de matter, and I'm quite clar we ought not to go dat ar way. I nebber been over it noways. It's despit lonesome, and we might lose our way—whar we'd come to, de Lord only knows."

"Nevertheless," said Haley, "I shall go that way."

"Now I think on't, I think I hearn 'em tell that dat ar road was all fenced up and down by der creek, and thar, an't it, Andy?"

Andy wasn't certain; he'd only "hearn tell" about that road, but never been over it. In short, he was strictly non-committal.

When, therefore, Sam indicated the road, Haley plunged briskly into it, followed by Sam and Andy.

Now, the road, in fact, was an old one that had formerly been a thoroughfare to the river, but abandoned for many years after the laying of the new pike. It was open for about an hour's ride, and after that it was cut across by various farms and fences. Sam knew this fact perfectly well—indeed, the road had been so long closed up that Andy had never heard of it. He therefore rode along with an air of dutiful submission, only groaning and vociferating occasionally that "'twas desp't rough, and bad for Jerry's foot".

"Now, I jest give yer warning," said Haley, "I know yer: yer won't get me to turn off this yer road with all yer fussin'—so you shet up!"

Sam was in wonderful spirits—professed to keep a very brisk look-out—at one time exclaiming that he saw "a gal's bonnet" on the top of some distant eminence, or calling to Andy "if that wasn't Lizy down in the hollow"; always making these exclamations in some rough or craggy part of the road, where the sudden quickening of speed was a special inconvenience to all parties concerned, and thus keeping Haley in a state of constant commotion.

After riding about an hour in this way, the whole party made a precipitate and tumultuous descent into a barnyard belonging to a large farming establishment. Not a soul was in sight, all the hands being employed in the fields; but, as the barn stood conspicuously and plainly square across the road, it was evident that their journey in that direction had reached a decided finale.

"Warn't dat ar what I telled mas'r?" said Sam, with an air of injured innocence. "How does strange gentlemen 'spect to know more about a country dan de natives born and raised?"

"You rascal!" said Haley, "you knew all about this."

"Didn't I tell yer I *know'd*, and yer wouldn't believe me? I telled mas'r 'twas all shet up and fenced up, and I didn't 'spect we could get through—Andy heard me."

In consequence of all the various delays, it was about three-quarters of an hour after Eliza had laid her child to sleep in the village tavern that the party came riding into the same place. Eliza was standing by the window, looking out in another direction, when Sam's quick eye caught a glimpse of her. Haley and Andy were two yards behind. At this crisis Sam contrived to have his hat blown off, and uttered a loud and characteristic ejaculation which startled her at once; she drew suddenly back; the whole train swept by the window round to the front door.

A thousand lives seemed to be concentrated in that one moment to Eliza. Her room opened by a side door to the river. She caught her child and sprang down the steps towards it. The trader caught a full glimpse of her just as she was disappearing down the bank; and throwing himself from his horse, and calling loudly on Sam and Andy, he was after her like a hound after a deer. In that dizzy moment her feet to her scarce seemed to touch the ground, and a moment brought her to the water's edge. Right on behind they came; and, nerved with strength such as God gives only to the desperate, with one wild cry and flying leap she vaulted sheer over the turbid current by the shore on to the raft of ice beyond. It was a desperate leap—impossible to anything but madness and despair; and Haley, Sam, and Andy instinctively cried out and lifted up their hands, as she did it.

The huge green fragment of ice on which she alighted pitched and creaked as her weight came on it, but she stayed there not a moment. With wild cries and desperate energy she leaped to another and still another cake; stumbling, leaping, slipping; springing upward again! Her shoes were gone—her stockings cut from her feet—while blood marked every step; but she saw nothing, felt nothing, till dimly, as in a dream, she saw the Ohio side, and a man helping her up the bank.

"Yer a brave gal, now, whoever ye ar!" said the man, with an oath.

Eliza recognized the voice and face of a man who owned a farm not far from her old home.

"Oh, Mr Symmes!—save me—do save me—do hide me!" said Eliza.

"Why, what's this?" said the man. "Why, if 'tan't Shelby's gal!"

"My child!—this boy!—he'd sold him! There is his mas'r," said she, pointing to the Kentucky shore. "Oh, Mr Symmes, you've got a little boy!"

"So I have," said the man, as he roughly but kindly drew her up the steep bank. "Besides, you're a right brave gal. I like grit wherever I see it!"

When they had gained the top of the bank the man paused. "I'd be glad to do something for ye," said he; "but then there's nowhar I could take ye. The best I can do is to tell ye to go *thar*," said he, pointing to a large white house which stood by itself, off the main street of the village. "Go thar; they're kind folks. Thar's no kind o' danger but they'll help you—they're up to all that sort o' thing."

"The Lord bless you!" said Eliza earnestly.

"No 'casion, no 'casion in the world," said the man. "What I've done's of no 'count."

"And oh, surely, sir, you won't tell any one!"

"Go to thunder, gal! What do you take a feller for? In course not," said the man. "Come, now, go along, like a likely, sensible gal, as you are. You've arnt your liberty, and you shall have it for all me."

The woman folded her child to her bosom, and walked firmly and swiftly away. The man stood and looked after her.

"Shelby, now, mebbe won't think this yer the most neighbourly thing in the world; but what's a feller to do? If he catches one of my gals in the same fix, he's welcome to pay back. Somehow I never could see no kind o' crittur a-strivin' and pantin', and trying to clar theirselves with the dogs arter 'em, and go agin 'em. Besides, I don't see no kind o' 'casion for me to be hunter and catcher fer other folks, neither."

Haley had stood, a perfectly amazed spectator of the scene, till Eliza had disappeared up the bank, when he turned a blank, inquiring look on Sam and Andy.

"That ar was a tol'able fair stroke of business," said Sam.

"The gal's got seven devils in her, I believe!" said Haley. "How like a wild cat she jumped!"

"Wal, now," said Sam, scratching his head, "I hope mas'r'll 'scuse us tryin' dat ar road. Don't think I feel spry enough for dat ar noway!" and Sam gave a hoarse chuckle.

"*You* laugh!" said the trader, with a growl.

"Lord bless you, mas'r, I couldn't help it, now," said Sam, giving way to the long pent-up delight of his soul. "She looked so curis a-leapin' and a-springin'—ice a-crackin'—and only to hear her— plump! ker-chunk! ker-splash! Spring! Lord! how she goes it!" and Sam and Andy laughed till the tears rolled down their cheeks.

"I'll make yer laugh t'other side of yer mouths!" said the trader, laying about their heads with his riding-whip.

Both ducked, and ran shouting up the bank, and were on their horses before he was up.

"Good evening, mas'r!" said Sam, with much gravity, "I bery much spect missis be anxious 'bout Jerry. Mas'r Haley won't want us no longer. Missis wouldn't hear of our ridin' the critters over Lizy's bridge tonight"; and with a facetious poke into Andy's ribs, he started off, followed by the latter at full speed—their shouts of laughter coming faintly on the wind.

8

Escape to Freedom

ELIZA made her desperate retreat across the river just in the dusk of twilight. The grey mist of evening, rising slowly from the river, enveloped her as she disappeared up the bank, and the swollen current and floundering masses of ice presented a hopeless barrier between her and her pursuer. Haley therefore slowly and discontentedly returned to the little tavern to ponder further what was to be done. Here he sat him down to meditate on the instability of human hopes and happiness in general.

"What did I want with the little cuss now," he said to himself, "that I should have got myself treed like a coon, as I am, this yer way?" and Haley relieved himself by repeating a not very select litany of curses on himself. He was startled by the loud and dissonant voice of a man who was apparently dismounting at the door. He hurried to the window.

"By the land! if this yer an't the nearest, now, to what I've heard folks call Providence," said Haley. "I do b'lieve that ar's Tom Loker."

Haley hastened out. Standing by the bar, in the corner of the room, was a brawny, muscular man full six feet in height, and broad in proportion. He was dressed in a coat of buffalo skin, made with the hair outward, which gave him a shaggy and fierce appearance, perfectly in keeping with the whole air of his physiognomy. In the head and face every organ and lineament expressive of brutal and unhesitating violence was in a state of the highest possible development. He was accompanied by a travelling companion, in many respects an exact contrast to himself. He was short and slender, lithe and catlike in his motions, and had a peering, mousing expression about his keen black eyes, with which every feature of his face seemed sharpened into sympathy; his thin, long nose ran out as if it was eager to bore into the nature of things in general; his sleek, thin black hair was stuck eagerly forward, and all his motions and evolutions expressed a dry, cautious acuteness.

"Wal, now, who'd a thought this yer luck 'ad come to me? Why, Loker, how are ye?" said Haley, coming forward and extending his hand to the big man.

"The devil!" was the civil reply. "What brought you here, Haley?"

The mousing man, who bore the name of Marks, poked his head forward.

"I say, Tom, this yer's the luckiest thing in the world. I'm in a devil of a hobble, and you must help me out."

"Ugh! aw! like enough!" grunted his complacent acquaintance. "A body may be pretty sure of that when *you're* glad to see 'em. What's the blow now?"

"You've got a friend here?" said Haley, looking doubtfully at Marks; "partner, perhaps?"

"Yes, I have. Here, Marks! here's that ar feller that I was in with in Natchez."

"Shall be pleased with his acquaintance," said Marks, thrusting out a long, thin hand, like a raven's claw. "Mr Haley, I believe?"

"The same, sir," said Haley. "And now, gentlemen, seein' as we've met so happily, I think I'll stand up to a small matter of a treat in this here parlour. So now, old coon," said he to the man at the bar, "get us hot water, and sugar, and cigars, and plenty of the *real stuff*, and we'll have a blow-out."

Haley began a pathetic recital of his peculiar troubles. Loker shut up his mouth and listened to him with gruff and surly attention. Marks, who was anxiously and with much fidgeting compounding a tumbler of punch to his own peculiar taste, occasionally looked up from his employment, and, poking his sharp nose and chin almost into Haley's face, gave the most earnest heed to the whole narrative. The conclusion of it appeared to amuse him extremely, for he shook his shoulders and sides in silence, and perked up his thin lips with an air of great internal enjoyment.

"So then, ye're fairly sewed up, an't ye?" he said. "He! he! he! It's neatly done, too. Now, Mr Haley, what is it? You want us to undertake to catch this yer gal?"

"The gal's no matter of mine—she's Shelby's; it's only the boy. I was a fool for buying the monkey!"

"You're generally a fool!" said Tom gruffly.

"Come, now, Loker, none of your huffs," said Marks, licking

his lips; "you see, Mr Haley's a-puttin' us in a way of a good job,
I reckon; just hold still—these yer arrangements is my forte. This
yer gal, Mr Haley, how is she? what is she?"

"Wal! white and handsome—well brought up. I'd a gin Shelby
eight hundred or a thousand and then made well on her."

"White and handsome—well brought up!" said Marks, his sharp
eyes, nose, and mouth all alive with enterprise. "Look here, now,
Loker, a beautiful opening. We'll do a business here on our own
account; we does the catchin'; the boy, of course, goes to Mr Haley—
we takes the gal to Orleans to speculate on. An't it beautiful?"

"But, gentlemen, an't I to come in for a share of the profits?"
said Haley.

"Not by a long chalk! We'll have the gal out and out, and you
keep quiet, or, ye see, we'll have both; what's to hinder? Han't
you show'd us the game? It's as free to us as you, I hope."

"Oh, wal, certainly, jest let it go at that," said Haley, alarmed:
"you catch the boy for the job."

"So now let's come to the particulars. Now, Mr Haley, you saw
this yer gal when she landed?"

"To be sure—plain as I see you."

"And a man helpin' her up the bank?" said Loker.

"To be sure, I did."

"Most likely," said Marks, "she's took in somewhere; but
where's a question. Tom, what do you say?"

"We must cross the river tonight, no mistake," said Tom.

"But there's no boat about," said Marks. "The ice is running
awfully, Tom, an't it dangerous?"

"Don'no nothing 'bout that—only it's got to be done," said
Tom decidedly.

"Dear me!" said Marks, fidgeting, "it'll be—I say," he said,
walking to the window, "it's dark as a wolf's mouth, and, Tom—"

"The long and short is, you're scared, Marks; but I can't help
that—you've got to go. Suppose you want to lie by a day or two,
till the gal's been carried on the underground line up to Sandusky
or so, before you start!"

"Oh, no; I an't a grain afraid," said Marks; "only—"

"Only what?" said Tom.

"Well, about the boat. Yer see there an't any boat."

"I heard the woman say there was one coming along this evening, and that a man was going to cross over in it. Neck or nothing, we must go with him," said Tom.

"I s'pose you've got good dogs?" said Haley.

"first-rate," said Marks. "But what's the use? you han't got nothing o' her to smell on."

"Yes, I have," said Haley triumphantly. "Here's her shawl she left on the bed in her hurry, she left her bonnet too."

"That ar's lucky," said Loker; "fork over."

After exchanging a few words of further arrangement, Haley, with visible reluctance, handed over the fifty dollars to Tom, and the worthy trio separated for the night.

*   *   *   *   *   *   *   *   *

WHILE this scene was going on at the tavern, Sam and Andy pursued their way home.

Sam was in the highest possible feather, and expressed his exultation by all sorts of supernatural howls and ejaculations, by divers odd motions and contortions of his whole system. With all these evolutions he contrived to keep the horses up to the top of their speed, until, between ten and eleven, their heels resounded on the gravel at the end of the balcony. Mrs Shelby flew to the railings.

"Is that you, Sam? Where are they?"

"Mas'r Haley's a-restin' at the tavern; he's drefful fatigued, missis."

"And Eliza, Sam?"

"Wal, she's clar 'cross Jordan. As a body may say, in the land o' Canaan."

"Why, Sam, what *do* you mean?" said Mrs Shelby, breathless, and almost faint, as the possible meaning of these words came over her.

"Wal, missis, de Lord He presar ves His own. Lizy's done gone over the river into 'Hio, as 'markably as if de Lord took her over in a charrit of fire and two hosses."

"Come up here, Sam," said Mr Shelby, who had followed on to the verandah, "and tell your mistress what she wants. Come, come, Emily," said he, passing his arm round her, "you are cold and all in a shiver; you allow yourself to feel too much."

"Feel too much! Am I not a woman—a mother? Are we not

both responsible to God for this poor girl? My God! lay not this sin to our charge."

"What sin, Emily? You see yourself that we have only done what we were obliged to."

"There's an awful feeling of guilt about it, though," said Mrs Shelby. "I can't reason it away."

"Here, Andy, you nigger, be alive!" called Sam, under the verandah; "take these yer hosses to de barn; don't ye hear mas'r a-callin'"; and Sam soon appeared, palm-leaf in hand, at the parlour door.

"Now, Sam, tell us distinctly how the matter was," said Mrs Shelby. "Where is Eliza, if you know?"

"Wal, mas'r, I saw her, with my own eyes, a'crossin' on the floatin' ice. She crossed most 'markably; it wasn't no less nor a miracle; and I saw a man help her up the 'Hio side, and then she was lost in the dusk."

"Sam, I think this rather doubtful—this miracle. Crossing on floating ice isn't so easily done," said Mr Shelby.

"Easy! couldn't nobody a done it, without de Lord. Why, now," said Sam, "'twas jist dis yer way; she went down de river bank; Mas'r Haley he seed her, and yelled out, and him, and me, and Andy, we took arter. Down she come to the river, and thar was the current running ten feet wide by the shore, and over t'other side ice a-sawin' and ajiggling up and down, kinder as 'twer a great island. We come right behind her, and I thought, my soul! he'd got her sure enough— when she gin sich a screech as I never hearn, and thar she was, clar over t'other side the current, on the ice, and then on she went, a-screeching and ajumpin'—the ice went crack—c'wallop! cracking! chunk! and she a-boundin' like a buck! Lord, the spring that ar gal's got in her an't common, I'm o' 'pinion."

Mrs Shelby sat perfectly silent, pale with excitement, while Sam told his story.

"God be praised, she isn't dead!" she said; "but where is the poor child now?"

"De Lord will pervide," said Sam, rolling up his eyes piously. "As I've been a-sayin', dis yer's a providence and no mistake, as missis has allers been a-instructin' on us. Thar's allers instruments ris up to do de Lord's will. Now, if't hadn't been for me today, she'd a been took a dozen times. Warn't it I started off de hosses, dis yer mornin', and kept 'em chasin' till nigh dinner-time? And didn't I car' Mas'r Haley nigh five miles out of de road, dis evening, or else he's a come up with Lizy as easy as a dog arter a coon? These yer's all providences."

"They are a kind of providences that you'll have to be pretty sparing of, Master Sam. I allow no such practices with gentlemen on my place," said Mr Shelby, with as much sternness as he could command, under the circumstances.

"Mas'r's quite right—quite; it was ugly on me—there's no disputin' that ar; and of course mas'r and missis wouldn't encourage no such works. I'm sensible of dat ar; but a poor nigger like me's 'mazin' tempted to act ugly sometimes, when fellers will cut up such shines as dat ar Mas'r Haley; he an't no gen'l'man noway."

"Well, Sam," said Mrs Shelby, "as you appear to have a proper sense of your errors, you may go now and tell Aunt Chloe she may get you some of that cold ham that was left of dinner today. You and Andy must be hungry."

"Missis is a heap too good for us," said Sam, making his bow with alacrity, and departing.

Sam soon found himself seated, happy and glorious, over a large tin pan containing a sort of *olla podrida* of all that had appeared on the table for two or three days past. Savoury morsels of ham, golden blocks of corn-cake, fragments of pie of every conceivable mathematical figure, chicken wings, gizzards, and drumsticks, all appeared in picturesque confusion; and Sam, as monarch of all he surveyed, sat with his palm-leaf cocked rejoicingly to one side, and patronizing Andy at his right hand.

The kitchen was full of all his compeers, who had hurried and crowded in, from the various cabins, to hear the termination of the day's exploits. Now was Sam's hour of glory. The story of the day was rehearsed with all kinds of ornament and varnishing which might be necessary to heighten its effect; for Sam, like some of our fashionable dilettanti, never allowed a story to lose any of its gilding by passing through his hands.

9

Senator Bird

THE LIGHT of the cheerful fire shone on the rug and carpet of a cosy parlour, and glittered on the sides of the tea cups and well-brightened teapot, as Senator Bird was drawing off his boots, preparatory to inserting his feet in a pair of new, handsome slippers which his wife had been working for him while away on his senatorial tour. Mrs Bird, looking the very picture of delight, was superintending the arrangements of the table, ever and anon mingling admonitory remarks to a number of frolicsome juveniles, who were effervescing in all those modes of untold gambol and mischief that have astonished mothers ever since the flood.

"Tom, let the door-knob alone—there's man! Mary! Mary! don't pull the cat's tail—poor pussy! Jim, you mustn't climb on that table—no, no!—You don't know, my dear, what a surprise it is to us all, to see you here tonight!" she said, at last, when she found a space to say something to her husband.

"Yes, yes, I thought I'd just make a run down, spend the night, and have a little comfort at home. I'm tired to death, and my head aches! A cup of your good, hot tea, and some of our good home living, is what I want. It's a tiresome business, this legislating!"

And the senator smiled, as if he rather liked the idea of considering himself a sacrifice to his country.

"Well," said his wife, after the business of the tea-table was getting rather slack, "and what have they been doing in the Senate?"

Now, it was a very unusual thing for gentle little Mrs Bird ever to trouble her head with what was going on in the house of the State, very wisely considering that she had enough to do to mind her own. Mr Bird, therefore, opened his eyes in surprise, and said:

"Not very much of importance."

"Well; but is it true that they have been passing a law, forbidding people to give meat and drink to those poor coloured folks that come along? I heard they were talking of some such law, but I didn't think any Christian legislature would pass it!"

"Why, Mary, you are getting to be a politician, all at once."

"No, nonsense! I wouldn't give a fig for all your politics, generally, but I think this is something downright cruel and unchristian. I hope, my dear, no such law has been passed."

"There has been a law passed for bidding people to help off the slaves that come over from Kentucky, my dear."

"And what is the law? It don't forbid us to shelter these poor creatures a night, does it, and to give 'em something comfortable to eat, and a few old clothes, and to send them quietly about their business?"

"Why, yes, my dear; that would be aiding and abetting, you know."

Mrs Bird was a timid, blushing little woman, about four feet in height, and with mild blue eyes, and a peach-blow complexion, and the gentlest, sweetest voice in the world; as for courage, a moderate-sized cock-turkey had been known to put her to rout at the very first gobble, and a stout housedog of moderate capacity would bring her into subjection merely by a show of his teeth. Her husband and children were her entire world, and in these she ruled more by entreaty and persuasion than by command or argument. There was only one thing that was capable of arousing her, and that provocation came in on the side of her unusually gentle and sympathetic nature; anything in the shape of cruelty would throw her into a passion, which was the more alarming and inexplicable in proportion to the general softness of her nature.

On the present occasion, Mrs Bird rose quickly with very red cheeks, which quite improved her general appearance, and walked up to her husband with quite a resolute air, and said, in a determined tone:

"Now, John, I want to know if you think such a law as this is right and Christian? You didn't vote for it?"

"Even so, my fair politician."

"You ought to be ashamed, John! Poor, homeless, houseless

creatures! It's a shameful, wicked, abominable law, and I'll break it, for one, the first time I get a chance; and I hope I *shall* have a chance, I do! Things have got to a pretty pass if a woman can't give a warm supper and a bed to poor starving creatures, just because they are slaves, and have been abused and oppressed all their lives, poor things!"

"But, Mary, just listen to me. Your feelings are all quite right, dear, and interesting, and I love you for them; but then, dear, we mustn't suffer our feelings to run away with our judgement; you must consider it's not a matter of private feeling—there are great public interests involved—there is such a state of public agitation rising that we must put aside our private feelings."

"Now, John, I don't know anything about politics, but I can read my Bible; and there I see that I must feed the hungry, clothe the naked, and comfort the desolate; and that Bible I mean to follow."

"But in cases where your doing so would involve a great public evil—"

"Obeying God never brings on public evils. I know it can't. It's always safest, all round, to *do as He* bids us."

"Now, listen to me, Mary, and I can state to you a very clear argument, to show—"

"Oh, nonsense, John! you can talk all night, but you wouldn't do it. I put it to you, John—would you, now, turn away a poor, shivering, hungry creature from your door, because he was a runaway? *Would you*, now?"

Our Senator said "Ahem", and coughed several times, took out his pocket handkerchief, and began to wipe his glasses.

"I should like to see you doing that, John—I really should. Turning a woman out of doors in a snow storm, for instance; or maybe you'd take her up and put her in jail, wouldn't you? You would make a great hand at that!"

"Of course, it would be a very painful duty," began Mr Bird, in a moderate tone.

"Duty, John! don't use that word! You know it isn't a duty—it can't be a duty! If folks want to keep their slaves from running away, let 'em treat 'em well—that's my doctrine. If I had slaves (as I hope I never shall have), I'd risk their wanting to run away from me, or you either, John. I tell you folks don't run away when they are happy; and when they do run, poor creatures! they suffer enough with cold and hunger and fear, without everybody's turning against them; and, law or no law, I never will, so help me God!"

"Mary! Mary! My dear, let me reason with you."

"I hate reasoning, John—especially reasoning on such subjects. I know *you* well enough, John. You don't believe it's right any more "than I do; and you wouldn't do it any sooner than I."

At this critical juncture old Cudjoe, the black man-of-allwork, put his head in at the door and wished "Missis would come into the kitchen".

After a moment her voice was heard at the door, in a quick, earnest tone—"John! John! I do wish you'd come here a moment."

He laid down his paper and went into the kitchen, and started, quite amazed at the sight that presented itself. A young and slender woman, with garments torn and frozen, with one shoe gone, and the stocking torn away from the cut and bleeding foot, was laid back in a deadly swoon upon two chairs. There was the impress of the despised race on her face, yet none could help feeling its mournful and pathetic beauty, while its stony sharpness, its cold, fixed, deadly aspect, struck a solemn chill over him. He drew his breath short, and stood in silence. His wife, and their only coloured domestic, old Aunt Dinah, were busily engaged in restorative measures; while old Cudjoe had got a boy on his knee, and was busy pulling off his shoes and stockings, and chafing his little cold feet.

"Sure, now, if she an't a sight to behold!" said old Dinah compassionately; "'pears like 'twas the heat that made her faint. She was tol'able peart when she cum in, and asked if she couldn't warm herself here a spell; and I was just a-askin' her where she cum from, and she fainted right down. Never done much hard work, guess, by the looks of her hands."

"Poor creature!" said Mrs Bird compassionately, as the woman slowly unclosed her large, dark eyes, and looked vacantly at her. Suddenly an expression of agony crossed her face, and she sprang up, saying, "Oh, my Harry! Have they got him?"

The boy at this jumped from Cudjoe's knee, and, running to

her side, put up his arms, "Oh, he's here! he's here!" she exclaimed. "Oh, ma'am!" said she wildly to Mrs Bird, "do protect us! don't let them get him!"

"Nobody shall hurt you here, poor woman," said Mrs Bird encouragingly. "You are safe; don't be afraid."

"God bless you!" said the woman, covering her face and sobbing; while the little boy, seeing her crying, tried to get into her lap.

With many gentle and womanly offices which none knew better how to render than Mrs Bird, the poor woman was, in time, rendered more calm. A temporary bed was provided for her on the settle, near the fire; and, after a short time, she fell into a heavy slumber, with the child, who seemed no less weary, soundly sleeping on her arm.

Mr and Mrs Bird had gone back to the parlour, where, strange as it may appear, no reference was made, on either side, to the preceding conversation; but Mrs Bird busied herself with her knitting work, and Mr Bird pretended to be reading the paper.

"I wonder who and what she is!" said Mr Bird at last, as he laid it down.

"When she wakes up and feels a little rested, we will see," said Mrs Bird.

"I say, wife!" said Mr Bird, after musing in silence over his paper. "She couldn't wear one of your gowns, could she, by any letting down, or such matter? She seems to be rather larger than you are."

A quite perceptible smile glimmered on Mrs Bird's face as she answered, "We'll see."

Another pause, and Mr Bird again broke out.

"I say, wife! There's that old bombazine cloak that you keep on purpose to put over me when I take my afternoon's nap; you might as well give her that—she needs clothes."

At that instant Dinah looked in to say that the woman was awake, and wanted to see missis.

Mr and Mrs Bird went into the kitchen, followed by the two eldest boys, the smaller fry having by this time been safely disposed of in bed.

The woman was now sitting up on the settle by the fire. She

was looking steadily into the blaze with a calm, heartbroken expression, very different from her former agitated wildness.

"Did you want me?" said Mrs Bird, in gentle tones. "I hope you feel better now, poor woman!"

A long-drawn, shivering sigh was the only answer; but she lifted her dark eyes and fixed them on her with such a forlorn and imploring expression that the tears came into the little woman's eyes.

"You needn't be afraid of anything; we are friends here, poor woman! Tell me where you came from, and what you want," said she.

"I came from Kentucky," said the woman.

"When?" said Mr Bird, taking up the interrogatory.

"Tonight."

"How did you come?"

"I crossed on the ice."

"Crossed on the ice!" said every one present.

"Yes," said the woman slowly, "I did. God helping me, I crossed on the ice; for they were behind me—right behind—and there was no other way!"

"Law, missis," said Cudjoe, "the ice is all in broken-up blocks, a-swinging and a-tettering up and down in the water."

"I know it was—I know it!" said she wildly; "but I did it! I wouldn't have thought I could—I didn't think I should get over, but I didn't care! I could but die if I didn't. The Lord helped me; nobody knows how much the Lord can help 'em till they try," said the woman, with a flashing eye.

"Were you a slave?" asked Mr Bird.

"Yes, sir; I belonged to a man in Kentucky."

"Was he unkind to you?"

"No, sir; he was a good master."

"And was your mistress unkind to you?"

"No, sir—no! my mistress was always good to me."

"What could induce you to leave a good home, then, and run away, and go through such dangers?"

The woman looked up at Mrs Bird with a keen, scrutinizing glance, and it did not escape her that she was dressed in deep mourning.

"Ma'am," she said suddenly, "have you ever lost a child?"

The question was unexpected, and it was a thrust on a new wound; for it was only a month since a darling child of the family had been laid in the grave.

Mr Bird turned around and walked to the window, and Mrs Bird burst into tears, but, recovering her voice, she said:

"Why do you ask that? I have lost a little one."

"Then you will feel for me. I have lost two, one after another— left 'em buried there when I came away; and I had only this one left. I never slept a night without him; he was all I had. He was my comfort and pride, day and night; and, ma'am, they were going to take him away from me—to *sell* him—sell him down South, ma'am, to go all alone—a baby that had never been away from his mother in his life! I couldn't stand it, ma'am. I knew I never should be good for anything if they did; and when I knew the papers were signed and he was sold, I took him and came off in the night; and they chased me—the man that bought him, and some of mas'r's folks—and they were coming down right behind me, and I heard 'em. I jumped right on to the ice; and how I got across I don't know—but, first I knew, a man was helping me up the bank."

The two little boys had thrown themselves disconsolately into the skirts of their mother's gown, where they were sobbing and wiping their eyes and noses to their hearts' content; Mrs Bird had her face fairly hidden in her pocket handkerchief; our senator was a statesman, and, of course, could not be expected to cry like other mortals; and so he turned his back to the company and looked out of the window, and seemed particularly busy in clearing his throat and wiping his spectacle glasses.

"How came you to tell me that you had a kind master?" he suddenly exclaimed.

"Because he *was* a kind master; I'll say that of him anyway; and my mistress was kind; but they couldn't help themselves. They were owing money; and there was some way, I can't tell how, that a man had a hold on them, and they were obliged to give him his will. I listened, and heard him telling mistress that, and she begging and pleading for me—and he told her he couldn't help himself, and that the papers were all drawn—and then it was I took him and left my home, and came away. I knew 'twas no use of my trying to live if they did it; for't 'pears like this child is all I have."

"Have you no husband?"

"Yes, but he belongs to another man. His master is real hard to him, and won't let him come to see me, hardly ever; and he's grown harder and harder upon us, and he threatens to sell him down South; it's like I'll never see *him* again."

"And where do you mean to go, my poor woman?" said Mrs Bird.

"To Canada, if I only knew where that was. Is it very far off, is Canada?" said she, looking up, with a simple, confiding air, to Mrs Bird's face.

"Much farther than you think, poor child!" said Mrs Bird; "but we will try to think what can be done for you.—Here, Dinah, make her up a bed in your own room, close by the kitchen, and I'll think what to do for her in the morning. Meanwhile, never fear, poor woman; put your trust in God; He will protect you."

Mrs Bird and her husband re-entered the parlour. She sat down in her little rocking chair before the fire, swaying thoughtfully to and fro. Mr Bird strode up and down the room, grumbling to himself. At length, striding up to his wife, he said:

"I say, wife, she'll have to get away from here, this very night. That fellow will be down on the scent bright and early tomorrow morning; if 'twas only the woman, she could lie quiet till it was over; but that little chap can't be kept still by a troop of horse and foot, I'll warrant me; he'll bring it all out, popping his head out of some window or door. A pretty kettle of fish it would be for me, too, to be caught with them both here, just now! No; they'll have to be got off tonight."

"Tonight! How is it possible?—where to?"

"Well, I know pretty well where to," said the senator, beginning to put on his boots, with a reflective air; and, stopping when his leg was half in, he embraced his knee with both hands, and seemed to go off in deep meditation.

"It's a confounded awkward, ugly business," said he at last, beginning to tug at his boot-straps again, "and that's a fact!" After one boot was fairly on, the senator sat with the other in his hand, profoundly studying the figure of the carpet. "It will have to be done, though, for aught I see—hang it all!" and he drew the other boot anxiously on, and looked out of the window.

"You see," he said, "there's my old client, Van Trompe, has come over from Kentucky, and set all his slaves free; and he has bought a place seven miles up the creek, here, back in the woods, where nobody goes, unless they go on purpose; and it's a place that isn't found in a hurry. There she'd be safe enough; but the plague of the thing is, nobody could drive a carriage there tonight but me."

"Why not? Cudjoe is an excellent driver."

"Ay, ay, but here it is. The creek has to be crossed twice; and the second crossing is quite dangerous, unless one knows it as I do. I have crossed it a hundred times on horseback, and know exactly the turns to take. And so, you see, there's no help for it. Cudjoe must put in the horses, as quietly as may be, about twelve o'clock, and I'll take her over; and then, to give colour to the matter, he must carry me on to the next tavern, to take the stage for Columbus, that comes by about three or four, and so it will look as if I had had the carriage only for that. I shall get into business bright and early in the morning."

"Your heart is better than your head, in this case, John," said the wife, laying her little white hand on his. "Could I ever have loved you had I not known you better than you know yourself?"

"Mary, I don't know how you'd feel about it, but there's that drawer full of things—of—of—poor little Henry's." So saying, he turned quickly on his heel, and shut the door after him.

His wife opened the little bedroom door adjoining her room, and taking the candle, set it down on the top of a bureau there; then from a small recess she took a key and put it thoughtfully in the lock of a drawer, and made a sudden pause, while two boys who, boy-like, had followed close on her heels, stood looking with silent, significant glances at their mother.

"Mamma," said one of the boys, gently touching her arm, "are you going to give away *those* things?"

"My dear boys," she said softly and earnestly, "if our dear, loving little Henry looks down from Heaven, he would be glad to have us do this. I give them to a mother more heartbroken and sorrowful than I am; and I hope God will send His blessings with them!"

After a while Mrs Bird opened a wardrobe, and, taking from thence a plain, serviceable dress or two, she sat down busily to her work-table, and, with needle, scissors, and thimble at hand, quietly commenced the "letting down" process which her husband had recommended, and continued busily at it till the old clock in the corner struck twelve, and she heard the low rattling of wheels at the door.

"Mary," said her husband, coming in with his overcoat in his hand, "you must wake her up now; we must be off."

Mrs Bird hastily deposited the various articles she had collected in a small, plain trunk, and, locking it, desired her husband to see it in the carriage, and then proceeded to call the woman. Soon, arrayed in a cloak, bonnet, and shawl that had belonged to her benefactress, she appeared at the door with her child in her arms. Mr Bird hurried her into the carriage, and Mrs Bird pressed on after her to the carriage steps. Eliza leaned out of the carriage and put out her hand—a hand as soft and beautiful as was given in return. She fixed her large, dark eyes, full of earnest meaning, on Mrs Bird's face, and seemed going to speak. Her lips moved— she tried once or twice, but there was no sound—and, pointing upward, with a look never to be forgotten, she fell back in the seat and covered her face. The door was shut, and the carriage drove on.

What a situation, now, for a patriotic senator that had been all the week before spurring up the legislature of his native State to pass more stringent resolutions against escaping fugitives, their harbourers and abettors!

The road was an Ohio railroad of the good old times. Over this our senator went stumbling along.

It was full late in the night when the carriage emerged, dripping and bespattered, out of the creek, and stood at the door of a large farmhouse.

It took no inconsiderable perseverance to arouse the inmates; but at last the respectable proprietor appeared, and undid the door. He was a great, tall, bristling Orson of a fellow, full six feet and some inches in his stockings, and arrayed in a red flannel hunting-shirt. A very heavy *mat* of sandy hair, in a decidedly tousled condition, and a beard of some days' growth, gave the worthy man an appearance, to say the least, not particularly prepossessing.

Honest old John Van Trompe was once quite a considerable land-holder and slave owner in the State of Kentucky. Having "nothing of the bear about him but the skin", and being gifted by nature with a great, honest, just heart, quite equal to his gigantic frame, he had been for some years witnessing with repressed uneasiness the workings of a system equally bad for oppressor and oppressed. At last, one day John's great heart had swelled altogether too big to wear his bonds any longer; so he just took his pocketbook out of his desk, and went over into Ohio, and bought a quarter of a township of good, rich land, made out free papers for all his people—men, women, and children— packed them up in wagons, and sent them off to settle down; and then honest John turned his face up the creek, and sat quietly down on a snug, retired farm, to enjoy his conscience and his reflections.

"Are you the man that will shelter a poor woman and child from slave-catchers?" said the senator explicitly.

"I rather think I am," said honest John, with some considerable emphasis. "If there's anybody comes here I'm ready for him; and I've got seven sons, each six foot high, and they'll be ready for 'em too."

Weary, jaded, and spiritless, Eliza dragged herself up to the door, with her child lying in a heavy sleep on her arm. The rough man held the candle to her face, and uttering a kind of compassionate grunt, opened the door of a small bedroom adjoining to the large kitchen where they were standing, and motioned her to go in.

"Now, I say, gal, you needn't be a bit afeard; let who will come here, I'm up to all that sort o' thing," said he, pointing to two or three goodly rifles over the mantelpiece; "and most people that know me know that 'twouldn't be healthy to try to get anybody out o' my house when I'm agin it. So now you just go to sleep now, as quiet as if yet mother was a'rockin' ye," said he, as he shut the door.

"Why, this is an uncommon handsome un," he said to the senator. "Ah, well; handsome uns has the greatest cause to run, sometimes."

The senator, in a few words, briefly, explained Eliza's history.

"Oh! ou! aw! now," said the good man, pitifully. "Poor crittur! Hunted down now like a deer, jest for havin' natural feelin's, and doin' what no kind o' mother could help a-doin'! I tell ye what, these yer things make me come the highest to swearin', now, o' most anything."

John equipped himself, and, with a lantern in hand, was soon seen guiding the senator's carriage towards a road that ran down in a hollow, back of his dwelling. When they parted, the senator put into his hand a ten-dollar bill.

"It's for her," he said briefly.

"Ay, ay," said John, with equal conciseness.

They shook hands and parted.

10

Uncle Tom's Departure

THE FEBRUARY morning looked grey and drizzling through the window of Uncle Tom's cabin. It looked on downcast faces, the images of mournful hearts. The little table stood out before the fire, covered with an ironing-cloth; a coarse but clean shirt or two, fresh from the iron, hung on the back of a chair by the fire, and Aunt Chloe had another spread out before her on the table. Carefully she rubbed and ironed every fold and every hem, with the most scrupulous exactness, every now and then raising her hand to her face to wipe off the tears that were coursing down her cheeks.

Tom sat by, with his Testament open on his knee, and his head leaning upon his hand; but neither spoke. It was yet early, and the children lay all asleep together in their little rude trundle-bed.

Tom, who had to the full the gentle, domestic heart, which, woe for them! has been a peculiar characteristic of his unhappy race, got up and walked silently to look at his children.

"It's the last time," he said.

Aunt Chloe did not answer, only rubbed away over and over on the coarse shirt, already as smooth as hands could make it; and finally setting her iron suddenly down with a despairing plunge, she sat down to the table, and "lifted up her voice and wept".

"S'pose we must be resigned; but, O Lord! how ken I? If I know'd anything whar you's goin', or how they'd sarve you! Missis says she'll try and 'deem ye, in a year or two; but Lor! nobody never comes up that goes down thar! They kills 'em! I've hearn 'em tell how dey works 'em up on dem ar plantations."

"There'll be the same God there, Chloe, that there is here."

"Well," said Aunt Chloe, "s'pose dere will; but de Lord lets dre'ful things happen, sometimes. I don't seem to get no comfort dat way."

"I'm in the Lord's hands," said Tom; "nothin' can go no furder than He lets it; and thar's *one* thing I can thank Him for. It's me that's sold and going down, and not you nur the chil'ren. Here you're safe—what comes will come only on me; and the Lord, He'll help me—I know He will."

Ah, brave, manly heart—smothering thine own sorrow, to comfort thy beloved ones!

"'Tan't right!" said Aunt Chloe. "Mas'r never ought ter left it so that ye *could* be took for his debts. Ye've arnt him all he gets for ye, twice over. He owed ye yer freedom, and ought ter gin't to yer years ago. Mebbe he can't help himself now, but I feel it's wrong. Nothing can't beat that ar out o' me. Sich a faithful crittur as ye've been—and allers sot his business 'fore yer own every way—and reckoned on him more than yer own wife and chil'ren! Them as sells heart's love and heart's blood, to get out thar scrapes, de Lord'll be up to 'em!"

"Chloe! now, if ye love me, ye won't talk so, when perhaps jest the last time we'll ever have together! And I'll tell ye, Chloe, it goes agin me to hear one word agin mas'r. Warn't he put in my arms a baby?—it's natur' I should think a heap of him. And he couldn't be spected to think so much of poor Tom. Mas'rs is used to havin' all these yer things done for 'em, and nat'lly they don't think so much on't. They can't be spected to, no way. Set him 'longside of other mas'rs—who's had the treatment and the livin' I've had? And he never would have let this yer come on me, if he could have seed it aforehand. I know he wouldn't."

"Wal, any way, thar's wrong about it *somewhar*," said Aunt Chloe, in whom a stubborn sense of justice was a predominant trait: "I can't jest make whar 'tis, but thar's wrong somewhar, I'm *clar* o' that."

"Yer ought ter look up to the Lord above—He's above all thar don't a sparrow fall without Him."

"It don't seem to comfort me, but I spect it orter," said Aunt Chloe. "But dar's no use talkin'; I'll jest wet up de corn-cake, and get ye one good breakfast, 'cause nobody knows when you'll get another."

The simple morning meal now smoked on the table, for Mrs Shelby had excused Aunt Chloe's attendance at the great house that morning. The poor soul had expended all her little energies on this farewell feast—had killed and dressed her choicest chicken, and prepared her corn-cake with scrupulous exactness, just to her husband's taste, and brought out certain mysterious jars on the mantelpiece, some preserves that were never produced except on extreme occasions.

"Now," said Aunt Chloe, bustling about after breakfast, "I must put up yer clothes. Jest like as not, he'll take 'em all away. I know thar ways mean as dirt, they is! Wal, now, yer flannels for rhumatis is in this corner; so be careful, 'cause there won't nobody make ye no more. Then here's yer old shirts, and these yer is new ones. I toed off these yer stockings last night, and put de ball in 'em to mend with. But Lor! who'll ever mend for ye?" and Aunt Chloe, again overcome, laid her head on the box side, and sobbed. "To think on't! no crittur to do for ye, sick or well! I don't railly think I ought ter be good now!"

The boys, having eaten everything there was on the breakfast-table, began now to take some thought of the case; and, seeing their mother crying, and their father looking very sad, began to whimper and put their hands to their eyes. Uncle Tom had the baby on his knee, and was letting her enjoy herself to the utmost extent, scratching his face and pulling his hair, and occasionally breaking out into clamorous explosions of delight, evidently arising out of her own internal reflections.

"Ay, crow away, poor crittur!" said Aunt Chloe; "ye'll have to come to it, too! ye'll live to see yer husband sold, or mebbe be sold yerself; and these yer boys, they's to be sold, I s'pose, too, jest like as not, when dey gets good for somethin'; ain't no use in niggers havin' nothing'!"

Here one of the boys called out, "Thar's missis a-comin' in!"

"She can't do no good; what's she coming for?" said Aunt Chloe.

Mrs Shelby entered. Aunt Chloe set a chair for her in a manner decidedly gruff and crusty. She did not seem to notice either the action or the manner. She looked pale and anxious.

"Tom," she said, "I come to—" and stopping suddenly, and regarding the silent group, she sat down in the chair, and, covering her face with her handkerchief, began to sob.

"Lor, now, missis, don't—don't!" said Aunt Chloe, bursting out in her turn; and for a few moments they all wept in company.

"My good fellow," said Mrs Shelby, "I can't give you anything to do you any good. If I give you money, it will only be taken from you. But I tell you solemnly, and before God, that I will keep trace of you, and bring you back as soon as I can command the money; and, till then, trust in God!"

Here the boys called out that Mas'r Haley was coming, and then an unceremonious kick pushed open the door. Haley stood there in very ill humour, having ridden hard the night before, and being not at all pacified by his ill success in recapturing his prey.

"Come," said he, "ye nigger, ye'r ready? Servant, ma'am!" said he, taking off his hat, as he saw Mrs Shelby.

Aunt Chloe shut and corded the box, and, getting up, looked gruffly on the trader, her tears seeming suddenly turned to sparks of fire.

Tom rose up meekly to follow his new master, and raised up his heavy box on his shoulder. His wife took the baby in her arms to go with him to the wagon, and the children, still crying, trailed on behind.

A crowd of all the old and young hands on the place stood gathered around it, to bid farewell to their old associate. Tom had been looked up to, both as a head servant and a Christian teacher, by all the place, and there was much honest sympathy and grief about him, particularly among the women.

"Get in!" said Haley to Tom, as he strode through the crowd of servants, who looked at him with lowering brows.

Tom got in, and Haley, drawing out from under the wagon seat a heavy pair of shackles, made them fast around each ankle.

A smothered groan of indignation ran through the whole circle, and Mrs Shelby spoke from the verandah:

"Mr Haley, I assure you that precaution is entirely unnecessary."

"Do'n know, ma'am; I've lost one five hundred dollars from this yer place, and I can't afford to run no more risks."

"What else could she spect on him?" said Aunt Chloe indignantly, while the two boys, who now seemed to comprehend at once their father's destiny, clung to her gown, sobbing and groaning vehemently.

"I'm sorry," said Tom, "that Mas'r George happened to be away."

George had gone to spend two or three days with a companion on a neighbouring estate, and having departed early in the morning, before Tom's misfortune had been made public, had left without hearing of it.

"Give my love to Mas'r George," he said earnestly.

Haley whipped up the horse, and, with a steady, mournful look, fixed to the last on the old place, Tom was whirled away.

Tom and Haley rattled on along the dusty road, whirling past every old familiar spot, until the bounds of the estate were fairly passed, and they found themselves out on the open pike. After they had ridden about a mile, Haley suddenly drew up at the door of a blacksmith's shop, when, taking out with him a pair of handcuffs, he stepped into the shop, to have a little alteration in them.

"These yer's a little too small for his build," said Haley, showing the fetters, and pointing out to Tom.

"Lor! now, if thar an't Shelby's Tom. He han't sold him, now?" said the smith.

"Yes, he has," said Haley.

"Now, ye don't! well, reely," said the smith, "who'd a thought it! Why, ye needn't go to fetterin' him up this yer way. He's the faithfullest, best crittur—"

"Yes, yes," said Haley; "but yer good fellers are just the criturs to want ter run off. Them stupid ones, as doesn't care whar they go, and shif'less, drunken ones, as don't care for nothin', they'll stick by, and like as not be rather pleased to be toted round; but these yer prime fellers, they hates it like sin. No way but to fetter 'em; got legs—they'll use 'em—no mistake."

"Well," said the smith, feeling among his tools, "them plantations down thar, stranger, an't jest the place a Kentuck nigger wants to go to; they dies thar tol'able fast, don't they? A feller can't help thinkin' it's a mighty pity to have a nice, quiet, likely feller, as good un as Tom is, go down to be fairly ground up on one of them ar sugar plantations."

"Wal, he's got a fa'r chance. I promised to do well by him. I'll get him in house servant in some good old family, and then, if he stands the fever and 'climating, he'll have a berth good as any nigger ought ter ask for."

"He leaves his wife and chil'en up here, s'pose?"

"Yes; but he'll get another thar. Lord, thar's women enough everywhar," said Haley.

Tom was sitting very mournfully on the outside of the shop while this conversation was going on. Suddenly he heard the quick, short click of a horse's hoof behind him; and, before he could fairly awake from his surprise, young Master George sprang into the wagon, threw his arms tumultuously round his neck, and was sobbing and scolding with energy.

"I declare, it's real mean! I don't care what they say, any of 'em! It's a nasty, mean shame! If I was a man, they shouldn't do it—they should not, *so*!" said George, with a kind of subdued howl.

"Oh! Mas'r George! this does me good!" said Tom, "I couldn't bar to go off without seein' ye! It does me real good, ye can't tell!" Here Tom made some movement of his feet, and George's eye fell on the fetters.

"What a shame!" he exclaimed, lifting his hands. "I'll knock that old fellow down—I will!"

"No, you won't, Mas'r George; and you must not talk so loud. It won't help me any, to anger him."

"Well, I won't, then, for your sake; but only to think of it—isn't it a shame? They never sent for me, nor sent me any word, and, if it hadn't been for Tom Lincoln, I shouldn't have heard it. I tell you, I blew 'em up well, all of 'em, at home!"

"That ar wasn't right, I'm 'feard, Mas'r George."

"Can't help it! I say it's a shame! Look here, Uncle Tom," said he, turning his back to the shop, and speaking in a mysterious tone, "*I've brought you my dollar!*"

"Oh I couldn't think o' takin' on't, Masr' George, no ways in the world!" said Tom, quite moved.

"But you *shall* take it!" said George; "look here—I told Aunt Chloe I'd do it, and she advised me just to make a hole in it, and put a string through, so you could hang it round your neck, and keep it out of sight; else this mean scamp would take it away. I tell ye, Tom, I want to blow him up! it would do me good!"

"No, don't, Mas'r George, for it won't do *me* any good."

"Well, I won't, for your sake," said George, busily tying his dollar round Tom's neck; "but there, now, button your coat tight over it, and keep it, and remember, every time you see it, that I'll come down after you, and bring you back. Aunt Chloe and I have been talking about it. I told her not to fear; I'll see to it, and I'll tease father's life out if he don't do it."

"Oh! Mas'r George, ye mustn't talk so 'bout yer father!"

"Lor, Uncle Tom, I don't mean anything bad."

"And now, Mas'r George," said Tom, "ye must be a good boy; 'member how many hearts is sot on ye. Al'ays keep close to yer mother. Don't be gettin' into any of them foolish ways boys has of gettin' too big to mind their mothers. Tell ye what, Mas'r George, the Lord gives good many things twice over; but he don't give ye a mother but once. Ye'll never see sich another woman, Mas'r George, if ye live to be a hundred years old. So, now, you hold on to her, and grow up and be a comfort to her, that's my own good boy—you will, now, won't ye?"

"Yes, I will, Uncle Tom," said George seriously.

"And be careful of yer speaking, Mas'r George. Young boys, when they comes to your age, is wilful, sometimes—it's natur' they should be. But real gentlemen, such as I hopes you'll be, never lets fall no words that isn't 'spectful to thar parents. Ye an't 'fended, Mas'r George?"

"No, indeed, Uncle Tom; you always did give me good advice."

"I's older, ye know," said Tom, stroking the boy's fine curly head with his large, strong hand, but speaking in a voice as tender as a woman's, "and I sees all that's bound up in you. Oh, Mas'r George, you has everything—larnin', privileges, readin', writin'— and you'll grow up to be a great, learned, good man, and all the people on the place and your mother and father'll be so proud on ye! Be a good mas'r, like yer father; and be a Christian, like yer mother. 'Member yer Creator in the days o' yer youth, Mas'r George."

"I'll be *real* good, Uncle Tom, I tell you," said George. "I'm going to be a *first-rater*; and don't you be discouraged. I'll have you back to the place yet. As I told Aunt Chloe this morning, I'll build your house all over, and you shall have a room for a parlour with a carpet on it, when I'm a man. Oh, you'll have good times yet!"

Haley now came to the door, with the handcuffs in his hands.

"Look here, now, Mister," said George, with an air of great superiority, as he got out, "I shall let father and mother know how you treat Uncle Tom!"

"You're welcome," said the trader.

"I should think you'd be ashamed to spend all your life buying men and women, and chaining them, like cattle! I should think you'd feel mean!" said George.

"So long as your grand folks wants to buy men and women, I'm as good as they is," said Haley, "'tan't any meaner sellin' on 'em, than 'tis buyin'!"

"I'll never do either, when I'm a man," said George; "I'm ashamed, this day, that I'm a Kentuckian. I always was proud of it before ... Well, good-bye, Uncle Tom; keep a stiff upper lip."

"Good-bye, Mas'r George," said Tom, looking fondly and admiringly at him. "God Almighty bless you! Ah! Kentucky han't got many like you!" he said, in the fullness of his heart, as the frank, boyish face was lost to his view. Away he went, and Tom looked till the clatter of his horse's heels died away—the last sound or sight of his home. But over his heart there seemed to be a warm spot, where those young hands had placed that precious dollar. Tom put up his hand, and held it close to his heart.

11

In Disguise

I T WAS late in a drizzly afternoon that a traveller alighted at the door of a small country hotel, in the village of N—, in Kentucky. In the bar-room he found assembled quite a miscellaneous company, whom stress of weather had driven to harbour, and the place presented the usual scenery of such reunions. Great, tall, raw-boned Kentuckians, attired in hunting-shirts, and trailing their loose joints over a vast extent of territory, with the easy lounge peculiar to the race—rifles stacked away in the corner, shot-pouches, game-bags, hunting-dogs, and little negroes, all rolled together in the corners—were the characteristic features in the picture. At each end of the fireplace sat a long-legged gentleman, with his chair tipped back, his hat on his head, and the heels of his muddy boots reposing sublimely on the mantelpiece.

Mine host, who stood behind the bar, like most of his countrymen, was great of stature, good-natured, and loose-jointed, with an enormous shock of hair on his head, and a great tall hat on the top of that.

Into such an assembly of the free-and-easy our traveller entered. He was a short, thick-set man, carefully dressed, with a round, good-natured countenance, and something rather fussy and particular in his appearance. He was very careful of his valise and umbrella, bringing them in with his own hands, and resisting, pertinaciously, all offers from the various servants to relieve him of them. He looked round the bar-room with rather an anxious air, and, retreating with his valuables to the warmest corner, disposed them under his chair, sat down, and looked rather apprehensively up at the worthy whose heels illustrated the end of the mantelpiece, who was spitting from right to left with a courage and energy rather alarming to gentlemen of weak nerves and particular habits.

"I say, stranger, how are ye?" said the aforesaid gentleman, firing an honorary salute of tobacco juice in the direction of the new arrival.

"Well, I reckon," was the reply of the other, as he dodged, with some alarm, the threatening honour.

"Any news?" said the respondent, taking out a strip of tobacco and a large hunting-knife from his pocket.

"Not that I know of," said the man.

"Chaw?" said the first speaker, handing the old gentleman a bit of his tobacco, with a decidedly brotherly air.

"No, thank ye—it don't agree with me," said the little man, edging off.

"Don't, eh?" said the other, easily, and stowing away the morsel in his own mouth.

The old gentleman uniformly gave a little start whenever his long-sided brother fired in his direction; and this being observed by his companion, he very good-naturedly turned his artillery to another quarter, and proceeded to storm one of the fire-irons with a degree of military talent fully sufficient to take a city.

"What's that?" said the old gentleman, observing some of the company formed into a group around a large handbill.

"Nigger advertised!" said one of the company, briefly.

Mr Wilson, for that was the old gentleman's name, rose up, and, after carefully adjusting his valise and umbrella, proceeded deliberately to take out his spectacles and fix them on his nose; and, this operation being performed, read as follows:

"Ran away from the subscriber, my mulatto boy, George. Said George six feet in height, a very light mulatto, brown curly hair; is very intelligent, speaks handsomely, can read and write; will probably try to pass for a white man; is deeply scarred on his back and shoulders; has been branded in his right hand with the letter H.

"I will give four hundred dollars for him alive, and the same sum for satisfactory proof that he has been killed."

The old gentleman read this advertisement from end to end, in a low voice, as if he were studying it.

The long-legged veteran, who had been besieging the fireiron, as before related, now took down his cumbrous length, and rearing aloft his tall form, walked up to the advertisement, and very deliberately spat a full discharge of tobaccojuice on it.

"There's my mind upon that!" said he, briefly, and sat down again.

"Why, now, stranger, what's that for?" said mine host.

"I'd do it all the same to the writer of that ar paper, if he was here," said the long man, coolly resuming his old employment of cutting tobacco. "Any man that owns a boy like that, and can't find any better way o' treating on him *deserves* to lose him. Such papers as these is a shame to Kentucky; that's my mind right out, if anybody wants to know!"

"Well, now, that's a fact," said mine host, as he made an entry in his book.

"I've got a gang of boys, sir," said the long man, resuming his attack on the fire-irons, "and I jest tell 'em—"Boys," says I, "*run* now! dig! put! jest when ye want to! I never shall come to look after you!" That's the way I keep mine. Let 'em know they are free to run any time, and it jest breaks up their wantin' to. Mor'n all, I've got free papers for 'em all recorded, in case I gets keeled up any o' these times, and they knows it; and I tell ye, stranger, there an't a fellow in our parts get more out of his niggers than I do. Treat 'em like dogs, and you'll have dogs' works and dogs' actions. Treat 'em like men, and you'll have men's works." And the honest drover, in his warmth, endorsed this moral sentiment by firing a perfect *feu de joie* at the fireplace.

"I think you're altogether right, friend," said Mr Wilson; "and this boy described here is a fine fellow—no mistake about that. He worked for me some half dozen years in my bagging factory, and he was my best hand, sir. He is an ingenious fellow, too; he invented a machine for the cleaning of hemp a really valuable affair; it's gone into use in several factories. His master holds the patent of it."

"I'll warrant ye," said the drover, "holds it and makes money out of it, and then turns round and brands the boy in his right hand. If I had a fair chance I'd mark him, I reckon, so that he'd carry it *one* while."

Here the conversation was interrupted by the approach of a small one-horse buggy to the inn. It had a genteel appearance, and a well-dressed, gentlemanly man sat on the seat, with a coloured servant driving.

The whole party examined the newcomer with the interest with which a set of loafers in a rainy day usually examine every newcomer. He was very tall, with a dark, Spanish complexion, fine, expressive black eyes, and close-curling hair, also of a glossy blackness. His well-formed aquiline nose, straight thin lips, and the admirable contour of his finely-formed limbs, impressed the whole company instantly with the idea of something uncommon. He walked easily in among the company, and with a nod indicated to his waiter where to place his trunk, bowed to the company, and, with his hat in his hand, walked up leisurely to the bar, and gave in his name as Henry Butler, Oaklands, Shelby County. Turning, with an indifferent air, he sauntered up to the advertisement and read it over.

"Jim," he said to his man, "seems to me we met a boy something like this up at Bernan's, didn't we?"

"Yes, mas'r," said Jim, "only I an't sure about the hand." "Well, I didn't look, of course," said the stranger, with a careless yawn. Then, walking up to the landlord, he desired him to furnish him with a private apartment, as he had some writing to do immediately.

The landlord was all obsequiousness, and a relay of about seven negroes, old and young, male and female, little and big, were soon whizzing about like a covey of partridges, bustling, hurrying, treading on each other's toes, and tumbling over each other in their zeal to get mas'r's room ready, while he seated himself easily on a chair in the middle of the room, and entered into conversation with the man who sat next to him.

The manufacturer, Mr Wilson, from the time of the entrance of the stranger, had regarded him with an air of disturbed and uneasy curiosity. He seemed to himself to have met and been acquainted with him somewhere, but he could not recollect. Every few moments, when the man spoke, or moved, or smiled, he would start and fix his eyes on him, and then suddenly withdraw them, as the bright, dark eyes met his with such unconcerned coolness. At last a sudden recollection seemed to flash upon him, for he stared at the stranger with such an air of blank amazement and alarm, that he walked up to him.

"Mr Wilson, I think," said he, in a tone of recognition, and extending his hand. "I beg your pardon, I didn't recollect you before. I see you remember me—Mr Butler of Oaklands, Shelby County."

"Ye—yes—yes, sir," said Mr Wilson, like one speaking in a dream.

Just then a negro boy entered and announced that mas'r's room was ready.

"Jim, see to the trunks," said the gentleman negligently; then addressing himself to Mr Wilson, he added—"I should like to have a few moments' conversation with you on business, in my room, if you please."

Mr Wilson followed him as one who walks in his sleep; and they proceeded to a large upper chamber, where a newmade fire was crackling, and various servants flying about, putting finishing touches to the arrangements.

When all was done, and the servants departed, the young man deliberately locked the door, and putting the key in his pocket, faced about, and folding his arms on his bosom, looked Mr Wilson full in the face.

"George!" said Mr Wilson.

"Yes, George," said the young man.

"I couldn't have thought it!"

"I am pretty well disguised, I fancy," said the young man with a smile. "A little walnut bark has made my yellow skin a genteel brown, and I've dyed my hair black; so you see I don't answer to the advertisement at all."

"Oh, George! but this is a dangerous game you are playing. I could not have advised you to it."

"I can do it on my own responsibility," said George, with the same proud smile.

We remark, *en passant*, that George was, by his father's side, of white descent. His mother was one of those unfortunates of her race, marked out by personal beauty to be the slave of the passions of her possessor, and the mother of children who may never know a father. From one of the proudest families in Kentucky he had inherited a set of fine European features, and a high, indomitable spirit. From his mother he had received only a slight mulatto tinge, amply compensated by its accompanying rich, dark eye.

Mr Wilson, a good-natured but extremely fidgety and cautious old gentleman, ambled up and down the room.

"Well, George, I s'pose you're running away—leaving your lawful master, George—(I don't wonder at it)—at the same time, I'm sorry, George—yes, decidedly—I think I must say that, George—it's my duty to tell you so."

"Why are you sorry, sir?" said George calmly.

"Why, to see you, as it were, setting yourself in opposition to the laws of your country."

"My country!" said George, with a strong and bitter emphasis; "what country have I but the grave—and I wish to God that I was laid there! Mr Wilson, you have a country, but what country have I, or anyone like me, born of slave mothers? What laws are there for us? We don't make them—we don't consent to them—we have nothing to do with them; all they do for us is to crush us and keep us down."

"George, this is bad. I must tell you, you know, as a friend, you'd better not be meddling with such notions; they are bad, George, very bad, for boys in your condition—very;" and Mr Wilson sat down to a table, and began nervously chewing the handle of his umbrella.

"See here, now, Mr Wilson," said George, coming up and sitting himself determinately down in front of him; "look at me, now. Don't I sit before you, every way, just as much a man as you are? Look at my face—look at my hands—look at my body," and the young man drew himself up proudly; "why am I *not* a man as much as anybody? Well, Mr Wilson, hear what I can tell you. I had a father—one of your Kentucky gentlemen—who didn't think enough of me to keep me from being sold with his dogs and horses, to satisfy the estate, when he died. I saw my mother put up at sheriff's sale, with her seven children. They were sold before her eyes, one by one, all to different masters; and I was the youngest. She came and kneeled down before old mas'r, and begged him to buy her with me, that she might have at least one child with her; and he kicked her away with his heavy boot. I saw him do it; and the last that I heard was her moans and screams, when I was tied to his horse's neck, to be carried off to his place."

"Well, then?"

"My master traded with one of the men, and bought my oldest sister. She was a pious, good girl—a member of the Baptist church—and as handsome as my poor mother had been. She was well brought up, and had good manners. At first I was glad the was bought, for I had one friend near me. I was soon sorry for it. Sir, I have stood at the door and heard her whipped, when it seemed as if every blow

cut into my naked heart, and I couldn't do anything to help her; and
she was whipped, sir, for wanting to live a decent Christian life,
such as your laws give no slave girl a right to live; and at last I saw
her chained with a trader's gang, to be sent to market in Orleans—
sent there for nothing else but that—and that's the last I know of
her. Well, I grew up—long years and years—no father, no mother,
no sister, not a living soul that cared for me more than a dog; nothing
but whipping, scolding, starving. Why, sir, I've been so hungry that
I have been glad to take the bones they threw to their dogs; and yet,
when I was a little fellow, and lain awake whole nights and cried, it
wasn't the hunger, it wasn't the whipping I cried for. No, sir; it was
for *my mother and my sisters*—it was because I hadn't a friend to
love me on earth. I never knew what peace or comfort was. I never
had a kind word spoken to me till I came to work in your factory. Mr
Wilson, you treated me well; you encouraged me to do well, and to
learn to read and write, and to try to make something of myself; and
God knows how grateful I am for it. Then, sir, I found my wife,
you've seen her—you know how beautiful she is. When I found she
loved me, when I married her, I scarcely could believe I was alive, I
was so happy; and, sir, she is as good as she is beautiful. But now
what? Why, now comes my master, takes me right away from my
work, and my friends, and all I like, and grinds me down in the very
dirt! And why? Because, he says, I forgot who I was; he says, to teach
me that I am only a nigger! After all, and last of all, he comes between
me and my wife, and says I shall give her up, and live with another
woman. And all this your laws give him power to do, in spite of God
or man. Mr Wilson, look at it! There isn't *one* of all these things that
have broken the hearts of my mother, and my sister, and my wife,
and myself, but your laws allow, and give every man power to do, in
Kentucky, and none can say to him nay! Do you call these the laws of
my country? Sir, I haven't any country, any more than I have any
father. But I am going to have one. I don't want anything of your
country, except to be let alone—to go peaceably out of it; and when
I get to Canada, where the laws will own me and protect me, *that*
shall be my country, and its laws I will obey. But if any man tries to
stop me, let him take care, for I am desperate. I'll fight for my liberty
to the last breath I breathe. You say your fathers did it; if it was right
for them, it is right for me!"

This speech, delivered partly while sitting at the table, and partly walking up and down the room—delivered with tears, and flashing eyes, and despairing gestures—was altogether too much for the good-natured old body to whom it was addressed, who had pulled out a great yellow silk pockethandkerchief and was mopping up his face with great energy.

"Blast 'em all!" he suddenly broke out. "Haven't I always said so—the infernal old cusses! I hope I an't swearing now. Well! go ahead, George, go ahead; but be careful, my boy; don't shoot anybody, George, unless—well—you'd *better* not shoot, I reckon; at least, I wouldn't *hit* anybody, you know. Where is your wife, George?" he added, as he nervously rose and began walking the room.

"Gone, sir, gone, with her child in her arms, the Lord only knows where—gone after the north star; and when we ever meet, or whether we meet at all in this world, no creature can tell."

"Is it possible? Astonishing! from such a kind family?"

"Kind families get in debt, and the laws of our country allow them to sell the child out of its mother's bosom to pay its master's debts," said George bitterly.

"Well, well," said the honest old man, fumbling in his pocket. "I s'pose, perhaps, I an't following my judgement—hang it, I *won't* follow my judgement!" he added suddenly; "so here, George," and taking out a roll of bills from his pocket-book, he offered them to George.

"No; my kind, good sir!" said George; "you've done a great deal for me, and this might get you into trouble. I have money enough, I hope, to take me as far as I need it."

"No! but you must, George. Money is a great help everywhere; can't have too much, if you get it honestly. Take it—*do* take it, *now*—do, my boy!"

"On condition, sir, that if I may repay it at some future time, I will," said George, taking up the money.

"And now, George, how long are you going to travel in this way?—not long or far, I hope. It's well carried on, but too bold. And this black fellow—who is he?"

"A true fellow, Jim Selden, who went to Canada more than a year ago. He heard, after he got there, that his master was so angry at him for going off, that he had whipped his poor old mother; and he has come all the way back to comfort her, and get a chance to get her away."

"Has he got her?"

"Not yet; he has been hanging about the place, and found no chance yet. Meanwhile he is going with me as far as Ohio, to put me among friends that helped him, and then he will come back after her."

"Dangerous, very dangerous," said the old man.

George drew himself up, and smiled disdainfully.

The old gentleman eyed him from head to foot, with a sort of innocent wonder.

"George, something has brought you out wonderfully. You hold up your head, and speak and move like another man," said Mr Wilson.

"Because I'm a *free* man!" said George proudly. "Yes, sir; I've said mas'r for the last time to any man. *I'm free!*"

"Take care! You are not sure—you may be taken."

"All men are free and equal *in the grave*, if it comes to that, Mr Wilson," said George.

"I'm perfectly dumfoundered with your boldness!" said Mr Wilson—"to come right here to the nearest tavern!"

"Mr Wilson, it is *so* bold, and this tavern is so near, that they will never think of it; they will look for me on ahead, and you yourself wouldn't know me. Jim's master don't live in this country; he isn't known in these parts. Besides, he is given up—nobody is looking after him; and nobody will take me up from the advertisement, I think."

"But the mark in your hand?"

George drew off his glove, and showed a newly healed scar in his hand.

"That is a parting proof of Mr Harris's regard," he said scornfully. "A fortnight ago he took it into his head to give it to me, because he said he believed I should try to get away one of these days. Looks interesting, doesn't it?" he said, drawing his glove on again.

"I declare, my very blood runs cold when I think of it—your conditions and your risks!" said Mr Wilson.

"Mine has run cold a good many years, Mr Wilson; at present, it's about up to the boiling point," said George.

"Well, my good sir," continued George, after a few moments' silence, "I saw you knew me; I thought I'd just have this talk with you, lest your surprised looks should bring me out. I leave early tomorrow morning, before daylight; by tomorrow night I hope to sleep safe in Ohio. I shall travel by daylight, stop at the best hotels, go to the dinner tables with the lords of the land. So, good-bye, sir; if you hear that I'm taken, you may know that I'm dead!"

George stood up like a rock, and put out his hand with the air of a prince. The friendly little old man shook it heartily, and after a little shower of caution, he took his umbrella, and began to fumble his way out of the room.

"Mr Wilson, one word more," called out George. "I want to ask one last deed of Christian kindness of you. I am running a dreadful risk. There isn't on earth a living soul to care if I die," he added, drawing his breath hard and speaking with a great effort. "I shall be kicked out and buried like a dog, and nobody'll think of it a day after—*only my poor wife*! Poor soul! she'll mourn and grieve; and if you'd only contrive, Mr Wilson, to send this little pin to her. She gave it to me for a Christmas present, poor child! Give it to her, and tell her I loved her to the last. Will you? *Will* you?" he added earnestly.

"Yes, certainly—poor fellow!" said the old gentleman, taking the pin, with watery eyes.

"Tell her one thing," said George; "it's my last wish, if she *can* get to Canada, to go there. No matter how kind her mistress is—no matter how much she loves her home; beg her not to go back—for slavery always ends in misery. Tell her to bring up her boy a free man, and then he won't suffer as I have. Tell her this, Mr Wilson, will you?"

"Yes, George, I'll tell her; but I trust you won't die; take heart—you're a brave fellow. Trust in the Lord, George, I wish in my heart you were safe through, though—that's what I do."

12

On Board

MR HALEY and Tom jogged onward in their wagon, each, for a time, absorbed in his own reflections.

Then Mr Haley pulled out of his pocket sundry newspapers, and began looking over their advertisements with absorbed interest. He was not a remarkably fluent reader, and was in the habit of reading in a sort of recitative half-aloud, by way of calling in his ears to verify the deductions of his eyes. In this tone he slowly recited the following paragraph:

"Executor's Sale.—Negroes!—Agreeably to order of court, will be sold, on Tuesday, February 20, before the Court-house door, in the town of Washington, Kentucky, the following negroes: Hagar, aged 60; John, aged 30; Ben, aged 21; Saul, aged 25; Albert, aged 14. Sold for the benefit of the creditors and heirs of the estate of Jesse Blutchford, Esq.

"Samuel Morris,
"Thomas Flint, } *Executors*."

"This yer I must look at," said he to Tom, for want of somebody else to talk to. "Ye see, I'm going to get up a prime gang to take down with ye, Tom; it'll make it sociable and pleasant like—good company will, ye know. We must drive right to Washington first and foremost, and then I'll clap you into jail while I does the business."

Tom received this agreeable intelligence quite meekly; simply wondering, in his own heart, how many of these doomed men had wives and children, and whether they would feel as he did about leaving them. It is to be confessed, too, that the naive, off-hand information that he was to be thrown into jail by no means produced an agreeable impression on a poor fellow who had always prided himself on a strictly honest and upright course of life. Yes, Tom, we must confess it, was rather proud of his honesty, poor fellow—not having very much else to be proud of; if he had belonged to some of the higher walks of society, he perhaps never would have been reduced to such straits. However, the day wore on, and the evening saw Haley and Tom comfortably accommodated in Washington—the one in a tavern, and the other in a jail.

A few days saw Haley, with his new possessions, safely deposited on one of the Ohio boats. It was the commencement of his gang, to be augmented, as the boat moved on, by various other merchandise of the same kind, which he, or his agent, had stored for him in various points along shore.

The *La Belle Rivière*, as brave and beautiful a boat as ever walked the waters of her namesake river, was floating gaily down the stream, under a brilliant sky, the Stripes and Stars of free America waving and fluttering overhead; the guards crowded with well-dressed ladies and gentlemen walking and enjoying the delightful day. All was full of life, buoyant and rejoicing—all but Haley's gang, who were stored, with other freight, on the lower deck, and who, somehow, did not seem to appreciate their various privileges, as they sat in a knot, talking to each other in low tones.

"Boys," said Haley, coming up briskly, "I hope you keep up good heart, and are cheerful. Now, no sulks, ye see; keep a stiff upper lip, boys; do well by me, and I'll do well by you."

The boys addressed responded the invariable "Yes, mas'r", for ages the watchword of poor Africa; but it is to be owned they did not look particularly cheerful.

Men talked, and loafed, and read, and smoked. Women sewed, and children played, and the boat passed on her way.

13

Among Friends

A QUIET scene now rises before us. A large, roomy, neatly-painted kitchen, its yellow floor glossy and smooth, and without a particle of dust; a neat, well-blacked cooking-stove; rows of shining tin, suggestive of unmentionable good things to the appetite; glossy green wood chairs, old and firm; a small flat-bottomed rocking-chair, with a patchwork cushion in it, neatly contrived out of small pieces of different coloured woollen goods, and a larger-sized one, motherly and old, whose wide arms breathed hospitable invitation, seconded by the solicitation of its feather cushions—a real comfortable, persuasive old chair, and worth, in the way of honest, homely enjoyment, a dozen of your plush or brocatelle drawing-room gentry; and in the chair, gently swaying back and forward, her eyes bent on some fine sewing, sat our old friend Eliza. Yes, there she is, paler and thinner than in her Kentucky home, with a world of quiet sorrow lying under the shadow of her long eyelashes, and marking the outline of her gentle mouth! It was plain to see how old and firm the girlish heart was grown under the discipline of heavy sorrow; and when, anon, her large dark eye was raised to follow the gambols of her little Harry, who was sporting, like some tropical butterfly, hither and thither over the floor, she showed a depth of firmness and steady resolve that was never there in her earlier and happier days.

By her side sat a woman with a bright tin pan in her lap, into which she was carefully sorting some dried peaches. She might be fifty-five or sixty; but hers was one of those faces that time seems to touch only to brighten and adorn. The snowy lisse crape cap, made after the straight Quaker pattern—the plain white muslin handkerchief, lying in placid folds across her bosom—the drab shawl and dress—showed at once the community to which she belonged. Her face was round and rosy, with a healthful downy softness suggestive of a ripe peach. Her hair, partially silvered by age, was parted smoothly back from a high, placid forehead; and beneath shone a large pair of clear, honest, loving brown eyes; you only needed to look straight into them to feel that you saw to the bottom of a heart as good and true as ever throbbed in woman's bosom.

"And so thee still thinks of going to Canada, Eliza?" she said, as she was quietly looking over her peaches.

"Yes, ma'am," said Eliza firmly. "I must go onward. I dare not stop."

"And what'll thee do, when thee gets there? Thee must think about that, my daughter."

"My daughter" came naturally from the lips of Rachel Halliday; for hers was just the face and form that made "mother" seem the most natural word in the world.

Eliza's hands trembled, and some tears fell on her fine work; but she answered firmly—

"I shall do—anything I can find. I hope I can find something."

"Thee knows thee can stay here as long as thee pleases," said Rachel.

"Oh, thank you," said Eliza; "but"—she pointed to Harry—"I can't sleep nights; I can't rest. Last night I dreamed I saw that man coming into the yard," she said, shuddering.

"Poor child!" said Rachel, wiping her eyes; "but thee mustn't feel so. The Lord hath ordered it so that never hath a fugitive been stolen from our village. I trust thine will not be the first."

The door here opened, and a little short, round, pincushiony woman stood at the door, with a cheery, blooming face, like a ripe apple. She was dressed, like Rachel, in sober grey, with the muslin folded neatly across her round, plump little chest.

"Ruth Stedman," said Rachel, coming joyfully forward; "how is thee, Ruth?" she said, heartily taking both her hands.

"Nicely," said Ruth, taking off her little drab bonnet, and dusting it with her handkerchief, displaying, as she did so, a round little head, on which the Quaker cap sat with a sort of jaunty air, despite all the stroking and patting of the small fat hands, which were busily applied to arranging it.

"Ruth, this friend is Eliza Harris; and this is the little boy I told thee of."

"I'm glad to see thee, Eliza—very," said Ruth, shaking hands, as if Eliza were an old friend she had long been expecting; "and this is thy dear boy—I brought a cake for him," she said, holding out a little heart to the boy, who came up gazing through his curls, and accepted it shyly.

"Where's thy baby, Ruth?" said Rachel.

"Oh, he's coming; but thy Mary caught him as I came in, and ran off with him to the barn, to show him to the children."

At this moment the door opened, and Mary, an honest, rosy-looking girl, with large brown eyes, like her mother's, came in with the baby.

"Ah! ha!" said Rachel, coming up, and taking the great, white, fat fellow in her arms; "how good he looks, and how he does grow!"

"To be sure, he does," said little bustling Ruth, as she took the child, and began taking off a little blue silk hood, and various layers and wrappers of outer garments; and having given a twitch here, and a pull there, and variously adjusted and arranged him, and kissed him heartily, she set him on the floor to collect his thoughts. Baby seemed quite used to this mode of proceeding, for he put his thumb in his mouth (as if it were quite a thing of course), and seemed soon absorbed in his own reflections, while the mother seated herself, and taking out a long stocking of mixed blue and white yarn, began to knit with briskness.

"Mary, thee'd better fill the kettle, hadn't thee?" gently suggested the mother.

Mary took the kettle to the well, and soon reappearing, placed it over the stove, where it was soon purring and steaming. The peaches, moreover, in obedience to a few gentle whispers from Rachel, were soon deposited, by the same hand, in a stew-pan over the fire.

Rachel now took down a snowy moulding-board, and tying on an apron, proceeded quietly to making up some biscuits, first saying to Mary—"Mary, hadn't thee better tell John to get a chicken ready?" and Mary disappeared as Simeon Halliday, a tall, straight, muscular man, in drab coat and pantaloons, and broad-brimmed hat, now entered.

"How is thee, Ruth?" he said warmly, as he spread his broad open hand for her little fat palm; "and how is John?"

"Oh! John is well, and all the rest of our folks," said Ruth cheerily.

"Any news, father?" said Rachel, as she was putting her biscuits into the oven.

"Peter Stebbins told me that they should be along tonight,

with *friends*," said Simeon significantly, as he was washing his hands at a neat sink, in a little back porch.

"Indeed!" said Rachel, looking thoughtfully, and glancing at Eliza.

"Did thee say thy name was Harris?" said Simeon to Eliza, as he re-entered.

Rachel glanced quickly at her husband, as Eliza tremulously answered "Yes"; her fears, ever uppermost, suggesting that possibly there might be advertisements out for her.

"Mother!" said Simeon, standing in the porch, and calling Rachel out.

"What does thee want, father?" said Rachel, rubbing her fioury hands, as she went into the porch.

"This child's husband is in the settlement, and will be here tonight," said Sirneon.

"Now, thee doesn't say that, father?" said Rachel, all her face radiant with joy.

"It's really true. Peter was down yesterday with the wagon, to the other stand, and there he found an old woman and two men, and one said his name was George Harris; and from what he told of his history, I am certain who he is. He is a bright, likely fellow, too. Shall we tell her now?" said Simeon.

"Let's tell Ruth," said Rachel. "Here, Ruth—come here."

Ruth laid down her knitting-work, and was in the back porch in a moment.

"Ruth, what does thee think?" said Rachel. "Father says Eliza's husband is in the last company, and will be here tonight."

A burst of joy from the little Quakeress interrupted the speech. She gave such a bound from the floor, as she clapped her little hands, that two stray curls fell from under her Quaker cap, and lay brightly on her white neckerchief.

"Hush thee, dear!" said Rachel gently; "hush, Ruth! Tell us, shall we tell her now?"

"Now! to be sure—this very minute. Why, now, suppose 'twas my John, how should I feel? Do tell her, right off."

"Thee uses thyself only to learn how to love thy neighbour, Ruth," said Simeon, looking with a beaming face on Ruth.

"To be sure. Isn't it what we are made for? If I didn't love John and the baby, I should not know how to feel for her. Come, now, do tell her—do!" and she laid her hands persuasively on Rachel's arm. "Take her into thy bedroom, there, and let me fry the chicken while thee does it."

Rachel came out into the kitchen, where Eliza was sewing, and opening the door of a small bedroom, said, gently, "Come in here with me, my daughter; I have news to tell thee."

"I should pay my fine," said Simeon quietly.

"But what if they put thee in prison?"

"Couldn't thee and mother manage the farm?" said Simeon, smiling.

"Mother can do almost everything," said the boy. "But isn't it a shame to make such laws?"

"Thee mustn't speak evil of thy rulers, Simeon," said his father gravely. "The Lord only gives us our wordly goods that we may do justice and mercy; if our rulers require a price of us for it, we must deliver it up."

"Well, I hate those old slaveholders!" said the boy, who felt as unchristian as became any modern reformer.

"I am surprised at thee, son," said Simeon; "thy mother never taught thee so. I would do even the same for the slaveholder as for the slave, if the Lord brought him to my door in affliction."

Simeon the second blushed scarlet; but his mother only smiled, and said, "Simeon is my good boy; he will grow older by and by, and then he will be like his father."

"I hope, my good sir, that you are not exposed to any difficulty on our account," said George anxiously.

"Fear nothing, George, for therefore are we sent into the world. If we would not meet trouble for a good cause, we were not worthy of our name."

"But for me," said George, "I could not bear it."

"Fear not, then, friend George; it is not for thee, but for God and man we do it," said Simeon. "And now thou must lie by quietly this day, and tonight, at ten o'clock, Phineas fletcher will carry thee onward to the next stand—thee and the rest of thy company. The pursuers are hard after thee; we must not delay."

"If that is the case, why wait till evening?" said George.

"Thou art safe here by daylight, for everyone in the settlement is a Friend, and all are watching. It has been found safer to travel by night."

14

Little Eva

THE MISSISSIPPI! The slanting light of the setting sun quivers on the sea-like expanse of the river; the shivery canes, and the tall, dark cypress, hung with wreaths of dark, funereal moss, glow in the golden ray, as the heavily-laden steamboat marches onward.

Piled with cotton-bales, from many a plantation, up over deck and sides, till she seems in the distance a square, massive block of grey, she moves heavily onward to the nearing mart. We must look some time among its crowded decks before we shall find again our humble friend Tom. High on the upper deck, in a little nook among the everywhere predominant cotton-bales, at last we may find him.

Partly from confidence inspired by Mr Shelby's representations, and partly from the remarkably inoffensive and quiet character of the man, Tom had insensibly won his way far into the confidence even of such a man as Haley.

At first he had watched him narrowly through the day, and never allowed him to sleep at night unfettered; but the uncomplaining patience and apparent contentment of Tom's manner led him gradually to discontinue these restraints, and for some time Tom had enjoyed a sort of parole of honour, being permitted to come and go freely where he pleased on the boat.

Ever quiet and obliging, and more than ready to lend a hand in every emergency which occurred among the workmen below, he had won the good opinion of all the hands, and spent many hours in helping them with as hearty a goodwill as ever he worked on a Kentucky farm.

When there seemed to be nothing for him to do, he would climb to a nook among the cotton-bales of the upper deck, and busy himself in studying over his Bible—and it is there we see him now.

For a hundred or more miles above New Orleans the river is

higher than the surrounding country, and rolls its tremendous
volume between massive levees twenty feet in height. The traveller
from the deck of the steamer, as from some floating castle-top,
overlooks the whole country for miles and miles around. Tom,
therefore, had spread out full before him, in plantation after
plantation, a map of the life to which he was approaching.

He saw the distant slaves at their toil; he saw afar their villages
of huts gleaming out in long rows on many a plantation distant
from the stately mansions and pleasure-grounds of the master;
and as the moving picture passed on, his poor, foolish heart would
be turning backward to the Kentucky farm, with its old shadowy
beeches—to the master's house, with its wide, cool halls, and,
near by, the little cabin, overgrown with the multiflora and
bignonia. There he seemed to see familiar faces of comrades,
who had grown up with him from infancy; he saw his busy wife,
bustling in her preparations for his evening meal; he heard the
merry laugh of his boys at their play, and the chirrup of the baby
at his knee: and then, with a start, all faded, and he saw again the
cane-brakes and cypresses and gliding plantations, and heard
again the creaking and groaning of machinery, all telling him too
plainly that all that phase of life had gone by for ever.

In such a case, you write to your wife, and send messages to
your children; but Tom could not write—the mail for him had
no existence, and the gulf of separation was unbridged by even a
friendly word or signal.

Is it strange, then, that some tears fall on the pages of his
Bible, as he lays it on the cotton-bale, and with patient finger,
threading his slow way from word to word, traces out its promises?
Having learned late in life, Tom was but a slow reader, and passed
on laboriously from verse to verse. Fortunate for him was it that
the book he was intent on was one which slow reading cannot
injure—nay, one whose words, like ingots of gold, seem often to
need to be weighed separately, that the mind may take in their
priceless value. Let us follow him a moment, as, pointing to each
word, and pronouncing each half aloud, he reads:

"Let—not—your—heart—be—troubled. In—my—Father's—
house—are—many—mansions. I—go—to—prepare—a—
place—for—you."

As for Tom's Bible, though it had no annotations and helps in margin from learned commentators, still it had been embellished with certain way-marks and guide-boards of Tom's own invention, and which helped him more than the most learned expositions could have done. It had been his custom to get the Bible read to him by his master's children, in particular by young Master George; and, as they read, he would designate, by bold, strong marks and dashes, with pen and ink, the passages which more particularly gratified his ear or affected his heart. His Bible was thus marked through, from one end to the other, with a variety of styles and designations; so he could in a moment seize upon his favourite passages without the labour of spelling out what lay between them; and while it lay there before him, every passage breathing of some old home scene, and recalling some past enjoyment, his Bible seemed to him all of this life that remained, as well as the promise of a future one.

Among the passengers on the boat was a young gentleman of fortune and family, resident in New Orleans, who bore the name of St. Clare. He had with him a daughter between five and six years of age, together with a lady who seemed to claim relationship to both, and to have the little one especially under her charge.

Tom had often caught glimpses of this little girl—for she was one of those busy, tripping creatures, that can be no more contained in one place than a sunbeam or a summer breeze— nor was she one that, once seen, could be easily forgotten.

But he watched the little lady a great deal before he ventured on any overtures towards acquaintanceship. He knew an abundance of simple acts to propitiate and invite the approaches of the little people, and he resolved to play his part right skilfully. He could cut cunning little baskets out of cherry-stones, could make grotesque faces on hickorynuts, or odd jumping figures out of elder pith, and he was a very Pan in the manufacture of whistles of all sizes and sorts. His pockets were full of miscellaneous articles of attraction, which he had hoarded in days of old for his master's children, and which he now produced, with commendable prudence and economy, one by one, as overtures for acquaintance and friendship.

The little one was shy, for all her busy interest in everything going on, and it was not easy to tame her. For a while, she would perch like a canary-bird on some box or package near Tom, while busy in the little arts aforenamed, and take from him, with a kind of grave bashfulness, the little articles he offered. But at last they got on quite confidential terms.

"What's little missy's name?" said Tom at last, when he thought matters were ripe to push such an inquiry.

"Evangeline St. Clare," said the little one, "though papa and everybody else call me Eva. Now, what's your name?"

"My name's Tom; the little chil'ren used to call me Uncle Tom, way back thar in Kentuck."

"Then I mean to call you Uncle Tom, because, you see, I like you," said Eva. "So, Uncle Tom, where are you going?"

"I don't know, Miss Eva."

"Don't know?" said Eva.

"No. I am going to be sold to somebody. I don't know who."

"My papa can buy you," said Eva quickly; "and if he buys you, you will have good times. I mean to ask him to, this very day."

"Thank you, my little lady," said Tom.

The boat here stopped at a small landing to take in wood, and Eva, hearing her father's voice, bounded nimbly away. Tom rose up, and went forward to offer his service in wooding, and soon was busy among the hands.

Eva and her father were standing together by the railings to see the boat start from the landing-place, the wheel had made two or three revolutions in the water, when, by some sudden movement, the little one suddenly lost her balance, and fell sheer over the side of the boat into the water. Her father, scarce knowing what he did, was plunging in after her, but was held back by some behind him, who saw that more efficient aid had followed his child.

Tom was standing just under her, on the lower deck, as she fell. He saw her strike the water, and sink, and was after her in a moment. A broad-chested, strong-armed fellow, it was nothing for him to keep afloat in the water, till, in a moment or two, the child rose to the surface, and he caught her in his arms, and, swimming with her to the boat-side, handed her up, all dripping, to the grasp of hundreds of hands, which, as if they had all

belonged to one man, were stretched eagerly out to receive her.
A few moments more, and her father bore her, dripping and
senseless, to the ladies' cabin, where, as is usual in cases of the
kind, there ensued a very well-meaning and kind-hearted strife
among the female occupants generally, as to who should do the
most things to make a disturbance, and to hinder her recovery
in every way possible.

*   *   *   *   *   *   *   *   *

IT WAS a sultry, close day, the next day, as the steamer drew
near to New Orleans. A general bustle of expectation and
preparation was spread through the boat; in the cabin, one and
another were gathering their things together, and arranging them,
preparatory to going ashore. The steward and chambermaid, and
all, were busily engaged in cleaning, furnishing, and arranging
the splendid boat, preparatory to a grand *entrée*.

On the lower deck sat our friend Tom, with his arms folded,
and anxiously, from time to time, turning his eyes towards a group
on the other side of the boat.

There stood the fair Evangeline, a little paler than the day
before, but otherwise exhibiting no traces of the accident which
had befallen her. A graceful, elegantly-formed young man stood
by her, carelessly leaning one elbow on a bale of cotton, while a
large pocket-book lay open before him. It was quite evident, at a
glance, that the gentleman was Eva's father. There was the same
noble cast of head, the same large blue eyes, the same golden-
brown hair; yet the expression was wholly different. In the large
clear blue eyes, though in form and colour exactly similar, there
was wanting that misty, dreamy depth of expression; all was clear,
bold, and bright, but with a light wholly of this world: the
beautifully-cut mouth had a proud and somewhat sarcastic
expression, while an air of free-and-easy superiority sat not
ungracefully in every turn and movement of his fine form. He
was listening, with a good-humoured, negligent air, half comic,
half contemptuous, to Haley.

"All the moral and Christian virtues bound in black morocco,
complete!" he said, when Haley had finished. "Well, now, my

good fellow, what's the damage, as they say in Kentucky; in short, what's to be paid out for this business? How much are you going to cheat me, now? Out with it!"

"Wal," said Haley, "if I should say thirteen hundred dollars for that ar fellow, I shouldn't but just save myself; I shouldn't now, raily."

Poor fellow!" said the young man, fixing his keen, mocking blue eye on him; "but I suppose you'd let me have him for that, out of a particular regard for me?"

"Well, the young lady here seems to be set on him, and nat'lly enough."

"Oh! certainly, there's a call on your benevolence, my friend. Now, as a matter of Christian charity, how cheap could you afford to let him go, to oblige a young lady that's particular set on him?"

"Wal, now, just think on't," said the trader; "just look at them limbs—broad-chested, strong as a horse. Look at his head; them high forrads allays shows calculatin' niggers, that'll do any kind o' thing. I've marked that ar. Now, a nigger of that ar heft and build is worth considerable, just, as you may say, for his body, supposin' he's stupid; but come to put in his calculatin' faculties, and them which I can show he has oncommon, why, of course, it makes him come higher. Why, that ar fellow managed his master's whole farm. He has a 'stror'nary talent for business."

"Bad, bad, very bad; knows altogether too much?" said the young man, with the same mocking smile playing about his mouth. "Never will do, in the world. Your smart fellows are always running off, stealing horses, and raising the devil generally. I think you'll have to take off a couple of hundred for his smartness."

"Wal, there might be something in that ar, if it warn't for his character; but I can show recommends from his master and others, to prove he is one of your real pious—the most humble, prayin', pious crittur ye ever did see. Why, he's been called a preacher in them parts he came from."

"And I might use him for a family chaplain, possibly," added the young man dryly. "That's quite an idea. Religion is a remarkably scarce article at our house."

If the trader had not been sure, by a certain good-humoured twinkle in the large blue eye, that all this banter was sure, in the long run, to turn out a cash concern, he might have been somewhat out of patience; as it was, he laid down a greasy pocket-book on the cotton-bales, and began anxiously studying over certain papers in it, the young man standing by, the while, looking down on him with an air of careless, easy drollery.

"Papa, do buy him! it's no matter what you pay," whispered Eva softly, getting up on a package, and putting her arm round her father's neck, "You have money enough, I know. I want him."

"What for, pussy? Are you going to use him for a rattle-box, or a rocking-horse, or what?"

"I want to make him happy."

"An original reason, certainly."

Here the trader handed up a certificate, signed by Mr Shelby, which the young man took with the tips of his long fingers, and glanced over carelessly.

"There, count your money, old boy!" he said, as he handed a roll of bills to the trader.

"All right," said Haley, his face beaming with delight; and pulling out an old inkhorn, he proceeded to fill out a bill of sale, which, in a few moments, he handed to the young man.

"I wonder, now, if I was divided up and inventoried," said the latter, as he ran over the paper, "how much I might bring. Say so much for the shape of my head, so much for a high forehead, so much for arms, and hands, and legs, and then so much for education, learning, talent, honesty, religion! Bless me! there would be small charge on that last, I'm thinking—But come, Eva," he said; and taking the hand of his daughter, he stepped across the boat, and carelessly putting the tip of his finger under Tom's chin, said good-humouredly, "Look up, Tom, and see how you like your new master."

Tom looked up. It was not in nature to look into that gay, young, handsome face, without a feeling of pleasure; and Tom felt the tears start in his eyes as he said, heartily, "God bless you, mas'r!"

"Well, I hope He will. What's your name? Tom? Quite as likely to do it for your asking as mine, from all accounts. Can you drive horses, Tom?"

"I've been allays used to horses," said Tom. "Mas'r Shelby raised heaps on 'em."

"Well, I think I shall put you in coachy, on condition that you won't be drunk more than once a week, unless in cases of emergency, Tom."

Tom looked surprised, and rather hurt, and said, "I never drink, mas'r."

"I've heard that story before, Tom; but then we'll see. It will be a special accommodation to all concerned, if you don't. Never mind, my boy," he added good-humouredly, seeing Tom still looked grave; "I don't doubt you mean to do well."

"I sartin do, mas'r," said Tom.

"And you shall have good times," said Eva. "Papa is very good to everybody, only he always will laugh at them."

"Papa is much obliged to you for his recommendations," said St. Clare, laughing, as he turned on his heel and walked away.

15

Uncle Tom's New Master

AUGUSTINE St. Clare was the son of a wealthy planter of Louisiana. The family had its origin in Canada.

His mother had been a woman of uncommon elevation and purity of character, and he gave to Eva his mother's name, fondly fancying that she would prove a reproduction of her image. The thing had been remarked with petulant jealousy by his wife, and she regarded her husband's absorbing devotion to the child with suspicion and dislike; all that was given to her seemed so much taken from herself. From the time of the birth of this child, her health gradually sunk.

There was no end to her various complaints; but her principal forte appeared to lie in sick-headache, which sometimes would confine her to her room three days out of six. As, of course, all family arrangements fell into the hands of servants, St. Clare found his *ménage* anything but comfortable. His only daughter was exceedingly delicate, and he feared that, with no one to look after her and attend to her, her health and life might yet fall a sacrifice to her mother's inefficiency. He had taken her with him on a tour to Vermont, and had persuaded his cousin, Miss Ophelia St. Clare, to return with him to his southern residence; and they are now returning on this boat, where we have introduced them to our readers.

And now the distant domes and spires of New Orleans rise to our view.

Miss Ophelia, as you now behold her, stands before you, in a very shining brown linen travelling-dress, tall, square-formed, and angular. Her face was thin, and rather sharp in its outlines; the lips compressed, like those of a person who is in the habit of making up her mind definitely on all subjects; while the keen, dark eyes had a peculiarly searching, advised movement, and travelled over everything, as if they were looking for something to take care of.

All her movements were sharp, decided, and energetic; and, though she was never much of a talker, her words were remarkably direct, and to the purpose, when she did speak.

But, how in the world can Miss Ophelia get along with Augustine St. Clare—gay, easy, unpunctual, unpractical, sceptical?

To tell the truth, then, Miss Ophelia loved him and she loved the lovely little girl; and though she regarded Augustine as very much of a heathen, yet she loved him, laughed at his jokes, and forebore with his failings, to an extent which those who knew him thought perfectly incredible.

There she is now, sitting in her stateroom, surrounded by a mixed multitude of little and big carpet-bags, boxes and baskets as the boat now began, with heavy groans, like some vast, tired monster, to prepare to push up among the multiplied steamers at the levee. Eva joyously pointed out the various spires, domes, and way-marks, by which she recognized her native city.

"Yes, yes, dear; very fine," said Miss Ophelia. "But mercy on us! the boat has stopped! Where is your father?"

And now ensued the usual turmoil of landing—waiters running twenty ways at once—men tugging trunks, carpetbags, boxes—women anxiously calling to their children, and everybody crowding in a dense mass to the plank towards the landing.

Miss Ophelia seated herself resolutely and marshalling all her goods and chattels in fine military order, seemed resolved to defend them to the last, wondering to Eva, in each interval, "what upon earth her papa could be thinking of; he couldn't have fallen over, now—but something must have happened"; and just as she had begun to work herself into a real distress, he came up, with his usually careless motion, and giving Eva a quarter of the orange he was eating, said:

"Well, Cousin Vermont, I suppose you are all ready?"

"I've been ready, waiting, nearly an hour," said Miss Ophelia; "I began to be really concerned about you."

"Well, the carriage is waiting, and the crowd are now off, so that one can walk out in a decent and Christian manner, and not be pushed and shoved. Here," he added to a driver who stood behind him, "take these things."

"I'll go and see to his putting them in," said Miss Ophelia. "Oh, pshaw, cousin, what's the use?" said St. Clare.

"Well, at any rate, I'll carry this, and this, and this," said Miss Ophelia, singling out three boxes and a small carpet-bag.

"My dear Miss Vermont, positively, you mustn't come the Green Mountains over us that way. You must adopt at least a piece of Southern principle, and not walk out under all that load; they'll take you for a waiting-maid. Give them to this fellow; he'll put them down as if they were eggs, now."

Miss Ophelia looked despairingly, as her cousin took all her treasures from her, and rejoiced to find herself once more in the carriage with them, in a state of preservation.

"Where's Tom?" said Eva.

"Oh, he's on the outside, pussy. I'm going to take Tom up to mother, for a peace-offering, to make up for that drunken fellow that upset the carriage."

"Oh, Tom will make a splendid driver, I know," said Eva; "he'll never get drunk."

The carriage stopped in front of an ancient mansion, built in that odd mixture of Spanish and French style, of which there are specimens in some parts of New Orleans.

Eva seemed like a bird ready to burst from a cage, with the wild eagerness of her delight.

"Oh, isn't it beautiful, lovely! my own dear, darling home!" she said to Miss Ophelia. "Isn't it beautiful?"

"'Tis a pretty place," said Miss Ophelia, as she alighted; "though it looks rather old and heathenish to me."

Tom got down from the carriage, and looked about with an air of calm, still enjoyment.

St. Clare smiled as Miss Ophelia made her remark on his premises, and, turning to Tom, who was standing looking round, his beaming black face perfectly radiant with admiration, he said:

"Tom, my boy, this seems to suit you."

"Yes, mas'r, it looks about the right thing," said Tom.

All this passed in a moment, while trunks were being hustled off, hackman paid, and while a crowd, of all ages and sizes— men, women, and children—came running through the galleries, both above and below, to see mas'r come in. Foremost among them was a highly-dressed young mulatto man, evidently a very *distingué* personage, attired in the ultra extreme of the mode, and gracefully waving a scented cambric handkerchief in his hand.

This personage had been exerting himself, with great alacrity, in driving all the flock of domestics to the other end of the verandah.

"Back, all of you! I am ashamed of you," he said in a tone of authority. "Would you intrude on master's domestic relations, in the first hour of his return?"

All looked abashed at this elegant speech, delivered with quite an air, and stood huddled together at a respectful distance, except two stout porters, who came up and began conveying away the baggage.

Owing to Mr Adolph's systematic arrangements, when St. Clare turned round from paying the hackman, there was nobody in view but Mr Adolph himself, conspicuous in satin vest, gold guard-chain, and white pants, and bowing with inexpressible grace and suavity.

"Ah, Adolph, is it you?" said his master, offering his hand to him; "how are you, boy?" while Adolph poured forth, with great fluency, an extemporary speech, which he had been preparing, with great care, for a fortnight before.

"Well, well," said St. Clare, passing on, with his usual air of negligent drollery, "that's very well got up, Adolph. See that the baggage is well bestowed. I'll come to the people in a minute;" and, so saying, he led Miss Ophelia to a large parlour that opened on to the verandah.

While this had been passing, Eva had flown like a bird, through the porch and parlour, to a little boudoir opening likewise on the verandah.

A tall, dark-eyed, sallow woman half-rose from a couch on which she was reclining.

"Mamma!" said Eva, in a sort of a rapture, throwing herself on her neck, and embracing her over and over again.

"That'll do—take care, child—don't, you make my head ache," said the mother, after she had languidly kissed her.

St. Clare came in, embraced his wife in true, orthodox, husbandly fashion, and then presented to her his cousin. Marie lifted her large eyes on her cousin with an air of some curiosity, and received her with languid politeness. A crowd of servants now pressed to the entry door, and among them a middle-aged mulatto woman, of very respectable appearance, stood foremost, in a tremor of expectation and joy, at the door.

"Oh, there's Mammy!" said Eva, as she flew across the room; and, throwing herself into her arms, she kissed her repeatedly.

This woman did not tell her that she made her head ache, but, on the contrary, she hugged her, and laughed, and cried, till her sanity was a thing to be doubted of; and when released from her, Eva flew from one to another, shaking hands and kissing, in a way that Miss Ophelia afterwards declared fairly turned her stomach.

"Well!" said Miss Ophelia, "you Southern children can do something that I couldn't."

"What, now, pray?" said St. Clare.

"Well, I want to be kind to everybody, and I wouldn't have anything hurt; but as to kissing

"Niggers," said St. Clare, "that you're not up to—hey?"

"Yes, that's it. How can she?"

St. Clare laughed, as he went into the passage. "Halloa, here, what's to pay out here? Here, you all—Mammy, Jimmy, Polly, Sukey—glad to see mas'r?" he said, as he went shaking hands from one to another. "Look out for the babies!" he added, as he stumbled over a sotty little urchin, who was crawling upon all-fours. "If I step upon anybody, let 'em mention it."

There was an abundance of laughing and blessing mas'r, as St. Clare distributed small pieces of change among them.

"Come, now, take yourselves off, like good boys and girls," he said; and the whole assemblage, dark and light, disappeared through a door into a large verandah, followed by Eva, who carried a large satchel, which she had been filling with apples, nuts, candy, ribbons, laces, and toys of every description, during the whole homeward journey.

As St. Clare turned to go back his eye fell upon Tom, who was standing uneasily, shifting from one foot to the other, while Adolph stood negligently leaning against the banisters, examining Tom through an opera-glass, with an air that would have done credit to any dandy living.

"Puh! you puppy," said his master, striking down the opera-glass; "is that the way you treat your company? Seems to me, Dolph," he added, laying his finger on the elegant figured satin vest that Adolph was sporting—"seems to me that's *my* vest."

"Oh! master, this vest all stained with wine; of course, a gentleman in master's standing never wears a vest like this. I understood I was to take it. It does for a poor nigger-fellow like me."

And Adolph tossed his head, and passed his fingers through his scented hair with a grace.

"So, that's it, is it?" said St. Clare carelessly. "Well, here, I'm going to show this Tom to his mistress, and then you take him to the kitchen; and mind you don't put on any of your airs to him. He's worth two such puppies as you."

"Master always will have his joke," said Adolph, laughing. "I'm delighted to see master in such spirits."

"Here, Tom," said St. Clare, beckoning.

Tom entered the room. He looked wistfully on the velvet carpets, and the before unimagined splendours of mirrors, pictures, statues, and curtains, and, like the Queen of Sheba before Solomon, there was no more spirit in him. He looked afraid even to set his feet down.

"See here, Marie," said St. Clare to his wife, "I've brought you a coachman at last, to order. I tell you, he's a regular hearse for blackness and sobriety, and will drive you like a funeral, if you want. Open your eyes, now, and look at him. Now, don't say I never think about you when I'm gone."

"Well, I hope he may turn out well," said the lady; "it's more than I expect, though."

"Dolph," said St. Clare, "show Tom downstairs; and mind yourself," he added; "remember what I told you."

Adolph tripped gracefully forward, and Tom, with lumbering tread, went after.

"Come, now, Marie," said St. Clare, seating himself on a stool beside her sofa, "be gracious, and say something pretty to a fellow."

"You've been gone a fortnight beyond the time," said the lady, pouting.

"Well, you know I wrote you the reason. See here, now," he added, drawing an elegant velvet case out of his pocket and opening it, "here's a present I got for you in New York."

It was a photograph, clear and soft as an engraving, representing Eva and her father sitting hand in hand.

Marie looked at it with a dissatisfied air.

"What made you sit in such an awkward position?" she said.

"Well, the position may be a matter of opinion; but what do you think of the likeness?"

"If you don't think anything of my opinion in one case, I suppose you wouldn't in another," said the lady, shutting the daguerreotype.

"Hang the woman!" said St. Clare mentally; but aloud he added, "Come, now, Marie, what do you think of the likeness? Don't be nonsensical, now."

"It's very inconsiderate of you, St. Clare," said the lady, "to insist on my talking and looking at things. You know I've been lying all day with the sick-headache; and there's been such a tumult made ever since you came, I'm half dead."

"You're subject to the sick-headache, ma'am?" said Miss Ophelia, suddenly rising from the depths of the large armchair, where she had sat quietly, taking an inventory of the furniture, and calculating its expense.

"Yes, I'm a perfect martyr to it," said the lady.

"Juniper-berry tea is good for sick-headache," said Miss Ophelia, "at least, Auguste, Deacon Abraham Perry's wife, used to say so; and she was a great nurse."

"I'll have the first juniper berries that get ripe in our garden by the lake brought in for that especial purpose," said St. Clare, gravely pulling the bell as he did so; "meanwhile, cousin, you must be wanting to retire to your apartment, and refresh yourself a little, after your journey—Dolph," he added, "tell Mammy to come here." The decent mulatto woman whom Eva had caressed so rapturously soon entered; she was dressed neatly, with a high red and yellow turban on her head, the recent gift of Eva, and which the child had been arranging on her head. "Mammy," said St. Clare, "I put this lady under your care; she is tired, and wants rest; take her to her chamber, and be sure she is made comfortable", and Miss Ophelia disappeared in the rear of Mammy.

16

Uncle Tom's New Mistress

"AND NOW, Marie," said St. Clare, "your golden days are dawning. Here is our practical, business-like New England cousin, who will take the whole budget of cares off your shoulders, and give you time to refresh yourself, and grow young and handsome. The ceremony of delivering the keys had better come off forthwith."

This remark was made at the breakfast-table, a few mornings after Miss Ophelia had arrived.

"I'm sure she's welcome," said Marie, leaning her head languidly on her hand. "I think she'll find one thing, if she does, and that is, that it's we mistresses that are the slaves down here."

"Oh, certainly, she will discover that, and a world of wholesome truths besides, no doubt," said St. Clare.

"Talk about our keeping slaves, as if we did it for our *convenience*," said Marie. "I'm sure, if we consulted *that*, we might let them all go at once."

Evangeline fixed her large, serious eyes on her mother's face, with an earnest and perplexed expression, and said, simply, "What do you keep them for, mamma?"

"I don't know, I'm sure, except for a plague; they are the plague of my life. I believe that more of my ill-health is caused by them than by any one thing; and ours, I know, are the very worst that ever anybody was plagued with."

"Oh, come, Marie, you've got the blues this morning," said St. Clare. "You know 'tisn't so. There's Mammy, the best creature living—what could you do without her?"

"Mammy is the best I ever knew," said Marie; "and yet Mammy, now, is selfish—dreadfully selfish; it's the fault of the whole race."

"Selfishness is a dreadful fault," said St. Clare gravely.

"Well, now, there's Mammy," said Marie, "I think it's selfish of her to sleep so sound at nights; she knows I need little attentions almost every hour, when my worst turns are on, and yet she's so hard to wake. I absolutely am worse, this very morning, for the efforts I had to make to wake her last night."

"Hasn't she sat up with you a good many nights lately, mamma?" said Eva.

"How should you know that?" said Marie sharply; "she's been complaining, I suppose."

"She didn't complain; she only told me what bad nights you'd had—so many in succession."

"Why don't you let Jane or Rosa take her place, a night or two," said St. Clare, "and let her rest?"

"How can you propose it?" said Marie. "St. Clare, you really are inconsiderate. So nervous as I am, the least breath disturbs me; and a strange hand about me would drive me absolutely frantic. If Mammy felt the interest in me she ought to, she'd wake easier—of course, she would. I've heard of people wno had such devoted servants, but it never was *my* luck"; and Marie sighed.

"Now Mammy has a *sort* of goodness," said Marie; "she's smooth and respectful, but she's selfish at heart. Now, she never will be done fidgeting and worrying about that husband of hers. You see, when I was married and came to live here, of course, I had to bring her with me, and her husband my father couldn't spare."

"Has she children?" said Miss Ophelia.

"Yes; she has two."

"I suppose she feels the separation from them?"

"Well, of course, I couldn't bring them. They were little dirty things—I couldn't have them about; and, besides, they took up too much of her time: but I believe that Mammy has always kept up a sort of sulkiness about this. She won't marry anybody else; and I do believe, now, though she knows how necessary she is to me, and how feeble my health is, she would go back to her husband tomorrow, if she only could. I *do*, indeed," said Marie; "they are just so selfish, now, the best of them."

"It's distressing to reflect upon," said St. Clare dryly.

Miss Ophelia looked keenly at him, and saw the sarcastic curl of the lip as he spoke.

"Now, Mammy has always been a pet with me," said Marie. "I

wish some of your Northern servants could look at her closets of dresses—silks and muslins, and one real linen cambric, she has hanging there. I've worked sometimes whole afternoons, trimming her caps, and getting her ready to go to a party. As to abuse, she don't know what it is. She never was whipped more than once or twice in her whole life. She has her strong coffee or her tea every day, with white sugar in it. It's abominable, to be sure; but St. Clare will have high life below-stairs, and they every one of them live just as they please. The fact is, our servants are over-indulged. I suppose it is partly our fault that they are selfish, and act like spoiled children, but I've talked to St. Clare till I am tired."

"And I, too," said St. Clare, taking up the morning paper.

Eva, the beautiful Eva, had stood listening to her mother, with that expression of deep and mystic earnestness which was peculiar to her. She walked softly round to her mother's chair, and put her arms round her neck.

"Well, Eva, what now?" said Marie.

"Mamma, couldn't I take care of you one night—just one? I know I shouldn't make you nervous, and I shouldn't sleep. I often lie awake nights, thinking—"

"Oh, nonsense, child—nonsense!" said Marie; "you are such a strange child!"

"But may I, mamma? I think," she said timidly, "that Mammy isn't well. She told me her head ached all the time, lately."

"Oh, that's just one of Mammy's fidgets! Mammy is just like all the rest of them—makes such a fuss about every little headache or fingerache; it'll never do to encourage it—never! I'm principled about this matter," said she, turning to Miss Ophelia; "you'll find the necessity of it. If you encourage servants in giving way to every little disagreeable feeling, and complaining of every little ailment, you'll have your hands full. I never complain myself—nobody knows what I endure. I feel it a duty to bear it quietly, and I do."

Miss Ophelia's round eyes expressed an undisguised amazement at this peroration, which struck St. Clare as so supremely ludicrous, that he burst into a loud laugh.

"St. Clare always laughs when I make the least allusion to my ill-health," said Marie, with the voice of a suffering martyr. "I only hope the day won't come when he'll remember it"; and Marie put her handkerchief to her eyes.

Of course, there was rather a foolish silence. finally, St. Clare got up, looked at his watch, and said he had an engagement down street. Eva tripped away after him, and Miss Ophelia and Marie remained at the table alone.

"Now, that's just like St. Clare!" said the latter, withdrawing her handkerchief with somewhat of a spirited flourish when the criminal to be affected by it was no longer in sight. "He never realizes—never can, never will—what I suffer, and have, for years. If I was one of the complaining sort, or ever made any fuss about my ailments, there would be some reason for it. Men do get tired, naturally, of a complaining wife. But I've kept things to myself, and borne, till St. Clare got in the way of thinking I can bear anything."

Miss Ophelia did not exactly know what she was expected to answer to this.

While she was thinking what to say, Marie gradually wiped away her tears, and smoothed her plumage in a general sort of way, as a dove might be supposed to make toilet after a shower, and began a housewifely chat with Miss Ophelia, concerning cupboards, closets, linen-presses, store-rooms, and other matters, of which the latter was, by common understanding, to assume the direction—giving her so many cautious directions and charges, that a head less systematic and business-like than Miss Ophelia's would have been utterly dizzied and confounded.

"And now," said Marie, "I believe I've told you everything; so that, when my next sick turns comes on, you'll be able to go forward entirely, without consulting me; only about Eva—she requires watching."

"She seems to be a good child—very," said Miss Ophelia; "I never saw a better child."

"Eva's peculiar," said her mother, "very. There are things about her so singular; she isn't like me, now, a particle"; and Marie sighed, as if this was a truly melancholy consideration.

Miss Ophelia in her own heart said, "I hope she isn't," but had prudence enough to keep it down.

"Eva always was disposed to be with servants; and I think that well enough with some children. Now, I always played with father's little negroes—it never did me any harm. But Eva somehow always seems to put herself on an equality with every creature that comes near her. It's a strange thing about the child. I never have been able to break her of it. St. Clare, I believe, encourages her in it. The fact is, St. Clare indulges every creature under this roof but his own wife."

Again Miss Ophelia sat in blank silence.

"Now, there's no way with servants," said Marie, "but to *put them down*, and keep them down. It was always natural to me, from a child. Eva is enough to spoil a whole houseful. What she will do when she comes to keep house herself, I'm sure I don't know. I hold to being *kind* to servants—I always am; but you must make 'em *know their place*. Eva never does; there's no getting into the child's head the first beginning of an idea what a servant's place is! You heard her offering to take care of me nights, to let Mammy sleep! That's just a specimen of the way the child would be doing all the time, if she was left to herself."

"Why," said Miss Ophelia bluntly, "I suppose you think your servants are human creatures, and ought to have some rest when they are tired?"

"Certainly, of course. I'm very particular in letting them have everything that comes convenient—anything that doesn't put one at all out of the way, you know. Mammy can make up her sleep, some time or other; there's no difficulty about that. She's the sleepiest concern that ever I saw; sewing, standing or sitting, that creature will go to sleep, and sleep anywhere and everywhere. No danger but Mammy gets sleep enough. But this treating servants as if they were exotic flowers, or china vases, is really ridicuious!"

Marie seemed wonderfully supported, always, when she got upon this topic; and she now opened her eyes, and seemed quite to forget her languor.

"You don't know, and you can't, the daily, hourly trials that beset a housekeeper from them, everywhere and every way. But it's no use to complain to St. Clair. He talks the strangest stuff. He says we have made them what they are, and ought to bear

with them. He says their faults are all owing to us, and that it
would be cruel to make the fault and punish it too. He says we
shouldn't do any better, in their place; just as if one could reason
from them to us, you know."

"Don't you believe that the Lord made them of one blood with
us?" said Miss Ophelia shortly.

"No, indeed not I! A pretty story, truly! They are a degraded
race"

"Don't you think they've got immortal souls?" said Miss
Ophelia, with increasing indignation.

"Oh, well," said Marie, yawning, "that, of course—nobody
doubts that. But as to putting them on any sort of equality with us,
you know, as if we could be compared, why, it's impossible! Now,
St. Clare has really talked to me as if keeping Mammy from her
husband was like keeping me from mine. There's no comparing
in this way. Mammy couldn't have the feelings that I should. It's a
different thing altogether—of course it is—and yet St. Clare
pretends not to see it. And just as if Mammy could love her little
dirty babies as I love Eva! Yet St. Clare once really and soberly
tried to persuade me that it was my duty, with my weak health, and
all I suffer, to let Mammy go back, and take somebody else in her
place. That was a little too much even for me to bear. I don't often
show my feelings. I make it a principle to endure everything in
silence; it's a wife's hard lot, and I bear it. But I did break out that
time; so that he has never alluded to the subject since."

Miss Ophelia looked very much as if she was afraid she should
say something; but she rattled away with her needles in a way
that had volumes of meaning in it, if Marie could only have
understood it.

"So, you just see," she continued, "what you've got to manage.
A household without any rule; where servants have it all their
own way, do what they please, and have what they please, except
so far as I, with my feeble health, have kept up government. I
keep my cowhide about, and sometimes I do lay it on; but the
exertion is always too much for me. If St. Clare would only have
this thing done as others do—"

"And how's that?"

"Why, send them to the calaboose, or some of the other places, to be flogged. That's the only way. If I wasn't such a poor, feeble piece, I believe I should manage with twice the energy that St. Clare does."

"And how does St. Clare contrive to manage?" said Miss Ophelia. "You say he never strikes a blow."

"Well, men have a more commanding way, you know; it is easier for them, besides, if you ever looked full in his eye, it's peculiar— that eye—and if he speaks decidedly, there's a kind of flash. I'm afraid of it myself; and the servants know they must mind. I couldn't do as much by a regular storrn and scolding as St. Clare can by one turn of his eye, if once he is in earnest. Oh, there's no trouble about St. Clare; that's the reason he's no more feeling for me. But you'll find, when you come to manage, that there's no getting along without severity—they are so bad, so deceitful, so lazy."

"The old tune," said St. Clare, sauntering in. "What an awful account these wicked creatures will have to settle, at last, especially for being lazy! You see, cousin," said he, as he stretched himself at full length on a lounge opposite to Marie, "it's wholly inexcusable in them, in the light of the example that Marie and I set them—this laziness."

"Come now, St. Clare, you are too bad!" said Marie.

"Am I, now? Why, I thought I was talking good, quite remarkably for me. I try to enforce your remarks, Marie, always."

"You do really try to be provoking," said Marie.

"Oh, come, Marie, the day is growing warm, and I have just had a long quarrel with Dolph, which has fatigued me excessively; so pray be agreeable, now, and let a fellow repose in the light of your smile."

"What's the matter about Dolph?" said Marie. "That fellow's impudence has been growing to a point that is perfectly intolerable to me."

"What you say, my dear, is marked with your usual acuteness and good sense," said St. Clare. "As to Dolph, the case is this: that he has so long been engaged in imitating my graces and perfections, that he has, at last, really mistaken himself for his master; and I have been obliged to give him a little insight into his mistake."

"How?" said Marie.

"Why, I was obliged to let him understand explicitly that I preferred to keep *some* of my clothes for my own personal wearing; also, I put his magnificence upon an allowance of cologne-water, and actually was so cruel as to restrict him to one dozen of my cambric handkerchiefs. Dolph was particularly huffy about it, and I had to talk to him like a father to bring him round."

"Oh, St. Clare, when will you learn how to treat your servants? It's aborninable, the way you indulge them!" said Marie.

"Why, after all, what's the harm of the poor dog's wanting to be like his master; and if I haven't brought him up any better than to find his chief good in cologne and cambric handkerchiefs, why shouldn't I give them to him?"

"And why haven't you brought him up better?" said Miss Ophelia, with blunt determination.

"Too much trouble; laziness, cousin, laziness—which ruins more souls than you can shake a stock at."

"I think you slaveholders have an awful responsibility upon you," said Miss Ophelia. "I wouldn't have it for a thousand worlds. You ought to educate your slaves, and treat them like reasonable creatures."

"Oh, come, come," said St. Clare, getting up quickly; "what do you know about us?" And he sat down to the piano, and rattled a lively piece of music. St. Clare had a decided genius for music. His touch was brilliant and firm, and his fingers flew over the keys with a rapid and bird-like motion, airy and yet decided. He played piece after piece, like a man who is trying to play himself into a good humour. After pushing the music aside, he rose up, and said gaily, "Well, now, cousin, you've given us a good talk, and done your duty; on the whole I think the better of you for it. I make no manner of doubt that you threw a very diamond of truth at me, though you see it hit me so directly in the face that it wasn't exactly appreciated at first."

"For my part, I don't see any use in such sort of talk," said Marie. "I'm sure, if anybody does more for servants than we do, I'd like to know who; and it don't do 'em a bit good—not a particle—they get worse and worse. As to talking to them, or anything like that, I'm sure I have talked till I was tired and hoarse, telling them their duty, and all that; and I am sure they can go to church when they like, though they don't understand a word of the sermon, more than so many pigs—so it isn't of any great use for them to go, as I see; but they do go, and so they have every chance; but, as I said before, they are a degraded race, and always will be, and there isn't any help for them: you can't make anything of them, if you try. You see, Cousin Ophelia, I've tried, and you haven't: I was born and bred among them, and I know."

Miss Ophelia thought she had said enough, and therefore sat silent. St. Clare whistled a tune.

A gay laugh from the court rang through the silken curtains of the verandah. St. Clare stepped out, and, lifting up the curtain, laughed too.

"What is it?" said Miss Ophelia, coming to the railing.

There sat Tom, on a little mossy seat in the court, every one of his button-holes stuck full of Cape jessamines, and Eva, gaily laughing, was hanging a wreath of roses round his neck; and then she sat down on his knee, like a chip-sparrow, still laughing.

"Oh, Tom, you look so funny!"

Tom had a sober, benevolent smile, and seemed, in his quiet way, to be enjoying the fun quite as much as his little mistress. He lifted his eyes, when he saw his master, with a half-deprecating, apologetic air.

"How can you let her?" said Miss Ophelia.

"Why not?" said St. Clare.

"Why, I don't know, it seems so dreadful!"

"You would think no harm in a child's caressing a large dog, even if he was black; but a creature that can think, and reason, and feel, and is immortal, you shudder at; confess it, cousin."

"Well, cousin," said Mis Ophelia thoughtfully, "there may be some truth in this."

"What would the poor and lowly do without children?" said St. Clare, leaning on the railing, and watching Eva, as she tripped off, leading Tom with her.

It was some time later that he found Tom and Eva in grave and anxious discussion before Tom's slate, composing between them a letter to Chloe, asking when his redemption money could be raised.

Tom's letter was written in due form for him that evening by St. Clare himself, and safely lodged in the post-office.

17

George Hits Out

THERE was a gentle bustle at the Quaker house, as the afternoon drew to a close. Rachel Halliday moved quietly to and fro, collecting from her household stores such needments as could be arranged in the smallest compass, for the wanderers who were to go forth that night. The afternoon shadows stretched eastward, and the round red sun stood thoughtfully on the horizon, and his beams shone yellow and calm into the little bedroom where George and his wife were sitting. He was sitting with his child on his knee, and his wife's hand in his. Both looked thoughtful and serious, and traces of tears were on their cheeks.

"Yes, Eliza," said George, "I know all you say is true. You are a good child—a great deal better than I am; and I will try to do as you say. I'll try to act worthy of a free man. I'll try to feel like a Christian. God Almighty knows that I've meant to do well—tried hard to do well—when everything has been against me; and now I'll forget all the past, and put away every hard and bitter feeling, and read my Bible, and learn to be a good man."

"And when we get to Canada," said Eliza, "I can help you. I can do dressmaking very well; and I understand fine washing and ironing; and between us we can find something to live on."

"Yes, Eliza, so long as we have each other and our boy. Oh! Eliza, if these people only knew what a blessing it is for a man to feel that his wife and child belong to *him*! I've often wondered to see men that could call their wives and children *their own* fretting and worrying about anything else. Why, I feel rich and strong, though we have nothing but our bare hands. I feel as if I could scarcely ask God for any more. Yes, though I've worked hard every day, till I am twenty-five years old, and have not a cent of money, nor a roof to cover me, nor a spot of land to call my own, yet, if they will only let me alone now, I will be satisfied—thankful; I will work, and send back the money for you and my boy. As to my old master, he has been paid five times over for all he ever spent for me. I don't owe him anything."

"But yet we are not quite out of danger," said Eliza; "we are not yet in Canada."

"True," said George, "but it seems as if I smelled the free air, and it makes me strong."

At this moment, voices were heard in the outer apartment in earnest conversation, and very soon a rap was heard on the door. Eliza started and opened it.

Simeon Halliday was there, and with him a Quaker brother, whom he introduced as Phineas fletcher. Phineas was tall and lathy, red-haired, with an expression of great acuteness and shrewdness in his face.

"Our friend Phineas has discovered something of importance to the interests of thee and thy party, George," said Simeon; "it were well for thee to hear it."

"That I have," said Phineas, "and it shows the use of a man's always sleeping with one ear open, in certain places, as I've always said. Last night I stopped at a little lone tavern back on the road. Thee remembers the place, Simeon, where we sold some apples, last year, to that fat woman, with the great earrings. Well, I was tired with hard driving; and, after my supper, I stretched myself down on a pile of bags in the corner, and pulled a buffalo over me, to wait till my bed was ready; and what does I do but get fast asleep."

"With one ear open, Phineas?" said Simeon quietly.

"No; I slept, ears and all, for an hour or two, for I was pretty well tired; but when I came to myself a little, I found that there were some men in the room, sitting round a table, drinking and talking; and I thought, before I made much muster, I'd just see what they were up to, especially as I heard them say something about the Quakers. "So," says one, "they are up in the Quaker settlement, no doubt," says he. Then I listened with both ears, and I found that they were talking about this very party. So I lay and heard them lay off all their plans. This young man, they said, was to be sent back to Kentucky, to his master, who was going to make an example of him, to keep all niggers from running away; and his wife two of them were going to run down to New Orleans to sell, on their own account, and they calculated to get sixteen or eighteen hundred dollars for her; and the child, they said, was going to a trader, who had bought him; and then there was the boy, Jim, and his mother, they were to go back to their masters in Kentucky. They said that there were two constables, in a town a little piece ahead, who would go in with 'em to get 'em taken up, and the young woman was to be taken before a judge; and one of the fellows, who is small and smooth-spoken, was to swear to her for his property, and get her delivered over to him to take South. They've got a right notion of the track we are going tonight; and they'll be down after us, six or eight strong. So, now, what's to be done?"

The group that stood in various attitudes, after this communication, were worthy of a painter. Rachel Halliday, who had taken her hands out of a batch of biscuits to hear the news, stood with them upraised and floury, and with a face of the deepest concern. Simeon looked profoundly thoughtful, Eliza had thrown her arms around her husband, and was looking up to him. George stood with clenched hands and glowing eyes, and looking as any other man might look, whose wife was to be sold at auction, and son sent to a trader, all under the shelter of a Christian nation's laws.

"What *shall* we do, George?" said Eliza faintly.

"I know what I shall do," said George, as he stepped into the little room, and began examining his pistols.

"Ay, ay," said Phineas, nodding his head to Simeon; "thou seest, Simeon, how it will work."

"I see," said Simeon, sighing: "I pray it come not to that."

"I don't want to involve anyone with or for me," said George. "If you will lend me your vehicle and direct me, I will drive alone to the next stand. Jim is a giant in strength, and brave as death and despair, and so am I."

"Ah, well, friend," said Phineas, "but thee'll need a driver, for all that. Thee's quite welcome to do all the fighting, thee knows; but I know a thing or two about the road that thee doesn't."

"But I don't want to involve you," said George.

"Involve!" said Phineas, with a curious and keen expression of face. "When thee does involve me, please to let me know."

"Phineas is a wise and skilful man," said Simeon. "Thee does well, George, to abide by his judgement; and," he added, laying his hand kindly on George's shoulder, and pointing to the pistols, "be not over-hasty with these—young blood is hot."

"I will attack no man," said George. "All I ask of this country is to be let alone, and I will go out peaceably."

"Friend Phineas will ever have ways of his own," said Rachel Halliday, smiling; "but we all think that his heart is in the right place, after all."

"Well," said George, "isn't it best that we hasten our flight?"

"I got up at four o'clock, and came on with all speed, full two or three hours ahead of them, if they start at the time they planned. It isn't safe to start till dark, at any rate; for there are some evil persons in the villages ahead, that might be disposed to meddle with us, if they saw our wagon, and that would delay us more than the waiting; but in two hours I think we may venture. I will go over to Michael Cross, and engage him to come behind on his swift nag, and keep a bright look-out on the road, and warn us if any company of men come on. Michael keeps a horse that can soon get ahead of most other horses; and he could shoot ahead and let us know, if there were any danger. I am going now to warn Jim and the old woman to be in readiness, and to see about the horse. We have a pretty fair start, and stand a good chance to get to the stand before they can come up with us. So, have good courage, friend George; this isn't the first ugly scrape that I've been in," said Phineas, as he closed the door.

"Phineas is pretty shrewd," said Simeon. "He will do the best that can be done for thee, George."

"All I am sorry for," said George, "is the risk to you."

"Thee'll much oblige us, friend George, to say no more about that. What we do we are conscience bound to do; we can do no other way.—And now, mother," said he, turning to Rachel, "hurry thy preparations for these friends, for we must not send them away fasting."

While Rachel and her children were busy making corn-cake, and cooking ham and chicken, and hurrying on the *et ceteras* of the evening meal, George and his wife sat in their little room, with their arms folded about each other, in such talk as husband

and wife have when they know that a few hours may part them for ever.

"Eliza," said George, "people that have friends, and houses, and lands, and money, and all those things, *can't* love as we do, who have nothing but each other. Till I knew you, Eliza, no creature ever had loved me, but my poor, heartbroken mother and sister. I saw poor Emily that morning the trader carried her off. She came to the corner where I was lying asleep, and said, "Poor George, your last friend is going. What will become of you, poor boy?" And I got up and threw my arms round her, and cried and sobbed, and she cried too; and those were the last kind words I got for ten long years; and my heart all withered up, and felt as dry as ashes, till I met you. And your loving me—why, it was almost like raising one from the dead! I've been a new man ever since. And now, Eliza, I'll give my last drop of blood, but they *shall not* take you from me. Whoever gets you must walk over my dead body."

"O Lord, have mercy!" said Eliza, sobbing. "If He will only let us get out of this country together, that is all we ask."

And now Rachel took Eliza's hand kindly, and led the way to the supper-table. As they were sitting down, a light tap sounded at the door, and Ruth entered.

"I just ran in," she said, "with these little stockings for the boy—three pair, nice, warm woollen ones. It will be so cold, thee knows, in Canada. Does thee keep up good courage, Eliza?" she added, tripping round to Eliza's side of the table, and shaking her warmly by the hand, and slipping a seed-cake into Harry's hand. "I brought a little parcel of these for him," she said, tugging at her pocket to get at the package. "Children, thee knows, will always be eating."

"Oh, thank you; you are too kind," said Eliza.

"Come, Ruth, sit down to supper," said Rachel.

"I couldn't, any way. I left John with the baby, and some biscuits in the oven; and I can't stay a moment, else John will burn up all the biscuits, and give the baby all the sugar in the bowl. That's the way he does," said the little Quakeress, laughing. "So, good-bye, Eliza; good-bye, George; the Lord grant thee a safe journey;" and, with a few tripping steps, Ruth was out of the apartment.

A little while after supper, a large covered wagon drew up before
the door; the night was clear starlight; and Phineas jumped briskly
down from his seat to arrange his passengers. George walked
out of the door, with his child on one arm and his wife on the
other. His step was firm, his face settled and resolute. Rachel
and Simeon came out after them.

"You get out, a moment," said Phineas to those inside, "and
let me fix the back of the wagon, there, for the womenfolks and
the boy."

"Here are the two buffaloes," said Rachel. "Make the seats as
comfortable as may be; it's hard riding all night."

Jim came out first, and carefully assisted out his old mother,
who clung to his arm, and looked anxiously about as if she
expected the pursuer every moment.

"Jim, are your pistols all in order?" said George, in a low, firm
voice.

"Yes, indeed," said Jim.

"And you've no doubt what you shall do, if they come?"

"I rather think I haven't," said Jim, throwing open his broad
chest, and taking a deep breath. "Do you think I'll let them get
mother again?"

During this brief colloquy, Eliza had been taking her leave of
her kind friend, Rachel, and was handed into the carriage by
Simeon, and creeping into the back part with her boy, sat down
among the buffalo-skins. The old woman was next handed in
and seated, and George and Jim placed on a rough board seat
front of them, and Phineas mounted in front.

"Farewell, my friends," said Simeon, from without.

"God bless you!" answered all from within.

And the wagon drove off, rattling and jolting over the frozen
road.

There was no opportunity for conversation, on account of the
roughness of the way and the noise of the wheels. On, on, on
they jogged, hour after hour. The child soon fell asleep, and lay
heavily in his mother's lap. The poor, frightened old woman at
last forgot her fears; and even Eliza, as the night waned, found
all her anxieties insufficient to keep her eyes from closing.
Phineas seemed, on the whole, the briskest of the company, and

beguiled his long drive with whistling certain very un-Quaker-like songs, as he went on.

But about three o'clock, George's ear caught the hasty and decided click of a horse's hoof coming behind them at some distance, and jogged Phineas by the elbow. Phineas pulled up his horses, and listened.

"That must be Michael," he said; "I think I know the sound of his gallop;" and he rose up and stretched his head anxiously back over the road.

A man riding in hot haste was now dimly descried at the top of a distant hill.

"There he is, I do believe!" said Phineas. George and Jim both sprang out of the wagon, before they knew what they were doing. All stood intensely silent, with their faces turned towards the expected messenger. On he came. Now he went down into a valley, where they could not see him; but they heard the sharp, hasty tramp, rising nearer and nearer; at last they saw him emerge on the top of an eminence, within hail.

"Yes, that's Michael!" said Phineas, and, raising his voice "Holloa, there, Michael!"

"Phineas, is that thee?"

"Yes; what news—they coming?"

"Right on behind, eight or ten of them, hot with brandy, swearing and foaming like so many wolves."

And, just as he spoke, a breeze brought the faint sound of galloping horsemen towards them.

"In with you—quick, boys, *in!*" said Phineas. "If you must fight, wait till I get you a piece ahead." And, with the word, both jumped in, and Phineas lashed the horses to a run, the horseman keeping close beside them. The wagon rattled, jumped, almost flew, over the frozen ground; but plainer, and still plainer, came the noise of pursuing horsemen behind. The women heard it, and, looking anxiously out, saw, far in the rear, on the brow of a distant hill, a party of men looming up against the red-streaked sky of early dawn. Another hill, and their pursuers had evidently caught sight of their wagon, whose white, cloth-covered top made it conspicuous at some distance, and a loud yell of brutal triumph came forward on the wind. Eliza sickened, and strained her child closer to her bosom; the old woman prayed and groaned, and George and Jim clenched their pistols with the grasp of despair. The pursuers gained on them fast; the carriage made a sudden turn, and brought them near a ledge of a steep, overhanging rock, that rose in an isolated ridge or clump in a large lot, which was, all around it, quite clear and smooth. This isolated pile, or range of rocks, rose up black and heavy against the brightening sky, and seemed to promise shelter and concealment. It was a place well known to Phineas, who had been familiar with the spot in his hunting days; and it was to gain this point he had been racing his horses.

"Now for it!" said he, suddenly checking his horses, and springing from his seat to the ground. "Out with you, in a twinkling, every one, and up into these rocks with me. Michael, thee tie thy horse to the wagon, and drive ahead to Amariah's, and get him and his boys to come back and talk to these fellows."

In a twinkling they were all out of the carriage.

"There," said Phineas, catching up Harry, "you, each of you, see to the women; and run, *now*, if you ever *did* run!"

There needed no exhortation. Quicker than we can say it, the whole party were over the fence, making with all speed for the rocks, while Michael, throwing himself from his horse, and fastening the bridle to the wagon, began driving it rapidly away.

"Come ahead!" said Phineas, as they reached the rocks, and saw, in the mingled starlight and dawn, the traces of a rude but plainly-marked footpath leading up among them; "this is one of our old hunting-dens. Come up!"

Phineas went before, springing up the rocks like a goat, with the boy in his arms. Jim came second, bearing his trembling old mother over his shoulder; and George and Eliza brought up the rear. The party of horsemen came up to the fence, and, with mingled shouts and oaths, were dismounting, to prepare to follow them. A few moments' scrambling brought them to the top of the ledge; the path then passed between a narrow defile, where only one could walk at a time, till suddenly they came to a rift or chasm more than a yard in breadth, and beyond which lay a pile of rocks, separate from the rest of the ledge, standing full thirty feet high, with its sides steep and perpendicular as those of a castle. Phineas easily leaped the chasm, and set down the boy on a smooth, flat platform of crisp white moss, that covered the top of the rock.

"Over with you!" he called; "spring, now, once, for your lives!" said he, as one after another sprang across. Several fragments of loose stone formed a kind of breastwork, which sheltered their position from the observation of those below.

"Well, here we all are," said Phineas, peeping over the stone breastwork to watch the assailants, who were coming tumultuously up under the rocks. "Let 'em get us, if they can. Whoever comes here has to walk single file between those two rocks, in fair range of your pistols, boys, d'ye see?"

"I do see," said George; "and now, as this matter is ours, let us take all the risk, and do all the fighting."

"Thee's quite welcome to do the fighting, George," said Phineas, chewing some checkerberry leaves as he spoke; "but I may have the fun of looking on, I suppose. But see, these fellows are kinder debating down there, and looking up, like hens when they are going to fly on to the roost. Hadn't thee better give 'em a word of advice, before they come up, just to tell 'em handsomely they'll be shot if they do?"

The party beneath, now more apparent in the light of the dawn, consisted of our old acquaintances, Tom Loker and Marks, with two constables, and a posse consisting of such rowdies at the last tavern as could be engaged by a little brandy to go and help the fun of trapping a set of niggers.

"Well, Tom, yer coons are farly treed," said one.

"Yes, I see 'em go up right here," said Tom; "and here's a path. I'm for going right up. They can't jump down in a hurry, and it won't take long to ferret 'em out."

"But, Tom, they might fire at us from behind the rocks," said Marks. "That would be ugly, you know."

"Ugh!" said Tom with a sneer. "Always for saving your skin, Marks! No danger! niggers are too plaguy scared!"

"I don't know why I *shouldn't* save my skin," said Marks. "It's the best I've got; and niggers *do* fight like the devil, sometimes."

At this moment, George appeared on the top of a rock above them, and, speaking in a calm, clear voice, said:

"Gentlemen, who are you, down there; and what do you want?"

"We want a party of runaway niggers," said Tom Loker. "One George Harris, and Eliza Harris, and their son, and Jim Selden, and an old woman. We've got the officers here, and a warrant to take 'em; and we're going to have 'em, too. D'ye hear? An't you George Harris, that belongs to Mr Harris, of Shelby County, Kentucky?"

"I am George Harris. A Mr Harris, of Kentucky, did call me his property. But now I'm a free man, standing on God's free soil; and my wife and my child I claim as mine. Jim and his mother are here. We have arms to defend ourselves, and we mean to do it. You can come up, if you like; but the first one of you that comes within the range of our bullets is a dead man, and the next, and the next; and so on till the last."

"Oh, come! come!" said a short, puffy man, stepping forward, and blowing his nose as he did so. "Young man, this an't no kind of talk at all for you. You see, we're officers of justice. We've got the law on our side, and the power, and so forth; so you'd better give up peaceably, you see; for you'll certainly have to give up at last."

"I know very well that you've got the law on your side, and the power," said George bitterly. "You mean to take my wife to sell in New Orleans, and put my boy like a calf in a trader's pen, and send Jim's old mother to the brute that whipped and abused her before, because he couldn't abuse her son. You want to send Jim and me back to be whipped and tortured, and ground down under the heels of them that you call masters; and your laws *will* bear you out in it—more shame for you and them! But you haven't got us. We don't own your laws; we don't own your country; we stand here as free, under God's sky, as you are; and, by the great God that made us, we'll fight for our liberty till we die."

Marks was the only one who remained wholly untouched. He was deliberately cocking his pistol, and, in the momentary silence that followed George's speech, he fired at him.

"Ye see, ye get jist as much for him dead as alive in Kentucky," he said coolly, as he wiped his pistol on his coat-sleeve.

George sprang backward—Eliza uttered a shriek—the ball had passed close to his hair, had nearly grazed the cheek of his wife, and struck in the tree above.

"It's nothing, Eliza," said George quickly.

"Thee'd better keep out of sight, with thy speechifying," said Phineas; "they're mean scamps."

"Now, Jim," said George, "look that your pistols are all right, and watch that pass with me. The first man that shows himself, I fire at; you take the second, and so on. It won't do, you know, to waste two shots on one."

"But what if you don't hit?"

"I *shall* hit," said George coolly.

"Good! now, there's stuff in that fellow," muttered Phineas between his teeth.

The party below, after Marks had fired, stood for a moment rather undecided.

"I think you must have hit some on 'em," said one of the men. "I heard a squeal!"

"I'm going right up for one," said Tom. "I never was afraid of niggers, and I an't going to be now. Who goes arter?" he said, springing up the rocks.

George heard the words distinctly. He drew up his pistol, examined it, pointed it towards that point in the defile where the first man would appear.

One of the most courageous of the party followed Tom, and the way being thus made, the whole party began pushing up the rock—the hindermost pushing the front ones faster than they would have gone of themselves. On they came, and in a moment the burly form of Tom appeared in sight, almost at the verge of the chasm.

George fired—the shot entered his side; but, though wounded, he would not retreat, but, with a yell like that of a mad bull, he was leaping right across the chasm into the party.

"Friend," said Phineas, suddenly stepping to the front, and meeting him with a push from his long arms, "thee isn't wanted here."

Down he fell into the chasm, crackling down among trees, bushes, logs, loose stones, till he lay, bruised and groaning, thirty feet below. The fall might have killed him, had it not been broken and moderated by his clothes catching in the branches of a large tree; but he came down with some force, however—more than was at all agreeable or convenient.

"Lord help us, they are perfect devils!" said Marks, heading the retreat down the rocks with much more of a will than he had joined the ascent, while all the party came tumbling precipitately after him—the fat constable, in particular, blowing and puffing in a very energetic manner.

"I say, fellers," said Marks, "you jist go round and pick up Tom there, while I run and get on to my horse, to go back for help—that's you;" and without minding the hootings and jeers of his company, Marks was as good as his word, and was soon seen galloping away.

"Was ever such a sneaking varmint?" said one of the men: "to come on his business, and he clear out and leave us this yer way!"

"Well, we must pick up that feller," said another. "Cuss me if I much care whether he is dead or alive."

The men, led by the groans of Tom, scrambled and crackled through stumps, logs, and bushes, to where that hero lay groaning and swearing with alternate vehemence.

"Ye keep it agoing pretty loud, Tom," said one. "Ye much hurt?"

"Don't know. Get me up, can't ye? Blast that infernal Quaker! If it hadn't been for him, I'd a pitched some on 'em down here, to see how they liked it."

With much labour and groaning, the fallen hero was assisted to rise; and, with one holding him up under each shoulder, they got him as far as the horses.

"If you could only get me a mile back to that ar tavern. Give me a handkerchief or something, to stuff into this place, and stop this infernal bleeding."

George looked over the rocks, and saw them trying to lift the burly form of Tom into the saddle. After two or three ineffectual attempts, he reeled, and fell heavily to the ground.

"Oh, I hope he isn't killed!" said Eliza, who, with all the party, stood watching the proceeding.

"Why not?" said Phineas; "serves him right."

"Because, after death comes the judgement," said Eliza.

"Yes," said the old woman, who had been groaning and praying, in her Methodist fashion, during all the encounter, "it's an awful case for the poor crittur's soul."

"On my word, they're leaving him, I do believe," said Phineas.

It was true; for after some appearance of irresolution and consultation, the whole party got on their horses and rode away. When they were quite out of sight, Phineas began to bestir himself.

"Well, we must go down and walk a piece," he said. "I told Michael to go forward and bring help, and be along back here with the wagon; but we shall have to walk a piece along the road, I reckon, to meet them. The Lord grant he be along soon! It's early in the day; there won't be much travel afoot yet awhile; we an't much more than two miles from our stopping-place. If the road hadn't been so rough last night, we could have outrun 'em entirely."

As the party neared the fence, they discovered in the distance, along the road, their own wagon coming back, accompanied by some men on horseback.

"Well, now, there's Michael, and Stephen, and Amariah," exclaimed Phineas joyfully. "Now we are made—as safe as if we'd got there."

"Well, do stop, then," said Eliza, "and do something for that poor man; he's groaning dreadfully."

"It would be no more than Christian," said George; "let's take him up and carry him on."

"And doctor him up among the Quakers!" said Phineas; "pretty well, that! Well, I don't care if we do. Here, let's have a look at him;" and Phineas, who, in the course of his hunting and backwoods life, had acquired some rude experience of surgery, kneeled down by the wounded man, and began a careful examination of his condition.

"Marks," said Tom feebly, "is that you, Marks?"

"No; I reckon 'tan't, friend," said Phineas. "Much Marks cares for thee, if his own skin's safe. He's off, long ago."

"I believe I'm done for," said Tom. "The cussed sneaking dog, to leave me to die alone! My poor old mother always told me 'twould be so."

"La sakes! jist hear the poor crittur. He's got a mammy, now," said the old negress. "I can't help kinder pityin' on him."

"Softly, softly; don't thee snap and snarl, friend," said Phineas, as Tom winced and pushed his hand away. "Thee has no chance, unless I stop the bleeding." And Phineas busied himself with making some off-hand surgical arrangements with his own pocket-handkerchief, and such as could be mustered in the company.

"You pushed me down there," said Tom faintly.

"Well, if I hadn't, thee would have pushed us down, thee sees," said Phineas, as he stooped to apply his bandage. "There, there—let me fix this bandage. We mean well to thee; we bear no malice. Thee shall be taken to a house where they'll nurse thee first-rate—as well as thy own mother could."

Tom groaned, and shut his eyes. In men of his class vigour and resolution are entirely a physical matter, and ooze out with the flowing of the blood; and the gigantic fellow really looked piteous in his helplessness.

The other party now came up. The seats were taken out of the wagon. The buffalo-skins, doubled in fours, were spread all along one side, and four men, with great difficulty, lifted the heavy form of Tom into it. Before he was gotten in, he fainted entirely. The old negress, in the abundance of her compassion, sat down on the bottom, and took his head in her lap. Eliza, George, and Jim bestowed themselves, as well as they could, in the remaining space, and the whole party set forward.

"What do you think of him?" said George, who sat by Phineas in front.

"Well, it's only a pretty deep flesh-wound; but, then, tumbling and scratching down that place didn't help him much. It has bled pretty freely—pretty much dreaned him out, courage and all—but he'll get over it, and maybe learn a thing or two by it."

"I'm glad to hear you say so," said George. "It would always be a heavy thought to me, if I'd caused his death, even in a just cause."

"Yes," said Phineas, "killing is an ugly operation; any way they'll fix it—man or beast."

"What shall you do with this poor fellow?" said George.

"Oh, carry him along to Amariah's. There's old Grandmam Stephens there—Dorcas they call her—she's most an amazin' nurse. She takes to nursing real natural, and an't never better suited than when she gets a sick body to tent. We may reckon on turning him over to her for a fortnight or so."

A ride of about an hour more brought the party to a neat farmhouse, where the weary travellers were received to an abundant breakfast. Tom Loker was soon carefully deposited in a much cleaner and softer bed than he had ever been in the habit of occupying. His wound was carefully dressed and bandaged, and he lay languidly opening and shutting his eyes on the white window-curtains and gentle-gliding figures of his sick-room, like a weary child. And here, for the present, we shall take our leave of one party.

18

Topsy

ONE morning, while Miss Ophelia was busy in some of her domestic cares, St. Clare's voice was heard, calling her at the foot of the stairs.

"Come down here, cousin; I've something to show you."

"What is it?" said Miss Ophelia, coming down.

"I've made a purchase for your department—see here," said St. Clare; and, with a word, he pulled along a little negro girl, about eight or nine years of age.

She was one of the blackest of her race; and her round, shining eyes, glittering as glass beads, moved with quick and restless glances over everything in the room. Her mouth, half open with astonishment at the wonders of the new mas'r's parlour, displayed a white and brilliant set of teeth. Her woolly hair was braided in sundry little tails, which stuck out in every direction. The expression of her face was an odd mixture of shrewdness and cunning, over which was oddly drawn, like a kind of veil, an expression of the most doleful gravity and solemnity. She was dressed in a single filthy, ragged garment, made of bagging; and stood with her hands demurely folded before her. Altogether, there was something odd and goblin-like about her appearance— something, as Miss Ophelia afterwards said, "so heathenish", as to inspire that good lady with utter dismay; and, turning to St. Clare, she said:

"Augustine, what in the world have you brought that thing here for?"

"For you to educate, to be sure, and train in the way she should go. I thought she was rather a funny specimen in the Jim Crow line.—Here, Topsy," he added, giving a whistle, as a man would to call the attention of a dog, "give us a song, now, and show us some of your dancing."

The black, glassy eyes glittered with a kind of wicked drollery, and the thing struck up, in a clear, shrill voice, an odd negro melody, to which she kept time with her hands and feet, spinning round, clapping her hands, knocking her knees together, in a wild, fantastic sort of time, and producing in her throat all those odd guttural sounds which distinguish the native music of her race; and finally, turning a summerset or two, and giving a prolonged closing note, as odd and unearthly as that of a steam-whistle, she came suddenly down on the carpet, and stood with her hands folded, and a most sanctimonious expression of meekness and solemnity over her face, only broken by the cunning glances which she shot askance from the corners of her eyes.

Miss Ophelia stood silent, perfectly paralysed with amazement. St. Clare, like a mischievous fellow as he was, appeared to enjoy her astonishment; and, addressing the child again, said:

"Topsy, this is your new mistress. I'm going to give you up to her; see now that you behave yourself."

"Yes, mas'r," said Topsy, with sanctimonious gravity, her wicked eyes twinkling as she spoke.

"You're going to be good, Topsy, you understand," said St. Clare.

"Oh, yes, mas'r," said Topsy, with another twinkle, her hands still devoutly folded.

"Now, Augustine, what upon earth is this for?" said Miss Ophelia. "Your house is so full of these little plagues, now, that a body can't set down their foot without treading on 'em. I get up in the morning, and find one asleep behind the door, and see one black head poking out from under the table, one lying on the door-mat—and they are moping and mowing and grinning between all the railings, and tumbling over the kitchen floor! What on earth did you want to bring this one for?"

"For you to educate—didn't I tell you? You're always preaching about educating. I thought I would make you a present of a fresh-caught specimen, and let you try your hand on her, and bring her up in the way she should go."

"*I* don't want her, I am sure; I have more to do with 'em now than I want to."

"That's you Christians all over!—you'll get up a society, and get some poor missionary to spend all his days among just such heathen. But let me see one of you that would take one into your house with you, and take the labour of their conversion on yourselves! No; when it comes to that, they are dirty and disagreeable, and it's too much care, and so on."

"Augustine, you know I didn't think of it in that light," said Miss Ophelia, evidently softening. "Well, it may be a real missionary work," said she, looking, rather more favourably on the child.

St. Clare had touched the right string. "But," she added, "I really didn't see the need of buying this one; there are enough now, in your house, to take all my time and skill."

"Well, then, cousin," said St. Clare, drawing her aside, "I ought to beg your pardon for my good-for-nothing speeches. You are so good, after all, that there's no sense in them. Why, the fact is, this concern belonged to a couple of drunken creatures that keep a low restaurant that I have to pass by every day, and I was tired of hearing her screaming, and them beating and swearing at her. She looked bright and funny, too, as if something might be made of her; so I bought her, and I'll give her to you. Try, now, and give her a good orthodox New England bringing up, and see what it'll make of her."

"Well, I'll do what I can," said Miss Ophelia; and she approached her new subject very much as a person might be supposed to approach a black spider, supposing them to have benevolent designs toward it.

"She's dreadfully dirty, and half naked," she said.

"Well, take her downstairs and make some of them clean and clothe her up."

Miss Ophelia carried her to the kitchen regions.

"Don't see what Mas'r St. Clare wants of 'nother nigger!" said Dinah, surveying the new arrival with no friendly air. "Won't have her round under *my* feet, *I* know!"

"Pah!" said Rosa and Jane, with supreme disgust; "let her keep out of the way! What in the world mas'r wanted another of these low niggers for, I can't see!"

"You go' long! No more nigger dan you be, Miss Rosa," said Dinah, who felt this last remark a reflection on herself. "You seem to tink yourself white folks. You an't nerry one, black *nor* white. I'd like to be one or turrer."

Miss Ophelia saw that there was nobody in the camp that would undertake to oversee the cleansing and dressing of the new arrival, and so she was forced to do it herself, with some very ungracious and reluctant assistance from Jane. Then she began to question her.

"How old are you, Topsy?"

"Dun'no, missis," said the image, with a grin that showed all her teeth.

"Don't know how old you are! Didn't anybody ever tell you? Who was your mother?"

"Never had none!" said the child, with another grin.

"Never had any mother! What do you mean? Where were you born?"

"Never was born!" persisted Topsy, with another grin, that looked so goblin-like, that, if Miss Ophelia had been at all nervous, she might have fancied that she had got hold of some sooty gnome from the land of Diablerie; but Miss Ophelia was not nervous, but plain and business-like, and she said, with some sternness:

"You mustn't answer me in that way, child; I'm not playing with you. Tell me where you were born, and who your father and mother were."

"Never was born," reiterated the creature, more emphatically; "never had no father nor mother, nor nothin'. I was raised by a speculator, with lots of others. Old Aunt Sue used to take car on us."

The child was evidently sincere; and Jane, breaking into a short laugh, said:

"Laws, missis, there's heaps of 'em. Speculators buys 'em up cheap, when they's little, and gets 'em raised for market."

"How long have you lived with your master and mistress?"

"Dun'no, missis."

"Is it a year, or more, or less?"

"Don'no, missis."

"Laws, missis, those low negroes—they can't tell; they don't know anything about time," said Jane; "they don't know what a year is; they don't know their own ages."

"Have you ever heard anything about God, Topsy?"

The child looked bewildered, but grinned as usual.

"Do you know who made you?"

"Nobody, as I knows on," said the child, with a short laugh. The idea appeared to amuse her considerably; for her eyes twinkled, and she added—

"I spect I grow'd. Don't think nobody ever made me."

"Do you know how to sew?" said Miss Ophelia.

"No, missis."

"What can you do?—what did you do for your master and mistress?"

"Fetch water, and wash dishes, and rub knives, and wait on folks."

"Were they good to you?"

"Spect they was," said the child, scanning Miss Ophelia cunningly.

Miss Ophelia rose from this encouraging colloquy; St. Clare was leaning over the back of her chair.

"You find virgin soil there, cousin; put in your own ideas—you won't find many to pull up."

Miss Ophelia began with Topsy by taking her into her chamber, the first morning, and solemnly commencing a course of instruction in the art and mystery of bed-making.

Behold, then, Topsy, washed and shorn of all the little braided tails wherein her heart had delighted, arrayed in a clean gown, with well-starched apron, standing reverently before Miss Ophelia, with an expression of solemnity well befitting a funeral.

"Now, Topsy, I'm going to show you just how my bed is to be made. I am very particular about my bed. You must learn exactly how to do it."

"Yes, ma'am," says Topsy, with a deep sigh, and a face of woeful earnestness.

"Now, Topsy, look here—this is the hem of the sheet—this is the right side of the sheet, and this is the wrong; will you remember?"

"Yes, ma'am," says Topsy, with another sigh.

"Well, now, the under sheet you must bring over the bolster—so—and tuck it clear down under the mattress nice and smooth—so—do you see?"

"Yes, ma'am," said Topsy, with profound attention.

"But the upper sheet," said Miss Ophelia, "must be brought down in this way, and tucked under firm and smooth at the foot— so—the narrow hem at the foot."

"Yes, ma'am," said Topsy, as before; but we will add, what Miss Ophelia did not see, that, during the time when the good lady's back was turned, the young disciple had contrived to snatch a pair of gloves and a ribbon, which she had adroitly slipped into her sleeves, and stood with her hands dutifully folded, as before.

"Now, Topsy, let's see you do this," said Miss Ophelia, pulling off the clothes, and seating herself.

Topsy, with great gravity and adroitness, went through the exercise completely to Miss Ophelia's satisfaction; smoothing the sheets, patting out every wrinkle, and exhibiting, through the whole process, a gravity and seriousness with which her instructress was greatly edified. By an unlucky slip, however, a fluttering fragment of the ribbon hung out of one of her sleeves, just as she was finishing, and caught Miss Ophelia's attention. Instantly she pounced upon it. "What's this? You naughty, wicked child—you've been stealing this!"

The ribbon was pulled out of Topsy's own sleeve, yet she was not in the least disconcerted; she only looked at it with an air of the most surprised and unconscious innocence.

"Laws! why, that ar's Miss Feely's ribbon, an't it? How could it a got caught in my sleeve?"

"Topsy, you naughty girl, don't you tell me a lie—you stole that ribbon!"

"Missis, I declar for't, I didn't—never seed it till dis yer blessed minnit."

"Topsy," said Miss Ophelia, "don't you know it's wicked to tell lies?"

"I never tells no lies, Miss Feely," said Topsy, with virtuous gravity; "it's jist the truth I've been a-tellin' now, and an't nothin' else."

"Topsy, I shall have to whip you, if you tell lies so."

"Laws, missis, if you's to whip all day, couldn't say no other way," said Topsy beginning to blubber. "I never seed that ar—it must a got caught in my sleeve. Miss Feely must have left it on the bed, and it got caught in the clothes, and so got in my sleeve."

Miss Ophelia was so indignant at the barefaced lie, that she caught the child and shook her.

"Don't you tell me that again!"

The shake brought the gloves on to the floor, from the other sleeve.

"There, you!" said Miss Ophelia; "will you tell me now, you didn't steal the ribbon?"

Topsy now confessed to the gloves, but still persisted in denying the ribbon.

"Now, Topsy," said Miss Ophelia, "if you'll confess all about it, I won't whip you this time." Thus adjured, Topsy confessed to the ribbon and gloves, with woeful protestations of penitence.

"Well, now, tell me. I know you must have taken other things since you have been in the house, for I let you run about all day yesterday. Now, tell me if you took anything, and I shan't whip you."

"Laws, missis! I took Miss Eva's red thing she wars on her neck."

"You did, you naughty child!—Well, what else?"

"I took Rosa's yer-rings—them red ones."

"Go bring them to me this minute, both of 'em."

"Laws, missis! I can't—they's burnt up!"

"Burnt up!—what a story! Go get 'em, or I'll whip you."

Topsy, with loud protestations, and tears, and groans, declared that she *could* not. "They's burnt up—they was."

"What did you burn 'em up for?" said Miss Ophelia.

"Cause I's wicked—I is. I's mighty wicked, anyhow. I can't help it."

Just at this moment, Eva came innocently into the room with the identical coral necklace on her neck.

"Why, Eva, where did you get your necklace?" said Miss Ophelia.

"Get it? why, I've had it on all day," said Eva.

"Did you have it on yesterday?"

"Yes; and what is funny, aunty, I had it on all night. I forgot to take it off when I went to bed."

Miss Ophelia looked perfectly bewildered; the more so, as Rosa, at that instant, came into the room, with a basket of newly-ironed linen poised on her head, and the coral eardrops shaking in her ears!

"I'm sure I can't tell anything what to do with such a child!" she said, in despair. "What in the world did you tell me you took those things for, Topsy?"

"Why, missis said I must 'fess; and I couldn't think of nothin' else to 'fess," said Topsy, rubbing her eyes.

"But, of course, I didn't want you to confess things you didn't do," said Miss Ophelia; "that's telling a lie, just as much as the other."

"Laws, now, is it?" said Topsy, with an air of innocent wonder.

"La, there an't any such thing as truth in that limb," said Rosa, looking indignantly at Topsy. "If I was Mas'r St. Clare, I'd whip her till the blood run, I would—I'd let her catch it!"

"No, no, Rosa," said Eva, with an air of command, which the child could assume at times; "you mustn't talk so, Rosa, I can't bear to hear it."

"La sakes! Miss Eva, you's so good, you don't know nothing how to get along with niggers. There's no way but to cut 'em well up, I tell ye."

"Rosa," said Eva, "hush! Don't you say another word of that sort!" and the eye of the child flashed, and her cheek deepened its colour.

Rosa was cowed in a moment.

"Miss Eva has got the St. Clare blood in her, that's plain. She can speak, for all the world, just like her papa," she said, as she passed out of the room.

Eva stood looking at Topsy.

"Poor Topsy, why need you steal? You're going to be taken good care of, now. I'm sure I'd rather give you anything of mine, than have you steal it."

It was the first word of kindness the child had ever heard in her life; and the sweet tone and manner struck strangely on the wild, rude heart, and a sparkle of something like a tear shone in the keen, round, glittering eye; but it was followed by the short laugh and habitual grin. No! the ear that has never heard anything but abuse is strangely incredulous of anything so heavenly as kindness; and Topsy only thought Eva's speech something funny and inexplicable—she did not believe it.

But what was to be done with Topsy?

"I don't see," said Miss Ophelia to St. Clare, "how I'm going to manage that child without whipping her."

"Well, whip her, then, to your heart's content, I'll give you full power to do as you like."

"Children always have to be whipped," said Miss Ophelia; "I never heard of bringing them up without."

"Oh, well, certainly," said St. Clare; "do as you think best. Only I'll make one suggestion: I've seen this child whipped with a poker, knocked down with the shovel or tongs, whichever came handiest; and, seeing that she is used to that style of operation, I think your whippings will have to be pretty energetic, to make much impression."

"What is to be done with her, then?" said Miss Ophelia.

"You have started a serious question," said St. Clare; "I wish you'd answer it. What is to be done with a human being that can be governed only by the lash—*that* fails—it's a very common state of things down here!"

"I'm sure I don't know; I never saw such a child as this."

"Such children are very common among us, and such men and women too. How are they to be governed? What *is* to be done with them?"

"Well, I can't say I thank you for the experiment. But, then, as it appears to be a duty, I shall persevere, and try, and do the best I can," said Miss Ophelia; and Miss Ophelia, after this, did labour, with a commendable degree of zeal and energy, on her new subject. She instituted regular hours and employments for her, and undertook to teach her to read and to sew.

In the former art the child was quick enough. She learned her letters as if by magic, and was very soon able to read plain reading; but the sewing was a more difficult matter. The creature was as lithe as a cat, and as active as a monkey, and the confinement of sewing was her abomination; so she broke her needles, threw them slyly out of windows, or down in chinks of the walls; she tangled, broke, and dirtied her thread, or, with a sly movement, would throw a spool away altogether. Her motions were almost as quick as those of a practised conjurer, and her command of her face quite as great.

Topsy was soon a noted character in the establishment. Her

talent for every species of drollery, grimace, and mimicry—for dancing, tumbling, climbing, singing, whistling, imitating every sound that hit her fancy—seemed inexhaustible. In her play-hours, she invariably had every child in the establishment at her heels, open-mouthed with admiration and wonder—not excepting Miss Eva, who appeared to be fascinated by her, as a dove is sometimes charmed by a glittering serpent. Miss Ophelia was uneasy that Eva should fancy Topsy's society so much, and implored St. Clare to forbid it.

"Poh! let the child alone," said St. Clare. "Topsy will do her good."

"But so depraved a child—are you not afraid she will teach her some mischief?"

"She can't teach her mischief; she might teach it to some children, but evil rolls off Eva's mind like dew off a cabbage leaf—not a drop sinks in."

"Don't be too sure," said Miss Ophelia. "I know I'd never let a child of mine play with Topsy."

"Well, your children needn't," said St. Clare, "but mine may; if Eva could have been spoiled, it would have been done years ago."

On one occasion, Miss Ophelia found Topsy with her very best scarlet India Canton crape shawl wound round her head for a turban, going on with her rehearsals before the glass in great style—Miss Ophelia having, with carelessness most unheard-of in her, left the key for once in her drawer.

"Topsy!" she would say, when at the end of all patience, "what does make you act so?"

"Dun'no, missis—I spects 'cause I's so wicked!"

"I don't know anything what I shall do with you, Topsy."

"Law, missis, you must whip me; my old missis allers whipped me. I an't used to workin' unless I gets whipped."

"Why, Topsy, I don't want to whip you. You can do well, if you've a mind to; what is the reason you won't?"

"Laws, missis, I's used to whippin', I spects it's good for me."

Miss Ophelia tried the recipe, and Topsy invariably made a terrible commotion, screaming, groaning, and imploring, though half an hour afterwards, when roosted on some projection of the balcony, and surrounded by a flock of admiring "young uns", she would express the utmost contempt of the whole affair.

"Law, Miss Feely whip!—wouldn't kill a skeeter, her whippin's. Oughter see how old mas'r made the flesh fly; old mas'r know'd how!"

Topsy always made great capital of her own sins and enormities, evidently considering them as something peculiarly distinguishing.

"Law, you niggers," she would say to some of her auditors, "does you know you's all sinners? Well, you is—everybody is. White folks is sinners too—Miss Feely says so; but I spects niggers is the biggest ones; but lor! ye an't any on ye up to me. I's so awful wicked there can't nobody do nothin' with me. I used to keep old missis a-swarin' at me half de time. I spects I's the wickedest crittur in the world"; and Topsy would cut a summerset, and come up brisk and shining on to a higher perch, and evidently plume herself on the distinction.

Miss Ophelia busied herself very earnestly on Sundays, teaching Topsy the catechism. Topsy had an uncommon verbal memory, and committed with a fluency, that greatly encouraged her instructress.

"What good do you expect it is going to do her?" said St. Clare.

"Why, it always has done children good. It's what children always have to learn, you know," said Miss Ophelia.

"Understand it or not?" said St. Clare.

"Oh, children never understand it at the time; but, after they are grown up, it'll come to them."

"Mine hasn't come to me yet," said St. Clare, "though I'll bear testimony that you put it into me pretty thoroughly when I was a boy."

"Ah, you were always good at learning, Augustine. I used to have great hopes of you," said Miss Ophelia.

"Well, haven't you now?" said St. Clare.

"I wish you were as good as you were when you were a boy, Augustine."

"So do I, that's fact, cousin," said St. Clare. "Well, go ahead and catechize Topsy; maybe you'll make out something yet."

Topsy, who had stood like a black statue during this discussion, with hands decently folded, now, at a signal from Miss Ophelia, went on:

"Our first parents, being left to the freedom of their own will, fell from the state wherein they were created."

Topsy's eyes twinkled, and she looked inquiringly.

"What is it, Topsy?" said Miss Ophelia.

"Please, missis, was dat ar state Kintuck?"

"What state, Topsy?"

"Dat state dey fell out of. I used to hear mas'r tell how we came down from Kintuck."

St. Clare laughed.

"You'll have to give her a meaning, or she'll make one," said he.

"Oh, Augustine, be still," said Miss Ophelia; "how can I do anything, if you will be laughing?"

"Well, I won't disturb the exercises again, on my honour"; and St. Clare took his paper into the parlour, and sat down, till Topsy had finished her recitations. They were all very well, only that now and then she would oddly transpose some important words, and persist in the mistake, in spite of every effort to the contrary; and St. Clare, after all his promises of goodness, took a wicked pleasure in these mistakes, calling Topsy to him whenever he had a mind to amuse himself, and getting her to repeat the offending passages, in spite of Miss Ophelia's remonstrances.

"How do you think I can do anything with the child, if you will go on so, Augustine?" she would say.

"Well, it is too bad—I won't again; but I do like to hear the droll little image stumble over those big words!"

"But you confirm her in the wrong way."

"What's the odds? One word is as good as another to her."

"You wanted me to bring her up right; and you ought to remember she is a reasonable creature, and be careful of your influence over her."

"Oh, dismal! so I ought; but, as Topsy herself says, 'I's so wicked!'"

In very much this way Topsy's training proceeded for a year or two.

19

My Old Kentucky Home

OUR readers may not be unwilling to glance back, for a brief interval, at Uncle Tom's cabin, on the Kentucky farm, and see what has been transpiring among those whom he had left behind.

It was late in the summer afternoon, and the doors and windows of the large parlour all stood open, to invite any stray breeze, that might feel in a good numour, to enter. Mr Shelby sat in a large hall opening into the room, and running through the whole length of the house to a balcony on either end. Leisurely tipped back in one chair, with his heels in another, he was enjoying his after-dinner cigar. Mrs Shelby sat in the door, busy about some fine sewing; she seemed like one who had something on her mind, which she was seeking an opportunity to introduce.

"Do you know," she said, "that Chloe has had a letter from Tom?"

"Ah! has she? Tom's got some friend there, it seems. How is the old boy?"

"He has been bought by a very fine family, I should think," said Mrs Shelby. "is kindly treated, and has not much to do."

"Ah! well, I'm glad of it—very glad," said Mr Shelby heartily. "Tom, I suppose, will get reconciled to a Southern residence—hardly want to come up here again."

"On the contrary, he inquires very anxiously," said Mrs Shelby, "when the money for his redemption is to be raised."

"I'm sure *I* don't know," said Mr Shelby. "Once get business running wrong, there does seem to be no end to it. It's like jumping from one bog to another, all through a swamp; borrow of one to pay another, and then borrow of another to pay one—and these confounded notes falling due before a man has time to smoke a cigar and turn round—dunning letters and dunning messages—all scamper and hurry-scurry."

"It does seem to me, my dear, that something might be done

to straighten matters. Suppose we sell off all the horses, and sell one of your farms, and pay up square?"

"Oh, ridiculous, Emily! You are the finest woman in Kentucky; but still you haven't sense to know that you don't understand business; women never do, and never can."

"But, at least," said Mrs Shelby, "could not you give me some little insight into yours; a list of all your debts, at least, and of all that is owed to you, and let me try and see if I can't help you to economize."

"Oh, bother! don't plague me, Emily!—I can't tell exactly. I know somewhere about what things are likely to be; but there's no trimming and squaring my affairs, as Chloe trims crust off her pies. You don't know anything about business, I tell you."

And Mr Shelby, not knowing any other way of enforcing his ideas, raised his voice—a mode of arguing very convenient and convincing, when a gentleman is discussing matters of business with his wife.

Mrs Shelby ceased talking, with something of a sigh. The fact was, that though her husband had stated she was a woman, she had a clear, energetic, practical mind, and a force of character every way superior to that of her husband; so that it would not have been so very absurd a supposition to have allowed her capable of managing, as Mr Shelby supposed. Her heart was set on performing her promise to Tom and Aunt Chloe, and she sighed as discouragements thickened around her.

"Don't you think we might in some way contrive to raise that money? Poor Aunt Chloe! her heart is so set on it!"

"I'm sorry, if it is. I think I was premature in promising. I'm not sure, now, but it's the best way to tell Chloe, and let her make up her mind to it. Tom'll have another wife, in a year or two; and she had better take up with somebody else."

"Mr Shelby, I have taught my people that their marriages are as sacred as ours. I never could think of giving Chloe such advice."

"It's a pity, wife, that you have burdened them with a morality above their condition and prospects. I always thought so."

"It's only the morality of the Bible, Mr Shelby."

"Well, well, Emily, I don't pretend to interfere with your religious notions; only they seem extremely unfitted for people in that condition."

"They are, indeed," said Mrs Shelby, "and that is why, from

my soul, I hate the whole thing. I tell you, my dear, I cannot absolve myself from the promises I make to these helpless creatures. If I can get the money no other way, I will take music scholars; I could get enough, I know, and earn the money myself."

"You wouldn't degrade yourself that way, Emily? I never could consent to it."

"Degrade! would it degrade me as much as to break my faith with the helpless? No indeed!"

"Well, you are always heroic and transcendental," said Mr Shelby, "but I think you had better think before you undertake such a piece of Quixotism."

Here the conversation was interrupted by the appearance of Aunt Chloe, at the end of the verandah.

"If you please, missis," said she.

"Well, Chloe, what is it?" said her mistress, rising, and going to the end of the balcony.

"If missis would come and look at dis yer lot o' poetry."

Chloe had a particular fancy for calling poultry poetry—an application of language in which she always persisted, notwithstanding frequent corrections and advising from the young members of the family.

"La sakes!" she would say, "I can't see; one jis good as turry—poetry suthin' good, anyhow;" and so poetry Chloe continued to call it.

Mrs Shelby smiled as she saw a prostrate lot of chickens and ducks, over which Chloe stood, with a very grave face of consideration.

"I'm a-thinkin" whether missis would be a-havin' a chicken pie o' dese yer."

"Really, Aunt Chloe, I don't much care; serve them any way you like."

Chloe stood handling them over abstractedly; it was quite evident that the chickens were not what she was thinking of. At last, with the short laugh with which her tribe often introduce a doubtful proposal, she said:

"Laws me, missis! what should mas'r and missis be atroublin' theirselves 'bout de money, and not a-usin' what's right in der hands?" and Chloe laughed again.

"I don't understand you, Chloe," said Mrs Shelby, nothing doubting, from her knowledge of Chloe's manner, that she had heard every word of the conversation that had passed between her and her husband.

"Why, laws me, missis!" said Chloe, laughing again, "other folks hires out der niggers and makes money on 'em? Don't keep sich a tribe eatin' 'em out of house and home."

"Well, Chloe, who do you propose that we should hire out?"

"Laws! I an't a-proposin' nothin'; only Sam he said der was one of dese yer *perfectioners*, dey calls 'em, in Louisville, said he wanted a good hand at cake and pastry; and said he'd give four dollars a week to one, he did."

"Well, Chloe."

"Well, laws, I's a-thinkin', missis, Sally's been under my care now, dis some time, and she does 'most as well as me, considerin'; and if missis would only let me go, I would help fetch up de money. I an't afraid to put my cake, nor pies nother, 'lonside no *perfectioner's*."

"Confectioner's, Chloe."

"Law sakes, missis! 'tan't no odds; words is so curis, can't never get 'em right."

"But, Chloe, do you want to leave your children?"

"Laws, missis! de boys is big enough to do day's works; dey does well enough; and Sally, she'll take de baby—she's such a peart young un, she won't take no lookin' arter."

"Louisville is a good way off."

"Law sakes! who afeard?—it's down river, somer near my old man, perhaps?" said Chloe, speaking the last in the tone of a question, and looking at Mrs Shelby.

"No, Chloe; it's many a hundred miles off," said Mrs Shelby. "Never mind; your going there shall bring you nearer, Chloe. Yes, you may go; and your wages shall, every cent of them, be laid aside for your husband's redemption."

As when a bright sunbeam turns a dark cloud to silver, so Chloe's dark face brightened immediately—it really shone.

"Laws! if missis isn't too good! I was thinking of dat ar very thing; 'cause I shouldn't need no clothes, nor shoes, nor nothin'—I could save every cent. How many weeks is der in a year, missis?"

"fifty-two," said Mrs Shelby.

"Laws! now, der is? and four dollars for each on 'em. Why, how much'd dat ar be?"

"Two hundred and eight dollars," said Mrs Shelby.

"Why-e!" said Chloe, with an accent of surprise and delight; "and how long would it take me to work it out, missis?"

"Some four or five years, Chloe; but, then, you needn't do it all—I shall add something to it."

"I wouldn't hear to missis givin' lessons nor nothin'. Mas'r's quite right in dat ar; 'twouldn't do, no ways. I hope none our family ever be brought to dat ar, while I's got hands."

"Don't fear, Chloe; I'll take care of the honour of the family," said Mrs Shelby, smiling, "But when do you expect to go?"

"Well, I warn't spectin' nothin'; only Sam, he's a-gwine to de river with some colts, and he said I could go 'long with him; so I jes put my things together. If missis was willin', I'd go with Sam tomorrow morning, if missis would write my pass, and write me a commendation."

"Well, Chloe, I'll attend to it, if Mr Shelby has no objections. I must speak to him."

Mrs Shelby went upstairs, and Aunt Chloe, delighted, went out to her cabin, to make her preparation.

"Law sakes, Mas'r George! ye didn't know I's a-gwine to Louisville tomorrow!" she said to George, as, entering her cabin, he found her busy in sorting over her baby's clothes. "I thought I'd jis look over sis's things, and get 'em straightened up. But I'm gwine, Mas'r George—gwine to have four dollars a week, and missis is gwine to lay it all up, to buy back my old man ag'in!"

"Whew!" said George, "here's a stroke of business, to be sure! How are you going?"

"Tomorrow, wid Sam. And now, Mas'r George, I knows you'll jis sit down and write to my old man, and tell him all about it—won't ye?"

"To be sure," said George; "Uncle Tom'll be right glad to hear from us. I'll go right in the house for paper and ink; and then, you know, Aunt Chloe, I can tell about the new colts and all."

"Sartin, sartin, Mas'r George; you go 'long, and I'll get ye up a bit o' chicken, or some sich; ye wo't have many more suppers wid yer poor old aunty."

20

Farewell, Eva!

LIFE passes with us all, a day at a time; so it passed with our friend Tom till two years were gone. In this time the friendship between Tom and Eva had grown with the child's growth, so his faithful old heart felt an intolerable ache as he noticed that Eva's little hand had grown thinner and her skin more transparent and her breath shorter. Miss Ophelia, too, had noted the slight dry cough and St. Clare himself, watching Eva feverishly day by day, grew so nervous and restless that at last he was compelled to call in medical advice—a thing from which he had always shrunk, because it was the admission of an unwelcome truth.

In a week or two, there was a great improvement of symptoms—one of those deceitful lulls, by which her inexorable disease so often beguiles the anxious heart, even on the verge of the grave. Eva's step was again in the garden—in the balconies; she played and laughed again—and her father, in a transport, declared that they should soon have her as hearty as anybody. Miss Ophelia and the physician alone felt no encouragement from this illusive truce. There was one other heart, too, that felt the same certainly, and that was the little heart of Eva. What is it that sometimes speaks in the soul so calmly, so clearly, that its earthly time is short? Is it the secret instinct of decaying nature, or the soul's impulsive throb, as immortality draws on? Be it what it may, it rested in the heart of Eva, a calm, sweet, prophetic certainty that heaven was near; calm as the light of sunset, sweet as the bright stillness of autumn, there her little heart reposed, only troubled by sorrow for those who loved her so dearly.

For the child, though nursed so tenderly, and though life was unfolding before her with every brightness that love and wealth could give, had no regret for herself in dying. The deceitful strength which had buoyed Eva up for a little while was fast passing away; seldom and more seldom her light footstep was heard in the verandah, and oftener and oftener she was found reclined on a little lounge by the open window, her large, deep eyes fixed on the rising and falling waters of the lake.

Eva, after this, declined rapidly; there was no more any doubt of the event; the fondest hope could not be blinded. Her beautiful room was avowedly a sick-room; and Miss Ophelia day and night performed the duties of a nurse—and never did her friends appreciate her value more than in that capacity. With so well-trained a hand and eye, such perfect adroitness and practice in every art which could promote neatness and comfort, and keep out of sight every disagreeable incident of sickness—with such a perfect sense of time, such a clear, untroubled head, such exact accuracy in remembering every prescription and direction of the doctor—she was everything to him. They who had shrugged their shoulders at her little peculiarities and setnesses, so unlike the careless freedom of Southern manners, acknowledged that now she was the exact person that was wanted.

Uncle Tom was much in Eva's room. The child suffered much from nervous restlessness, and it was a relief to her to be carried; and it was Tom's greatest delight to carry her little frail form in his arms, resting on a pillow, now up and down her room, now out into the verandah; and when the fresh sea-breezes blew from the lake—and the child felt freshest in the morning—he would sometimes walk with her under the orange-trees in the garden, or, sitting down in some of their old seats, sing to her their favourite old hymns.

Her father often did the same thing; but his frame was slighter, and when he was weary, Eva would say to him:

"Oh, papa, let Tom take me. Poor fellow! it pleases him and you know it's all he can do now, and he wants to do something!"

"So do I, Eva!" said her father.

"Well, papa, you can do everything, and are everything to me. You read to me—you sit up nights—and Tom has only this one thing, and his singing; and I know, too, he does it easier than you can. He carries me so strong!"

The desire to do something was not confined to Tom. Every servant in the establishment showed the same feeling, and in their way did what they could.

Poor Mammy's heart yearned towards her darling; but she found no opportunity, night or day, as Marie declared that the state of her mind was such, it was impossible for her to rest; and, of course, it was against her principles to let anyone else rest. Twenty times in a night, Mammy would be roused to rub her feet, to bathe her head, to find her pocket-handkerchief, to see what the noise was in Eva's room, to let down a curtain because it was too light, or to put it up because it was too dark; and in the daytime, when she longed to have some share in the nursing of her pet, Marie seemed unusually ingenious in keeping her busy anywhere and everywhere all over the house, or about her own person; so that stolen interviews and momentary glimpses were all she could obtain.

"I feel it my duty to be particularly careful of myself, now," she would say, "feeble as I am, and with the whole care and nursing of that dear child upon me."

"Indeed, my dear," said St. Clare, "I thought our cousin relieved you of that."

"You talk like a man, St. Clare—just as if a mother *could* be relieved of the care of a child in that state, but, then, it's all alike—no one ever knows what I feel! I can't throw things off, as you do."

The friend who knew most of Eva's own imaginings and fore-shadowings was her faithful bearer, Tom. To him she said what she would not disturb her father by saying. To him she imparted those mysterious intimations which the soul feels as the cords begin to unbind, ere it leaves its clay for ever.

Tom, at last, would not sleep in his room, but lay all night in the outer verandah, ready to rouse at every call.

At midnight—strange, mystic hour!—when the veil between the frail present and the eternal future grows thin—came the messenger!

There was a sound in that chamber, first of one who stepped quickly. It was Miss Ophelia, who had resolved to sit up all night with her little charge, and who, at the turn of the night, had discerned what experienced nurses significantly call "a change". The outer door was quickly opened, and Tom, who was watching outside, was on the alert in a moment.

"Go for the doctor, Tom! lose not a moment," said Miss Ophelia; and, stepping across the room, she rapped at St. Clare's door.

"Cousin," she said, "I wish you would come."

Those words fell on his heart like clods upon a coffin. Why did they? He was up and in the room in an instant, and bending over Eva, vho still slept.

What was it he saw that made his heart stand still? Why was no word spoken between the two? Thou canst say, who hast seen that same expression on the face dearest to thee—that look indescribable, hopeless, unmistakable, that says to thee that thy beloved is no longer thine.

On the face of the child, however, there was no ghastly imprint—only a high and almost sublime expression—the overshadowing presence of spiritual natures, the dawning of immortal life in that childish soul.

They stood there so still, gazing upon her, that even the ticking of the watch seemed too loud. In a few moments, Tom returned with the doctor. He entered, gave one look, and stood silent as the rest.

"When did this change take place?" said he, in a low whisper, to Miss Ophelia.

"About the turn of the night," was the reply.

Marie, roused by the entrance of the doctor, appeared, humedly, from the next room.

"Augustine! Cousin!—Oh!—what!" she hurriedly began.

"Hush!" said St. Clare hoarsely; "*she is dying!*"

Marnmy heard the words, and flew to awaken the servants. The house was soon roused—lights were seen, footsteps heard, anxious faces thronged the verandah, and looked tearfully through the glass doors; but St. Clare heard and said nothing—he saw only *that look* on the face of the little sleeper.

"Oh, if she would only wake, and speak once more!" he said; and stooping over her, he spoke in her ear—"Eva, darling!"

The large blue eyes unclosed—a smile passed over her face; she tried to raise her head, and to speak.

"Do you know me, Eva?"

"Dear papa," said the child, with a last effort, throwing her arms round his neck. In a moment they dropped again, and, as St. Clare raised his head, he saw a spasm of mortal agony pass over the face—she struggled for breath, and threw up her little hands.

"O God, this is dreadful!" he said, turning away in agony, and wringing Tom's hand, scarce conscious what he was doing. "Oh, Tom, my boy, it is killing me!"

Tom had his master's hands between his own; and, with tears streaming down his dark cheeks, looked up for help where he had always been used to look.

"Pray that this may be cut short!" said St. Clare—"this wrings my heart."

"Oh, bless the Lord! it's over—it's over, dear master!" said Tom; "look at her."

The child lay panting on her pillows, as one exhausted—the large clear eyes rolled up and fixed. Ah, what said those eyes, that spoke so much of heaven? Earth was past, and earthly pain; but so solemn, so mysterious was the triumphant brightness of that face, that it checked even the sobs of sorrow. They pressed around her, in breathless stillness.

"Eva," said St. Clare gently.

She did not hear.

"Oh, Eva, tell us what you see! What is it?" said her father.

A bright, a glorious smile passed over her face, and she said brokenly—"Oh! love—joy—peace!" gave one sigh, and passed from death unto life!

Farewell, beloved child! The bright, eternal doors have closed after thee; we shall see thy sweet face no more. Oh, woe for them who watched thy entrance into heaven, when they shall wake and find only the cold grey sky of daily life, and thou gone for ever!

21

St. Clare Goes Home

WEEK after week glided away in the St. Clare mansion, and the waves of life settled back to their usual flow, where that little bark had gone down.

All the interests and hopes of St. Clare's life had unconsciously wound themselves around this child. It was for Eva that he had managed his property; it was for Eva that he had planned the disposal of his time; and to do this and that for Eva—to buy, improve, alter, and arrange, or dispose something for her—had been so long his habit, that now she was gone, there seemed nothing to be thought of, and nothing to be done.

He had never pretended to govern himself by any religious obligation, but now he was, in many respects, another man. He read his little Eva's Bible seriously and honestly; he thought more soberly and practically of his relations to his servants—enough to make him extremely dissatisfied with both his past and present course; and one thing he did, soon after his return to New Orleans, and that was to commence the legal steps necessary to Tom's emancipation, which was to be perfected as soon as he could get through the necessary formalities. Meantime, he attached himself to Tom more and more every day. In all the wide world, there was nothing that seemed to remind him so much of Eva; and he would insist on keeping him constantly about him, and, fastidious and unapproachable as he was with regard to his deeper feelings, he almost thought aloud to Tom. Nor would any one have wondered at it, who had seen the expression of affection and devotion with which Tom continually followed his young master.

"Well, Tom," said St. Clare, the day after he had commenced the legal formalities for his enfranchisement, "I'm going to make a free man of you; so, have your trunk packed, and get ready to set out for Kentucky"

The sudden light of joy that shone in Tom's face as he raised his hands to heaven, his emphatic "Bless the Lord!" rather discomposed St. Clare; he did not like it that Tom should be so ready to leave him.

"You haven't had such very bad times, here, that you need be in such a rapture, Tom," he said dryly.

"No, no, mas'r! 'tan't that—it's bein' a *free man!* That's what I'm joyin' for."

"Why, Tom, don't you think, for your own part, you've been better off than to be free?"

"*No, indeed*, Mas'r St. Clare," said Tom, with a flash of energy. "No, indeed!"

"Why, Tom, you couldn't possibly have earned, by your wvork, such clothes and such living as I have given you."

"Knows all that, Mas'r St. Clare; mas'r's been too good; but, mas'r, I'd rather have poor clothes, poor house, poor everything, and have 'em *mine*, than have the best, and have 'em any man's else—I had *so*, mas'r; I think it's natur, mas'r."

"I suppose so, Tom; and you'll be going off and leaving me in a month or so," he added rather discontentedly. "Though why you shouldn't, no mortal knows," he said, in a gayer tone; and, getting up, he began to walk the floor.

"Not while mas'r is in trouble," said Tom. "I'll stay with mas'r as long as he wants me—so as I can be any use."

"Not while I'm in trouble, Tom?" said St. Clare, looking sadly out of the window. "And when will my trouble be over?"

"When Mas'r St. Clare's a Christian," said Tom.

"And you really mean to stay by till that day comes?" said St. Clare, half smiling, as he turned from the window, and laid his hand on Tom's shoulder. "Ah, Tom, you soft, silly boy! I won't keep you till that day. Go home to your wife and children, and give my love to all."

"I's faith to believe that day will come," said Tom earnestly, and with tears in his eyes; "the Lord has a work for mas'r."

"A work, hey?" said St. Clare; "well, now, Tom, give me your views on what sort of a work it is—let's hear."

"Why, even a poor fellow like me has a work from the Lord; and Mas'r St. Clare, that has larnin', and riches and, friends—how much he might do for the Lord!"

"Tom, you seem to think the Lord needs a great deal done for him," said St. Clare, smiling.

"We does for the Lord when we does for his critturs," said Tom.

"Good theology, Tom; better than Dr B. preaches, I dare swear," said St. Clare.

Tom did not answer.

St. Clare rose up and walked thoughtfully up and down the verandah, seeming to forget everything in his own thoughts; so absorbed was he, that Tom had to remind him twice that the tea-bell had rung, before he could get his attention.

St. Clare was absent and thoughtful all tea-time. After tea, he and Marie and Miss Ophelia took possession of the parlour, almost in silence.

"I believe I'll go down street, a few moments, and hear the news tonight," he said at last.

Taking his hat, he passed out.

Tom followed him to the passage, out of the court, and asked if he should attend him.

"No, my boy," said St. Clare. "I shall be back in an hour."

Tom sat down in the verandah. It was a beautiful moonlight evening, and he sat watching the rising and falling spray of the fountain, and listening to its murmur. Tom thought of his home, and that he should soon be a free man, and able to return to it at will. He thought how he should work to buy his wife and boys. He felt the muscles of his brawny arms with a sort of joy, as though they would soon belong to himself, and how much they could do to work out the freedom of his family. Then he thought of his noble young master, and, ever second to that, came the habitual prayer that he had always offered for him; and then his thoughts passed on to the beautiful Eva, whom he now thought of among the angels; and he thought till he almost fancied that that bright face and golden hair were looking upon him, out of the spray of the fountain. And, so musing, he fell asleep, and dreamed he saw her coming bounding towards him, just as she used to come, with a wreath of jessamine in her hair; her cheeks wore a paler hue—her eyes had a deep, divine radiance, a golden halo seemed around her head—and she vanished from his sight; and Tom was awakened by a loud knocking, and a sound of many voices at the gate.

He hastened to undo it; and, with smothered voices and heavy tread, came several men, bringing a body, wrapped in a cloak, and lying on a shutter. The light of the lamp fell full on the face; and Tom gave a wild cry of amazement and despair, that rang through all the galleries, as the men advanced, with their burden, to the open parlour door, where Miss Ophelia still sat knitting.

St. Clare had turned into a cafe, to look over an evening paper. As he was reading, an affray arose between two gentlemen in the room, who were both partially intoxicated. St. Clare and one or two others made an effort to separate them, and St. Clare received a fatal stab in the side with a bowie-knife, which he was attempting to wrest from one of them.

The house was full of cries and lamentations, shrieks and screams; servants frantically tearing their hair, throwing themselves on the ground, or running distractedly about, lamenting. Tom and Miss Ophelia alone seemed to have any presence of mind; for Marie was in strong hysteric convulsions. At Miss Ophelia's direction, one of the lounges in the parlour was hastily prepared, and the bleeding form laid upon it. St. Clare had fainted through pain and loss of blood; but, as Miss Ophelia applied restoratives, he revived, opened his eyes, looked fixedly on them, looked earnestly around the room, his eyes travelling wistfully over every object, and finally they rested on his mother's picture.

The physician now arrived, and made his examination. It was evident, from the expression of his face, that there was no hope; but he applied himself to dressing the wound, and he and Miss Ophelia and Tom proceeded composedly with this work, amid the lamentations and sobs and cries of the affrightened servants, who had clustered about the doors and windows of the verandah.

"Now," said the physician, "we must turn all these creatures out; all depends on his being kept quiet."

St. Clare opened his eyes, and looked fixedly on the distressed beings whom Miss Ophelia and the doctor were trying to urge from the apartment. "Poor creatures!" he said, and an expression of bitter self-reproach passed over his face. Adolph absolutely refused to go. Terror had deprived him of all presence of mind; he threw himself along on the floor, and nothing could persuade him to rise. The rest yielded to Miss Ophelia's urgent representations, that their master's safety depended on their stillness and obedience.

St. Clare could say but little; he lay with his eyes shut, but it was evident that he wrestled with bitter thoughts. After a while, he laid his hand on Tom's, who was kneeling beside him, and said, "Tom! poor fellow!"

"What, mas'r?" said Tom earnestly.

"I am dying!" said St. Clare, pressing his hand; "pray!"

And Tom did pray, with all his mind and strength, for the soul that was passing—the soul that seemed looking so steadily and mournfully from those large melancholy blue eyes. It was literally prayer offered with strong crying and tears.

When Tom ceased to speak, St. Clare reached out and took his hand, looking earnestly at him, but saying nothing. He closed his eyes, but still retained his hold; for, in the gates of eternity, the black hand and the white hold each other with an equal clasp. He murmured softly to himself, at broken intervals.

"His mind is wandering," said the doctor.

"No! it is coming HOME, at last!" said St. Clare energetically; "at last! at last!"

The effort of speaking exhausted him. The sinking paleness of death fell upon him; but with it there fell, as if shed from the wings of some pitying spirit, a beautiful expression of peace, like that of a wearied child who sleeps.

So he lay for a few moments. They saw that the mighty hand was on him. Just before the spirit parted, he opened his eyes, with a sudden light, as of joy and recognition, and said, "*Mother!*" and then he was gone.

22

For Sale

WE HEAR often of the distress of the negro servants, on the loss of a kind master; and with good reason, for no creature on God's earth is left more utterly unprotected and desolate than the slave in these circumstances.

When St. Clare breathed his last, terror and consternation took hold of all his household. He had been stricken down so in a moment, in the flower and strength of his youth! Every room and gallery of the house resounded with sobs and shrieks of despair.

But the funeral passed, with all its pageant of black crape, and prayers, and solemn faces; and back rolled the cool muddy waves of everyday life; and up came the everlasting hard inquiry of "What is to be done next?"

A few days later, Tom was standing musing by the balconies, when he was joined by Adolph, who, since the death of his master, had been entirely crestfallen and disconsolate. Adolph knew that he had always been an object of dislike to Marie; but while his master lived he had paid but little attention to it. Now that he was gone, he had moved about in daily dread and trembling, not knowing what might befall him next. Marie had held several consultations with her lawyer; after communicating with St. Clare's brother, it was determined to sell the place, and all the servants, except her own personal property, and these she intended to take with her, and go back to her father's plantation.

"Do ye know, Tom, that we've all got to be sold?" said Adolph.

"How did you hear that?" said Tom.

"I hid myself behind the curtain when missis was talking with the lawyer. In a few days, we shall all be sent off to auction, Tom."

"The Lord's will be done!" said Tom, folding his arms, and sighing heavily.

"We'll never get another such a master," said Adolph apprehensively; "but I'd rather be sold than take my chance under missis."

Tom turned away; his heart was full. The hope of liberty, the thought of distant wife and children, rose up before his patient soul. He drew his arms tightly over his bosom, and choked back the bitter tears, and tried to pray, but the more he said "Thy will be done", the worse he felt.

He sought Miss Ophelia, who, ever since Eva's death, had treated him with marked and respectful kindness.

"Miss Feely," he said, "Mas'r St. Clare promised me my freedom. He told me that he had begun to take it out for me; and now, perhaps, if Miss Feely would be good enough to speak about it to missis, she would feel like goin' on with it, as it was Mas'r St. Clare's wish."

"I'll speak for you, Tom, and do my best," said Miss Ophelia; "but, if it depends on Mrs St. Clare, I can't hope much for you;—nevertheless, I will try."

So the good soul gathered herself up, and, taking her knitting, resolved to go into Marie's room, be as agreeable as possible, and negotiate Tom's case with all the diplomatic skill of which she was mistress.

She found Marie reclining at length upon a lounge, supporting herself on one elbow by pillows, while Jane, who had been out shopping, was displaying before her certain samples of thin black stuffs.

"The fact is," said Marie, "that I haven't a dress in the world that I can wear; and, as I am going to break up the establishment, and go off, next week, I must decide upon something."

"Are you going so soon?" asked Miss Ophelia.

"Yes, St. Clare's brother has written, and he and the lawyer think that the servants and furniture had better be put up at auction, and the place left with our lawyer."

"There's one thing I wanted to speak with you about," said Miss Ophelia. "Augustine promised Tom his liberty, and began the legal forms necessary to it. I hope you will use your influence to have it perfected."

"Indeed, I shall do no such thing!" said Marie sharply. "Tom is one of the most valuable servants on the place—it couldn't be afforded, any way. Besides, what does he want of liberty? He's a great deal better off as he is."

"But he does desire it, very earnestly, and his master promised it," said Miss Ophelia.

"I dare say he does want it," said Marie; "they all want it, just because they are a discontented set—always wanting what they haven't got. Now, I'm principled against emancipating, in any case. Keep a negro under the care of a master, and he does well enough, and is respectable; but set them free, and they get lazy, and won't work, and take to drinking, and go all down to be mean, worthless fellows. I've seen it tried, hundreds of times. It's no favour to set them free."

"But Tom is so steady, industrious, and pious."

"Oh, you needn't tell me! I've seen a hundred like him. He'll do very well, as long as he's taken care of."

"But, then, consider," said Miss Ophelia, "when you set him up for sale, the chances of his getting a bad master."

"Oh, that's all humbug!" said Marie; "it isn't one time in a hundred that a good fellow gets a bad master; most masters are good, for all the talk that is made. I've lived and grown up here in the South, and I never yet was acquainted with a master that didn't treat his servants well—quite as well as is worth while. I don't feel any fears on that head."

"Well," said Miss Ophelia energetically, "I know it was one of the last wishes of your husband that Tom should have his liberty. I should not think you would feel at liberty to disregard it."

Marie had her face covered with her handkerchief at this appeal, and began sobbing and using her smelling-bottle, with great vehemence.

"Everybody goes against me!" she said. "Everybody is so inconsiderate! I shouldn't have expected that you would bring up all these remembrances of my troubles to me—it's so inconsiderate! But nobody ever does consider—my trials are so peculiar! It's so hard, that when I had only one daughter, she should have been taken!—and when I had a husband that just exactly suited me—and I'm so hard to be suited!—he should be taken! And you seem to have so little feeling for me, and keep bringing it up to me so carelessly, when you know how it overcomes me! I suppose you mean well; but it is very inconsiderate—very!" And Marie sobbed, and gasped for breath, and called Mammy to open the window, and to bring her the camphor-bottle, and to bathe her head and unhook her dress. And, in the general confusion that ensued, Miss Ophelia made her escape to her apartment.

She saw, at once, that it would do no good to say anything more; for Marie had an indefinite capacity for hysteric fits; and, after this, whenever her husband's or Eva's wishes with regard to the servants were alluded to, she always found it convenient to set one in operation. Miss Ophelia, therefore, did the next best thing she could for Tom—she wrote a letter to Mrs Shelby for him, stating his trouble, and urging them to send to his relief.

The next day, Tom and Adolph, and some half-dozen other servants, were marched down to a slave warehouse, to await the convenience of the trader, who was going to make up a lot for auction.

23

Slave Market

A SLAVE warehouse! Beneath a splendid dome were men of all nations, moving to and fro, over the marble pavé. On every side of the circular area were stations, for the use of speakers and auctioneers. Two of these, on opposite sides of the area, were now occupied by brilliant and talented gentlemen, enthusiastically forcing up, in English and French commingled, the bids of connoisseurs in their various wares. A third one, on the other side, still unoccupied, was surrounded by a group, waiting the moment of sale to begin. And here we may recognize the St. Clare servants—Tom, Adolph, and others; and there, too, is a respectably-dressed mulatto woman with soft eyes and a gentle face. By her side, nestling close to her, is a young girl of fifteen, her daughter Emmeline, a quadroon as may be seen from her fairer complexion. All await their turn with anxious and dejected faces. Various spectators, intending to purchase, or not intending, as the case might be, gathered around the group, handling, examining, and commenting on their various points and faces with the same freedom that a set of jockeys discuss the merits of a horse.

Tom had been standing wistfully examining the multitude of faces thronging around him for one whom he would wish to call master. He saw abundance of men—great, burly, gruff men; little, chirping, dried men; long-favoured, lank, hard men; and every variety of stubbed-looking, commonplace men, who pick up their fellow-men as one picks up chips, putting them into the fire or a basket with equal unconcern, according to their convenience; but he saw no St. Clare.

A little before the sale commenced, a short, broad, muscular man, in a checked shirt considerably open at the bosom, and pantaloons much the worse for dirt and wear, elbowed his way through the crowd, like one who is going actively into a business; and, coming up to the group, began to examine them systematically. From the moment that Tom saw him approaching, he felt an immediate and revolting horror at him, that increased as he came near. He was evidently, though short, of gigantic strength. His round, bullet head, large, light-grey eyes, with their shaggy, sandy eyebrows, and stiff, wiry, sunburned hair, were rather unprepossessing items, it is to be confessed; his large, coarse mouth was distended with tobacco, the juice of which, from time to time, he ejected from him with great decision and explosive force; his hands were immensely large, hairy sunburned, freckled, and very dirty, and garnished with long nails in a very foul condition. This man proceeded to a very free personal examination of the lot. He seized Tom by the jaw, and pulled open his mouth to inspect his teeth; made him strip up his sleeve, to show his muscle; turned him round, made him jump and spring, to show his paces.

"Where was you raised?" he added, briefly, to these investigations.

"In Kintuck, mas'r," said Tom, looking about, as if for deliverance.

"What have you done?"

"Had care of mas'r's farm," said Tom.

"Likely story!" said the other shortly, as he passed on. He paused a moment before Dolph, then spitting a discharge of tobacco-juice on his well-blacked boots, and giving a contemptuous umph, he walked on. Again he stopped before Emmeline. He put out his heavy, dirty hand, and drew the girl towards him; passed it over her neck and bust, felt her arms, looked at her teeth, and then pushed her back against her mother, whose patient face showed the suffering she had been going through at every motion of the hideous stranger.

The girl was frightened, and began to cry.

"Stop that, you minx!" said the salesman; "no whimpering here—the sale is going to begin." And accordingly the sale began.

Adolph was knocked off, at a good sum, to a young gentleman who had previously stated his intentions of buying him; and the other servants of the St. Clare lot went to various bidders.

"Now, up with you, boy! d'ye hear?" said the auctioneer to Tom.

Tom stepped upon the block, gave a few anxious looks round, all seemed mingled in a common, indistinct noise—the clatter of the salesman, crying off his qualifications in French and English, the quick fire of French and English bids; and almost in a moment came the final thump of the hammer, and the clear ring on the last syllable of the word *"dollars"*, as the auctioneer announced his price, and Tom was made over. He has a master in the short bullet-headed man, Simon Legree, who owns a cotton plantation on the Red River.

Down goes the hammer again. Legree has also got the girl Emmeline, body and soul, unless God helps her! She is pushed along into the same lot with Tom, and goes off, weeping as she goes.

24

Simon Legree

I T TOOK but a short time to familiarize Tom with all that
was to be hoped or feared in his new way of life. He was an
expert and efficient workman in whatever he undertook; and
was, both from habit and principle, prompt and faithful. Quiet
and peaceable in his disposition, he hoped, by unremitting
diligence, to avert from himself at least a portion of the evils of
his condition. He saw enough of abuse and misery to make him
sick and weary; but he determined to toil on with religious
patience, committing himself to Him that judgeth righteously,
not without hope that some way of escape might yet be opened
to him.

Simon Legree, his master, took silent note of Tom's availability.
He rated him as a first-class hand; and yet he felt a secret dislike
to him—the native antipathy of bad to good. He saw plainly that
when, as was often the case, his violence and brutality fell on the
helpless, Tom took notice of it; for, so subtle is the atmosphere
of opinion, that it will make itself felt without words; and the
opinion even of a slave may annoy a master. Tom in various ways
manifested a tenderness of feeling, a commiseration for his
fellow-sufferers, strange and new to them, which was watched
with a jealous eye by Legree. He had purchased Tom with a view
of eventually making him a sort of overseer, with whom he might
at times entrust his affairs in short absences; and, in his view,
the first, second, and third requisite for that place was *hardness*.
Legree made up his mind that, as Tom was not hard to his hand,
he would harden him forthwith; and some few weeks after Tom
had been on the place, he determined to commence the process.

Slowly the weary, dispirited creatures made to serve Legree
wound their way into the weighing-room, and, with crouching
reluctance, presented their baskets to be weighed.

Tom's basket was weighed and approved; and he looked, with
an anxious glance, for the success of Lucy, a mulatto woman

whom he had befriended who had been bought in the same lot with himself. Tottering with weakness, she came forward, and delivered her basket. It was of full weight, as Legree well perceived; but, affecting anger, he said:

"What, you lazy beast! short again! Stand aside, you'll catch it, pretty soon!"

The woman gave a groan of utter despair, and sat down on a board.

A person called Misse Cassy now came forward, and, with a haughty, negligent air, delivered her basket. She was a tall woman, slenderly formed and might have been between thirty-five and forty. Her face was one that once seen could never be forgotten, with high forehead, straight well-formed nose, firmly cut mouth and a graceful contour of head and neck; but it was also a face that was deeply wrinkled with lines of pain, and of proud and bitter endurance.

As she delivered her basket, Legree looked in her eyes with a sneering yet inquiring glance. She fixed her black eyes steadily on him, her lips moved slightly and she said something in French. What it was, no one knew; but Legree's face became perfectly demoniacal in its expression as she spoke, he half raised his hand, as if to strike—a gesture which she regarded with fierce disdain, as she turned and walked away.

"And now," said Legree, "come here, you Tom. You see, I telled ye I didn't buy ye jest for the common work; I mean to promote ye, and make a driver of ye; and tonight ye may jest as well begin to get yer hand in. Now, ye jest take this yer gal Lucy and flog her; ye've seen enough on't to know how."

"I beg mas'r's pardon," said Tom; "hopes mas'r won't set me at that. It's what I an't used to—never did—and can't do, no way possible."

"Ye'll larn a pretty smart chance of things ye never did know, before I've done with ye!" said Legree, taking up a cow-hide, and striking Tom a heavy blow across the cheek, and following up the affliction by a shower of blows.

"There!" he said, as he stopped to rest; "now, will ye tell me ye can't do it?"

"Yes, mas'r," said Tom, putting up his hand to wipe the blood that trickled down his face. "I'm willin' to work, night and day, and work while there's life and breath in me; but this yer thing I can't feel it right to do; and, mas'r, I *never* shall do it—*never*!"

Tom had a remarkably smooth, soft voice, and a habitually respectful manner, that had given Legree an idea that he would be cowardly, and easily subdued. When he spoke these last words, a thrill of amazement went through everyone; the poor woman clasped her hands, and said, "O Lord!" and everyone involuntarily looked at each other and drew in their breath, as if to prepare for the storm that was about to burst.

Legree looked stupefied and confounded; but at last burst forth:

"What! ye blasted black beast! tell *me* ye don't think it *right* to do what I tell ye! What have any of you cussed cattle to do with thinking what's right? I'll put a stop to it! Why, what do ye think ye are? Maybe ye think ye'r a gentleman, Master Tom, to be telling your master what's right, and what an't! So you pretend it's wrong to flog the gal?"

"I think so, mas'r," said Tom; "the poor crittur's sick and feeble; 'twould be downright cruel, and it's what I never will do, nor begin to. Mas'r, if you mean to kill me, kill me; but, as to my raising my hand agin anyone here, I never shall—I'll die first."

Tom spoke in a mild voice, but with a decision that could not be mistaken. Legree shook with anger; his greenish eyes glared fiercely, and his very whiskers seemed to curl with passion; but, like some ferocious beast, that plays with its victim before he devours it, he kept back his strong impulse to proceed to immediate violence, and broke out into bitter raillery.

"Well, here's a pious dog, at last, let down among us sinners!— a saint, a gentleman, and no less, to talk to us sinners about our sins! Powerful holy crittur, he must be! Here, you rascal, you make believe to be so pious—didn't you never hear, out of yer Bible, "Servants, obey yer masters"? An't I yer master? Didn't I pay down twelve hundred doilars, cash, for all there is of inside yer old cussed black shell? An' yer mine, now, body and soul?" he said, giving Tom a violent kick with his heavy boot; "tell me!"

In the very depth of physical suffering, bowed by brutal oppression, this question shot a gleam of joy and triumph through

Tom's soul. He suddenly stretched himself up, and looking earnestly to heaven, while the tears and blood that flowed down his face mingled, he exclaimed:

"No! no! no! my soul an't yours, mas'r! You haven't bought it—ye can't buy it! It's been bought and paid for by One that is able to keep it; no matter, no matter, you can't harm me!"

"I can't!" said Legree, with a sneer; "we'll see—we'll see! Here, Sambo, Quimbo, give this dog such a breakin' in as he won't get over this month!"

The two gigantic negroes that now laid hold of Tom, with fiendish exultation in their faces, might have formed no unapt personification of the powers of darkness. The poor woman screamed with apprehension, and all rose, as by a general impulse, while they dragged him unresisting from the place.

25

Misse Cassy Helps

IT WAS late at night, and Tom lay groaning and bleeding alone, in an old forsaken room of the gin-house, among pieces of broken machinery, piles of damaged cotton, and other rubbish which had there accumulated.

The night was damp and close, and the thick air swarmed with myriads of mosquitoes, which increased the restless torture of his wounds; whilst a burning thirst—a torture beyond all others—filled up the uttermost measure of physical anguish.

"Oh, good Lord! *Do* look down—give me the victory!—give me the victory over all!" prayed poor Tom, in his anguish.

A footstep entered the room behind him, and the light of a lantern flashed on his eyes.

"Who's there? Oh, for the Lord's massy, please give me some water!"

The woman Cassy—for it was she—set down her lantern, and pouring water from a bottle, raised his head, and gave him drink. Another and another cup were drained, with feverish eagerness.

"Drink all ye want," she said; "I knew how it would be. It isn't the first time I've been out in the night, carrying water to such as you."

"Thank you, missis," said Tom, when he had done drinking.

"Don't call me missis! I'm a miserable slave, like yourself—a lower one than you can ever be!" she said bitterly; "but now," said she, going to the door, and dragging in a small palliasse, over which she had spread linen cloths wet with cold water, "try, my poor fellow, to roll yourself on to this."

Stiff with wounds and bruises, Tom was a long time in accomplishing this movement; but when done, he felt a sensible relief from the cooling application to his wounds.

The woman, whom long practice with the victims of brutality had made familiar with many healing arts, went on to make many applications to Tom's wounds, by means of which he was soon somewhat relieved.

"Now," said the woman, when she had raised his head on a roll of damaged cotton, which served for a pillow, "there's the best I can do for you."

Tom thanked her, and the woman, sitting down on the floor, drew up her knees, and embracing them with her arms, looked fixedly before her, with a bitter and painful expression of countenance. Her bonnet fell back, and long wavy streams of black hair fell around her singular and melancholy face.

"It's no use, my poor fellow!" she broke out at last—"it's of no use, this you've been trying to do. You were a brave fellow—you had the right on your side; but it's all in vain, and out of the question, for you to struggle. You are in the devil's hands; he is the strongest, and you must give up!"

Give up! and had not human weakness and physical agony whispered that before? Tom started; for the bitter woman, with her wild eyes and melancholy voice, seemed to him an embodiment of the temptation with which he had been wrestling.

"O Lord! O Lord!" he groaned, "how can I give up?"

"There's no use calling on the Lord—He never hears," said the woman steadily; "there isn't any God, I believe; or, if there is, He's taken sides against us. All goes against us, heaven and earth. Everything is pushing us into hell. Why shouldn't we go?"

Tom closed his eyes, and shuddered at the dark, atheistic words.

"You see," said the woman, "you don't know anything about it; I do. I've been on this place five years, body and soul under this man's foot; and I hate him as I do the devil! Here you are, on a lone plantation, ten miles from any other, in the swamps; not a white person here who could testify if you were burned alive—if you were scalded, cut into inch-pieces, set up for the dogs to tear, or hung up and whipped to death. There's no law here, of God or man, that can do you, or any one of us, the least good; and this man! there's no earthly thing that he's too good to do. I could make anyone's hair rise, and their teeth chatter, if I should only tell what I have seen and been knowing to here—and it's no use resisting! Did I *want* to live with him? Wasn't I a woman delicately bred; and he—God in heaven! what was he, and is he? And yet I've lived with him these five years, and cursed every moment of my life—night and day! And now he's got a new one—a young thing, only fifteen, and she brought up, she says, piously. Her good mistress taught her to read the Bible; and she's brought her Bible here—to hell with her!" And the woman laughed a wild and doleful laugh, that rung, with a strange, supernatural sound, through the old ruined shed.

Tom folded his hands; all was darkness and horror.

"O Jesus! Lord Jesus! have you quite forgot us poor critturs?" burst forth, at last. "Help, Lord, I perish!"

The woman sternly continued:

"And what are these miserable low dogs you work with, that you should suffer on their account? Every one of them would turn against you the first time they got a chance. They are all of 'em as low and cruel to each other as they can be; there's no use in your suffering to keep from hurting them."

"Poor critturs!" said Tom—"what made 'em cruel?—and, if I give out, I shall get used to 't, and grow, little by little, just like 'em. No, no, missis! I've lost everything—wife, and children, and home, and a kind mas'r—and he would have set me free, if he'd only lived a week longer; I've lost everything in this world, and it's clean gone for ever—and now I *can't* lose heaven too; no, I can't get to be wicked, besides all!"

"But it can't be that the Lord will lay sin to our account," said the woman; "He won't charge it on us, when we're forced to it. He'll charge it to them that drove us to it."

"Yes," said Tom; "but that won't keep us from growing wicked. If I get to be as hard-hearted as that ar Sambo, and as wicked, it won't make much odds to me how I come so; it's the *bein' so*— that ar's what I'm a-dreadin'."

The woman fixed a wild and startled look on Tom, as if a new thought had struck her; and then, heavily groaning, said:

"O God a' mercy! you speak the truth! Oh—oh—oh!"—and, with groans, she fell on the floor, like one crushed and writhing under the extremity of mental anguish.

There was a silence a while, in which the breathing of both parties could be heard, when Tom faintly said, "Oh, please, missis!"

The woman suddenly rose up, with her face composed to its usual stern, melancholy expression.

"Please, missis, I saw 'em throw my coat in that ar corner, and in my coat-pocket is my Bible—if missis would please get it for me."

Cassy went and got it. Tom opened at once to a heavily-marked passage, much worn, of the last scenes in the life of Him by whose stripes we are healed.

"If missis would only be so good as to read that ar—it's better than water."

Cassy took the book, with a dry, proud air, and looked over the passage. She then read aloud, in a soft voice, and with a beauty of intonation that was peculiar, that touching account of anguish and of glory. Often, as she read, her voice faltered, and sometimes failed her altogether, when she would stop, with an air of frigid composure, till she had mastered herself. When she came to the touching words, "Father, forgive them, for they know not what they do", she threw down the book, and burying her face in the heavy masses of her hair, she sobbed aloud, with a convulsive violence.

Tom was weeping also, and occasionally uttering a smothered ejaculation.

"If we could only keep up to that ar!" said Tom; "it seemed to come so natural to Him, and we have to fight so hard for't!—O Lord, help us! O blessed Lord Jesus, do help us!"

"Missis," said Tom, after a while, "I can see that, somehow, you're quite 'bove me in everything; but there's one thing missis might learn even from poor Tom. Ye said the Lord took sides against us, because He let us be 'bused and knocked round; but ye see what came on His own Son—the blessed Lord of Glory—wan't he allays poor? and have we, any of us, yet come so low as He come? The Lord han't forgot us—I'm sartin o' that ar. If we suffer with Him, we shall also reign, Scripture says; but if we deny Him, He also will deny us. Didn't they all suffer?—the Lord and all His? It tells how they was stoned and sawn asunder, and wandered about in sheep-skins and goat skins, and was destitute, afflicted, tormented. Sufferin' an't no reason to make us think the Lord's turned agin us; but jest the contrary, if only we hold on to Him, and doesn't give up to sin."

"But why does He put us where we can't help but sin?" said the woman.

"I think we *can* help it," said Tom.

"You'll see," said Cassy; "what'll you do? Tomorrow they'll be at you again. I know 'em; I've seen all their doings; I can't bear to think of all they'll bring you to;—and they'll make you give out at last!"

"Lord Jesus!" said Tom, "you *will* take care of my soul? O Lord, do!—don't let me give out!"

"Oh, dear!" said Cassy; I've heard all this crying and prayer before; and yet, they've been broken down, and brought under. There's Emmeline, she's trying to hold on, and you're trying— but what use? You must give up, or be killed by inches."

"Well, then, I *will* die!" said Tom. "Spin it out as long as they can, they can't help my dying some time!—and, after that, they can't do no more. I'm clar, I'm set! I *know* the Lord'll help me, and bring me through."

The woman spoke very rapidly.

"But those that have given up, there's no hope for them! You see me now, in filth, grown loathsome. Well, I was brought up in luxury though my mother was a slavewoman. For seven years I loved the man who bought me. Everything that money could buy he gave me and we had two beautiful children—Henry, the image of his father; little Elise, he said, looked like me.

"Oh, those were happy days. I thought I was as happy as anyone can be, but then came evil times. To clear off his family debts, *he sold us* to a cousin and this cursed wretch made me as submissive as he desired. *And then he sold those children*. I passed from hand to hand, faded and wrinkled—and here I am.

"You tell me that there is a God! In the judgement day I will stand up before God, a witness against those that have ruined me and my children, body and soul! I used to love God and prayer. Now I am a lost soul, pursued by devils."

Tom looked earnestly and pitifully into her face.

"Oh, missis, I wish you'd go to Him that can give you living waters!"

"Go to Him! Where is He? Who is He?" said Cassy.

"Him that you read of to me—the Lord."

"I used to see the picture of Him, over the altar, when I was a girl," said Cassy, her dark eyes fixing themselves in an expression of mournful reverie; "but *He isn't here*! there's nothing here but sin, and long, long, long despair!"

Tom looked as if he would speak again; but she cut him short with a decided gesture.

"Don't talk, my poor fellow. Try to sleep if you can." And placing water in his reach, and making whatever little arrangements for his comfort she could, Cassy left the shed.

26

To Canada

A WHILE we must leave Tom in the hands of his persecutors, while we turn to pursue the fortunes of George and his wife, whom we left in friendly hands, in a farmhouse on the roadside.

Tom Loker we left groaning and tousling in a most immaculately clean Quaker bed, under the motherly supervision of Aunt Dorcas, who found him to the full as tractable a patient as a sick bison.

Imagine a tall, dignified, spiritual woman, whose clear muslin cap shades waves of silvery hair, parted on a broad, clear forehead, which overarches thoughtful grey eyes. A snowy handkerchief of lisse crape is folded neatly across her bosom; her glossy brown silk dress rustles peacefully, as she glides up and down the chamber.

"The devil!" says Tom Loker, giving a great throw to the bed-clothes. "It's so cursedly hot!"

Dorcas removed a comforter from the bed, straightened the clothes again, and tucked them in till Tom looked something like a chrysalis; remarking, as she did so:

"I wish, friend, thee would leave off cursing and swearing, and think upon thy ways."

"What the devil," said Tom, "should I think of *them* for? Last thing ever I want to think of—hang it all!" And Tom flounced over, untucking and disarranging everything.

"That fellow and gal are here, I s'pose?" said he sullenly, after a pause.

"They are so," said Dorcas.

"They'd better be off up to the lake," said Tom; "the quicker the better."

"Probably they will do so," said Aunt Dorcas, knitting peacefully.

"And hark ye," said Tom; "we've got correspondents in

Sandusky that watch the boats for us. I don't care if I tell now. I hope they *will* get away, just to spite Marks—the cursed puppy!—d—n him!"

"Thomas!" said Dorcas.

"I tell you, granny, if you bottle a fellow up too tight, I shall split," said Tom. "But about the gal—tell 'em to dress her up some way, so's to alter her. Her description's out in Sandusky."

"We will attend to that matter," said Dorcas, with characteristic composure.

As we at this place take leave of Tom Loker, we may as well say that, having lain three weeks at the Quaker dwelling, sick with a rheumatic fever, which set in, in company with his other afflictions, Tom arose from his bed a somewhat sadder and wiser man; and, in place of slave-catching, betook himself to life in one of the new settlements, where his talents developed themselves more happily in trapping bears, wolves, and other inhabitants of the forest, in which he made himself quite a name in the land. Tom always spoke reverently of the Quakers. "Nice people," he would say; "wanted to convert me, but couldn't come it, exactly."

As Tom had informed them that their party would be looked for in Sandusky, it was thought prudent to divide them. Jim, with his old mother, was forwarded separately; and a night or two after, George and Eliza, with their child, were driven privately into Sandusky, and lodged beneath a hospitable roof, preparatory to taking their last passage on the lake.

Their night was now far spent, and the morning-star of liberty rose fair before them. Liberty!—electric word! Is there anything in it glorious and dear for a nation, that is not also glorious and dear for a man? What is freedom to a nation, but freedom to the individuals in it? What is freedom to that young man who sits there, with his arms folded over his broad chest, the tint of African blood in his cheeks, its dark fires in his eyes—what is freedom to George Harris? To your fathers, freedom was the right of a nation to be a nation. To him, it is the right of a man to be a man, and not a brute; the right to call the wife of his bosom his wife, and to protect her from lawless violence; the right to protect and educate his child; the right to have a home of his own, a religion of his own, a character of his own, unsubject to the will of another. All these thoughts were rolling and seething in George's breast, as he was pensively leaning his head on his hand, watching his wife, as she was adapting to her slender and pretty form the articles of man's attire, in which it was deemed safest she should make her escape.

"Now for it," said she, as she stood before the glass, and shook down her silky abundance of black curly hair. "I say, George, it's almost a pity, isn't it," she said, as she held up some of it playfully—"pity it's all got to come off?"

George smiled sadly, and made no answer.

Eliza turned to the glass, and the scissors glittered as one long lock after another was detached from her head.

"There now, that'll do," she said, taking up a hair-brush; "now for a few fancy touches." She kneeled on one knee, and laid her hand on his. "We are only within twenty-four hours of Canada, they say. Only a day and a night on the lake, and then—oh, then!"

"Oh, Eliza!" said George, drawing her towards him; "that is it! Now my fate is all narrowing down to a point. To come so near, to be almost in sight, and then lose all. I should never live under it, Eliza."

"Don't fear," said his wife hopefully. "The good Lord would not have brought us so far, if He didn't mean to carry us through. I seem to feel Him with us, George."

"You are a blessed woman, Eliza!" said George, clasping her with a convulsive grasp. "But—oh, tell me! can this great mercy be for us? Will these years and years of misery come to an end?— shall we be free?"

"I am sure of it, George," said Eliza, looking upward, while tears of hope and enthusiasm shone on her long, dark lashes. "I feel it in me, that God is going to bring us out of bondage this very day."

"I will believe you, Eliza," said George, rising suddenly up. "I will believe—come, let's be off. Well, indeed!" said he, holding her off at arm's-length, and looking admiringly at her, "you *are* a pretty little fellow. That crop of little, short curls is quite becoming. Put on your cap. So—a little to one side. I never saw you look quite so pretty. But it's almost time for the carriage; I wonder if Mrs Smyth has got Harry rigged?"

The door opened, and a respectable, middle-aged woman entered, leading little Harry, dressed in girl's clothes.

"What a pretty girl he makes!" said Eliza, turning him round. "We call him Harriet, you see; don't the name come nicely?"

The child stood gravely regarding his mother in her new and strange attire, observing a profound silence, and occasionally drawing deep sighs, and peeping at her from under his dark curls.

"Does Harry know mamma?" said Eliza, stretching her hands towards him.

The child clung shyly to the woman.

"Come, Eliza, why do you try to coax him, when you know that he has got to be kept away from you?"

"I know it's foolish," said Eliza; "yet I can't bear to have him turn away from me. But come—where's my cloak? Here—how is it men put on cloaks, George?"

"You must wear it so," said her husband, throwing it over his shoulders.

"So, then," said Eliza, imitating the motion—"and I must stamp, and take long steps, and try to look saucy."

"Don't exert yourself," said George. "There is, now and then, a modest young man; and I think it would be easier for you to act that character."

"And these gloves—mercy upon us!" said Eliza; "why, my hands are lost in them."

"I advise you to keep them on pretty strictly," said George. "Your little slender paw might bring us all out.—Now, Mrs Smyth, you are to go under our charge, and be our aunty—you mind."

"I've heard," said Mrs Smyth, "that there have been men down, warning all the packet captains against a man and woman, with a little boy."

"They have!" said George. "Well, if we see any such people, we can tell them."

A hack now drove to the door, and the friendly family who had received the fugitives crowded around them with farewell greetings.

The disguises the party had assumed were in accordance with the hints of Tom Loker. Mrs Smyth, a respectable woman from the settlement in Canada, whither they were fleeing, being fortunately about crossing the lake to return thither, had consented to appear as the aunt of little Harry; and, in order to attach him to her, he had been allowed to remain, the last two days, under her sole charge; and an extra amount of petting, joined to an indefinite amount of seed-cakes and candy, had cemented a very close attachment on the part of the young gentleman.

The hack drove to the wharf. The two young men, as they appeared, walked up the plank into the boat, Eliza gallantly giving her arm to Mrs Smyth, and George attending to their baggage.

George was standing at the captain's office, settling for his party, when he overheard two men talking by his side.

"I've watched every one that came on board," said one, "and I know they're not on this boat."

The voice was that of the clerk of the boat. The speaker whom he addressed was our sometime friend Marks, who, with that valuable perseverance which characterized him, had come on to Sandusky, seeking whom he might devour.

"You would scarcely know the woman from a white one," said Marks. "The man is a very light mulatto; he has a brand in one of his hands."

The hand with which George was taking the tickets and change trembled a little; but he turned coolly around, fixed an unconcerned glance on the face of the speaker, and walked leisurely toward another part of the boat, where Eliza stood waiting for him.

Mrs Smyth, with little Harry, sought the seclusion of the ladies' cabin, where the dark beauty of the supposed little girl drew many flattering comments from the passengers.

George had the satisfaction, as the bell rang out its farewell peal, to see Marks walk down the plank to the shore, and drew a long sigh of relief when the boat had put a returnless distance between them.

It was a superb day. The blue waves of Lake Erie danced, rippling and sparkling in the sunlight. A fresh breeze blew from the shore, and the lordly boat ploughed her way right gallantly onward.

Oh, what an untold world there is in one human heart! Who

thought, as George walked calmly up and down the deck of the
steamer, with his shy companion at his side, of all that was
burning in his bosom? The mighty good that seemed approaching
seemed too good, too fair, even to be a reality; and he felt a jealous
dread, every moment of the day, that something would rise to
snatch it from *him*.

But the boat swept on. Hours fleeted, and, at last, clear and
full rose the blessed English shores; shores charmed by a mighty
spell—with one touch to dissolve every incantation of slavery, no
matter in what language pronounced, or by what national power
confirmed.

George and his wife stood arm in arm, as the boat neared the
small town of Amherstberg, in Canada. His breath grew thick
and short; a mist gathered before his eyes; he silently pressed
the little hand that lay trembling on his arm. The bell rang; the
boat stopped. Scarcely seeing what he did, he looked out his
baggage, and gathered his little party. The little company were
landed on the shore. They stood still till the boat had cleared;
and then, with tears and embracings, the husband and wife, with
their wondering child in their arms, knelt down and lifted up
their hearts to God!

> "'Twas something like the burst from death to life;
> From the grave's cerements to the robes of heaven;
> From sin's dominion, and from passion's strife,
> To the pure freedom of a soul forgiven;
> Where all the bonds of death and hell are riven,
> And mortal puts on immortality,
> When Mercy's hand hath turned the golden key,
> And Mercy's voice hath said, *Rejoice, thy soul is free*."

The little party were soon guided by Mrs Smyth to the hospitable
abode of a good missionary, whom Christian charity had placed
here as a shepherd to the outcast and wandering, who are
constantly finding an asylum on this shore.

27

Uncle Tom Triumphs

WHEN Tom stood face to face with his persecutor, and
heard his threats, and thought in his very soul that his
hour was come, his heart swelled bravely in him, and
he thought he could bear torture and fire, bear anything, with
the vision of Jesus and heaven but just a step beyond; but when
he was gone, and the present excitement passed off, came back
the pain of his bruised and weary limbs, came back the sense of
his utterly degraded, hopeless, forlorn estate; and the day passed
wearily enough.

Long before his wounds were healed, Legree insisted that he
should be put to the regular fieldwork; and then came day after
day of pain and weariness, aggravated by every kind of injustice
and indignity that the ill-will of a mean and malicious mind could
devise. Tom no longer wondered at the habitual surliness of his
associates; nay, he found the placid, sunny temper, which had been
the habitude of his life, broken in on, and sorely strained by the
inroads of the same thing. He had flattered himself on leisure to
read his Bible; but there was no such thing as leisure there. In the
height of the season, Legree did not hesitate to press all his hands
through, Sundays and week-days alike. Why shouldn't he?—he
made more cotton by it, and gained his wager; and if it wore out a
few more hands, he could buy better ones. At first, Tom used to
read a verse or two of his Bible, by the flicker of the fire, after he
had returned from his daily toil; but, after the cruel treatment he
received, he used to come home so exhausted, that his head swam
and his eyes failed when he tried to read; and he was fain to stretch
himself down with the others, in utter exhaustion.

One evening, he was sitting, in utter dejection and prostration,
by a few decaying brands, where his coarse supper was baking.
He put a few bits of brushwood on the fire, and strove to raise
the light, and then drew his worn Bible from his pocket. There
were all the marked passages, which had thrilled his soul so

often—words of patriarchs and seers, poets and sages, who from early time had spoken courage to man—voices from the great cloud of witnesses who ever surround us in the race of life. Had the word lost its power, or could the failing eye and weary sense no longer answer to the touch of that mighty inspiration? Heavily sighing, he put it in his pocket. A coarse laugh roused him; he looked up—Legree was standing opposite to him.

"Well, old boy," he said, "you find your religion don't work, it seems! I thought I should get that through your wool, at last!"

The cruel taunt was more than hunger and cold and nakedness. Tom was silent.

"You were a fool," said Legree; "for I meant to do well by you when I bought you. You might have been better off than Sambo, or Quimbo either, and had easy times; and, instead of getting cut up and thrashed, every day or two, ye might have had liberty to lord it round, and cut up the other niggers; and ye might have had, now and then, a good warming of whisky punch. Come, Tom, don't you think you'd better be reasonable?—heave that ar old pack of trash in the fire, and join my church!"

"The Lord forbid!" said Tom fervently.

"You see the Lord an't going to help you; if He had been, He wouldn't have let me get you! This yer religion is all a mess of lying trumpery, Tom. I know all about it. Ye'd better hold to me: I'm somebody, and can do something!"

"No, mas'r," said Tom; "I'll hold on. The Lord may help me, or not help; but I'll hold to Him, and believe Him to the last!"

"The more fool you!" said Legree, spitting scornfully at him, and spurning him with his foot. "Never mind; I'll chase you down yet, and bring you under—you'll see!" and Legree turned away.

How long Tom lay there, he knew not. When he came to himself, the fire was gone out, his clothes were wet with the chill and drenching dews; but the dread soul-crisis was past, and, in the joy that filled him, he no longer felt hunger, cold, degradation, disappointment, wretchedness. From his deepest soul, he that hour loosed and parted from every hope in the life that now is, and offered his own will an unquestioning sacrifice to the Infinite. Tom looked up to the silent, ever-living stars—types of the angelic hosts who ever look down on man; and the solitude of the night

rung with the triumphant words of a hymn, which he had sung
often in happier days, but never with such feeling as now:

> "The earth shall be dissolved like snow,
>   The sun shall cease to shine;
> But God, who call'd me here below,
>   Shall be for ever mine.
>
> "And when this mortal life shall fail,
>   And flesh and sense shall cease,
> I shall possess within the veil
>   A life of joy and peace.
>
> "When we've been there ten thousand years,
>   Bright shining like the sun,
> We've no less days to sing God's praise
> Than when we first begun."

From this time, an inviolable sphere of peace encompassed the
lowly heart of the oppressed one.

All noticed the change in his appearance. Cheerfulness and
alertness seemed to return to him, and a quietness which no
insult or injury could ruffle seemed to possess him.

"What the devil's got into Tom?" Legree said to Sambo. "A
while ago he was all down in the mouth, and now he's peart as a
cricket."

"Dun'no, mas'r; gwine to run off, mebbe."

"Like to see him try that," said Legree with a savage grin;
"wouldn't we, Sambo? Sambo, you look sharp. If the nigger's got
anything of this sort going, trip him up."

"Mas'r, let me alone for dat," said Sambo. "I'll tree de coon.
Ho, ho, ho!"

This was spoken as Legree was getting on to his horse, to go
to the neighbouring town. That night, as he was returning, he
thought he would turn his horse and ride round the quarters,
and see if all was safe.

It was a superb moonlight night, and the shadows of the
graceful China trees lay minutely pencilled on the turf below,

and there was that transparent stillness in the air which it seems almost unholy to disturb. Legree was at a little distance from the quarters, when he heard the voice of someone singing. It was not a usual sound there, and he paused to listen. A musical tenor voice sang:

> "Let cares like a wild deluge come,
>   And storms of sorrow fall,
> May I but safely reach my home,
>   My God, my Heaven, my All!"

"So ho!" said Legree to himself, "he thinks so, does he? How I hate these cursed Methodist hymns!—Here, you nigger," said he, coming suddenly out upon Tom, and raising his riding-whip, "how dare you be gettin' up this yer row, when you ought to be in bed? Shut yer old black gash, and get along with you!"

"Yes, mas'r," said Tom, with ready cheerfulness, as he rose to go in.

Legree was provoked beyond measure by Tom's evident happiness; and, riding up to him, belaboured him over his head and shoulders.

"There, you dog," he said, "see if you'll feel so comfortable, after that!"

But the blows fell now only on the outer man, and not, as before, on the heart. Tom stood perfectly submissive; and yet Legree could not hide from himself that his power over his bond-thrall was somehow gone.

Tom's whole soul overflowed with compassion and sympathy for the poor wretches by whom he was surrounded. To him it seemed as if his life-sorrows were now over, and as if, out of that strange treasury of peace and joy with which he had been endowed from above, he longed to pour out something for the relief of their woes. It is true, opportunities were scanty; but on the way to the fields and back again, and during the hours of labour, chances fell in his way of extending a helping hand to the weary, the disheartened and discouraged. The poor, worn-down, brutalized creatures at first could scarcely comprehend this; but when it was continued week after week, and month after month, it began to awaken long-silent chords in their benumbed hearts. Gradually and imperceptibly the strange, silent, patient man, who was ready to bear everyone s burden, and sought help from none—the man who, in cold nights would give up his tattered blanket to add to the comfort of some woman who shivered with sickness, and who filled the baskets of the weaker ones in the field, at the terrible risk of coming short in his own measure, and who, though pursued with unrelenting cruelty by their common tyrant, never joined in uttering a word of reviling or cursing—this man at last began to have a strange power over them; and when the more pressing season was past, and they were allowed again their Sundays for their own use, many would gather together to hear from him of Jesus. They would gladly have met to hear, and pray, and sing, in some place, together; but Legree would not permit it, and more than once broke up such attempts with oaths and brutal execrations, so that the blessed news had to circulate from individual to individual.

Stung to madness and despair by the crushing agonies of her life, Cassy had often resolved in her soul an hour of retribution, when her hand should avenge on her oppressor all the injustice and cruelty to which she had been witness, or which *she* had in her own person suffered.

One night, after all in Tom's cabin were sunk in sleep, he was suddenly aroused by seeing her face at the hole between the logs that served for a window. She made a silent gesture for him to come out.

Tom came out to the door. It was between one and two o'clock at night—broad, calm, still moonlight. Tom remarked, as the light of the moon fell upon Cassy's large, black eyes, that there was a wild and peculiar glare in them, unlike their wonted fixed despair.

"Come here, Father Tom," she said, laying her small hand on his wrist, and drawing him forward with a force as if the hand were of steel; "come here—I've news for you."

"What, Misse Cassy?" said Tom anxiously.

"Tom, wouldn't you like your liberty?"

"I shall have it, misse, in God's time," said Tom.

"Ay, but you may have it tonight," said Cassy, with a flash of sudden energy. "Come on. He's asleep—sound. I put enough into his brandy to keep him so. I wish I'd had more—I shouldn't have wanted you. But come, the back door is unlocked; there's an axe there. I put it there—his room door is open; I'll show you the way. I'd a done it myself, only my arms are so weak. Come along."

"Not for ten thousand worlds, misse!" said Tom firmly, stopping and holding her back, as she was pressing forward.

"But think of all these poor creatures," said Cassy. "We might set them all free, and go somewhere in the swamps and find an island, and live by ourselves; I've heard of its being done. Any life is better than this."

"No!" said Tom firmly. "No! Good never comes of wickedness. I'd sooner chop my right hand off!"

"Then *I* shall do it," said Cassy, turning.

"Oh, Misse Cassy!" said Tom, throwing himself before her, "for the dear Lord's sake that died for ye, don't sell your precious soul to the devil that way! Nothing but evil will come of it. The Lord hasn't called us to wrath. We must suffer, and wait His time."

"Wait!" said Cassy. "Haven't I waited?—waited till my head is dizzy and my heart sick? What has he made me suffer? What has he made hundreds of poor creatures suffer? Isn't he wringing the life-blood out of you? I'm called on! They call me! His time's come, and I'll have his heart's blood!"

"No, no, no!" said Tom, holding her small hands, which were clenched with spasmodic violence. "No, ye poor, lost soul, that ye mustn't do. The dear, blessed Lord never shed no blood but His own, and that He poured out for us when we was enemies. Lord, help us to follow His steps, and love our enemies."

"Love!" said Cassy, with a fierce glare; "love *such* enemies! It isn't in flesh and blood."

"No, misse, it isn't," said Tom, looking up; "but *He* gives it to us, and that's the *victory*. When we can love and pray over all and through all, the battle's past and the victory's come—glory be to God!" And, with streaming eyes and choking voice, the black man looked up to heaven.

The deep fervour of Tom's feelings, the softness of his voice, his tears, fell like dew on the wild, unsettled spirit of the poor woman. A softness gathered over the lurid fires of her eye; she looked down, and Tom could feel the relaxing muscles of her hands, as she said:

"Didn't I tell you that evil spirits followed me? Oh! Father Tom,

I can't pray—I wish I could. I never have prayed since my children were sold! What you say must be right, I know it must; but when I try to pray, I can only hate and curse, I can't pray!"

"Poor soul!" said Tom compassionately. "Satan desires to have ye, and sift ye as wheat. I pray the Lord for ye. Oh, Misse Cassy, turn to the dear Lord Jesus. He came to bind up the broken-hearted, and comfort all that mourn."

Cassy stood silent, while large, heavy tears dropped from her downcast eyes.

"Misse Cassy," said Tom, in a hesitating tone, after surveying her a moment in silence, "if ye only could get away from here—if the thing was possible—I'd 'vise ye and that young Emmeline to do it; that is, if ye could go without blood-guiltiness—not otherwise."

"Would you try it with us, Father Tom?"

"No," said Tom; "time was when I would; but the Lord's given me a work among these yer poor souls, and I'll stay with 'em and bear my cross with 'em till the end. It's different with you; it's a snare to you—it's more'n you can stand—and you'd better go, if you can."

"I know no way but through the grave," said Cassy. "There's no beast or bird but can find a home somewhere; even the snakes and the alligators have their places to lie down and be quiet; but there's no place for us. Down in the darkest swamps, their dogs will hunt us out, and find us. Everybody and everything is against us; even the very beasts side against us—and where shall we go?"

Tom stood silent; at length he said:

"Him that saved Daniel in the den of lions—that saved the children in the fiery furnace—Him that walked on the sea, and bade the winds be still—He's alive yet; and I've faith to believe He can deliver you. Try it, and I'll pray with all my might for you."

By what strange law of mind is it that an idea long overlooked, and trodden under foot as a useless stone, suddenly sparkles out in new light, as a discovered diamond?

Cassy had often revolved, for hours, all possible or probable schemes of escape, and dismissed them all as hopeless and impracticable; but at this moment there flashed through her mind a plan so simple and feasible in all its details as to awaken an instant hope.

"Father Tom, I'll try it!" she said suddenly. "Amen!" said Tom; "the Lord help ye!"

28

Is it Haunted?

THE GARRET of the house that Legree occupied, like most other garrets, was a great, desolate space, dusty, hung with cobwebs, and littered with cast-off lumber. The opulent family that had inhabited the house in the days of its splendour had imported a great deal of splendid furniture, some of which they had taken away with them, while some remained standing desolate in mouldering, unoccupied rooms, or stored away in this place. One or two immense packing-boxes, in which this furniture was brought, stood against the sides of the garret. There was a small window there, which let in, through its dingy, dusty panes, a scanty, uncertain light on the tall, high-backed chairs and dusty tables, that had once seen better days. Altogether, it was a weird and ghostly place; but, ghostly as it was, it wanted not in legends among the superstitious negroes, to increase its terrors. Some few years before, a negro woman who had incurred Legree's displeasure was confined there for several weeks. What passed there, we do not say; the negroes used to whisper darkly to each other; but it was known that the body of the unfortunate creature was one day taken down from there, and buried; and, after that, it was said that oaths and cursings, and the sound of violent blows, used to ring through that old garret, and mingled with wailings and groans of despair.

Gradually the staircase that led to the garret, and even the passageway to the staircase, were avoided by everyone in the house and it suddenly occurred to Cassy to make use of the superstitious excitability, which was so great in Legree, for the purpose of her liberation and that of her fellow-sufferer.

The sleeping-room of Cassy was directly under the garret. One day, without consulting Legree, she suddenly took it upon her, with some considerable ostentation, to change all the furniture and appurtenances of the room to one at some considerable distance. The under-servants, who were called on to effect this movement, were running and bustling about with great zeal and confusion, when Legree returned from a ride.

"Hollo! you Cass!" said Legree; "what's in the wind now?"

"Nothing; only I choose to have another room," said Cassy doggedly.

"And what for, pray?" said Legree.

"I'd like to get some sleep, now and then."

"Sleep! Well, what hinders your sleeping?"

"Oh! nothing. I suppose it wouldn't disturb you! Only groans, and people scuffing, and rolling round on the garret floor half the night, from twelve to morning!"

"People up garret!" said Legree uneasily, but forcing a laugh. "Who are they, Cassy?"

Cassy raised her sharp, black eyes, and looked in the face of Legree, with an expression that went through his bones, as she said, "To be sure, Simon, who are they? I'd like to have you tell me. You don't know, I suppose!"

With an oath Legree struck at her with his riding-whip; but she glided to one side, and passed through the door, and looking back said, "If you'll sleep in that room, you'll know all about it. Perhaps you'd better try it!" and then immediately she shut and locked the door.

Legree blustered and swore, and threatened to break down the door; but apparently thought better of it, and walked uneasily into the sitting-room. Cassy perceived that her shaft had struck home; and from that hour, with the most exquisite address, she never ceased to continue the train of influences she had begun.

In a knot-hole in the garret she had inserted the neck of an old bottle, in such a manner that when there was the least wind, most doleful and lugubrious wailing sounds proceeded from it, which, in a high wind, increased to a perfect shriek, such as to credulous and superstitious ears might easily seem to be that of horror and despair.

These sounds were from time to time heard by the servants, and revived in full force the memory of the old ghost legend. A superstitious creeping horror seemed to fill the house; and though no one dared to breathe it to Legree, he found himself encompassed by it.

A night or two after this, Legree was sitting in the old sitting-room, by the side of a flickering wood fire, that threw uncertain glances round the room. It was a stormy, windy night, such as raises whole squadrons of nondescript noises in rickety old houses. Windows were rattling, shutters flapping, the wind carousing, rumbling, and tumbling down the chimney, and every once in a while puffing out smoke and ashes, as if a legion of spirits were coming after them. Legree had been casting up accounts and reading newspapers for some hours, while Cassy sat in the corner, sullenly looking into the fire. Legree laid down his paper, and seeing an old book lying on the table, which he had noticed Cassy reading the first part of the evening, took it up, and began to turn it over. It was one of those collections of stories of bloody murders, ghostly legends, and supernatural visitations, which, coarsely got up and illustrated, have a strange fascination for one who once begins to read them.

Legree turned page after page, till, finally, after reading some way, he threw down the book with an oath.

"You don't believe in ghosts, do you, Cassy?" said he, taking the tongs and settling the fire. "I thought you'd more sense than to let noises scare you."

"No matter what I believe," said Cassy sullenly.

"Fellows used to try to frighten me with their yarns at sea," said Legree. "Never come it round me that way. I'm too tough for any such trash, tell ye."

Cassy sat looking intensely at him in the shadow of the corner. There was that strange light in her eyes that always impressed Legree with uneasiness.

"Them noises was nothing but rats and the wind," said Legree. "rats will make a devil of a noise. I used to hear 'em sometimes down in the hold of the ship; and wind—Lord's sake! ye can make anything out o' wind."

Cassy knew Legree was uneasy under her eyes, and therefore she made no answer, but sat fixing them on him.

"Can rats walk down stairs, and come walking through the entry, and open a door when you've locked it and set a chair against it?" she said; "and come walk, walk, walking right up to your bed, and put out their hand so?"

Cassy kept her glittering eyes fixed on Legree as she spoke, and he stared at her like a man in a nightmare, till, when she finished by laying her hand, icy cold, on his, he sprang back with an oath.

"Woman! what do you mean? Nobody did!"

"Oh, no—of course not—did I say they did?" said Cassy, with a smile of chilling derision.

"But—did—have you really seen?—Come, Cass, what is it, now?—speak out!"

"You may sleep there yourself," said Cassy, "if you want to know."

Legree walked up and down the room uneasily.

"I'll have this yer thing examined. I'll look into it this very night. I'll take my pistols.

"Do," said Cassy; "sleep in that room. I'd like to see you doing it. Fire your pistols—do!"

Legree stamped his foot, and swore violently.

"Don't swear," said Cassy; "nobody knows who may be hearing you. Hark! What was that?"

"What?" said Legree, starting.

A heavy old Dutch clock, that stood in the corner of the room, began, and slowly struck twelve.

For some reason or other, Legree neither spoke nor moved; a vague horror fell on him; while Cassy, with a keen, sneering glitter in her eyes, stood looking at him, counting the strokes.

"Twelve o'clock; well, *now* we'll see," said she, turning and opening the door into the passage-way, and standing as if listening.

"Hark! What's that?" said she, raising a finger.

"It's only the wind," said Legree. "Don't you hear how cursedly it blows?"

"Simon, come here," said Cassy in a whisper, laying her hand on his, and leading him to the foot of the stairs; "do you know what *that* is? Hark!"

A wild shriek came pealing down the stairway. It came from the garret. Legree's knees knocked together; his face grew white with fear.

"Hadn't you better get your pistols?" said Cassy, with a sneer that froze Legree's blood. "It's time this thing was looked into, you know. I'd like to have you to go up now; *they're at it*."

"I won't go!" said Legree, with an oath.

"Why not? There an't any such thing as ghosts, you know! Come!" and Cassy flitted up the winding stairway, laughing, and looking back after him, "Come on!"

"I believe you *are* the devil!" said Legree. "Come back, you hag—come back. Cass! You shan't go!"

But Cassy laughed wildly, and fled on. He heard her open the entry doors that led to the garret. A wild gust of wind swept down, extinguishing the candle he held in his hand, and with it the fearful, unearthly screams; they seemed to be shrieked in his very ear.

Legree fled frantically into the parlour, whither, in a few moments, he was followed by Cassy, pale, calm, cold as an avenging spirit, and with that same fearful light in her eye.

"I hope you are satisfied," said she.

"Blast you, Cass!" said Legree.

"What for?" said Cassy. "I only went up and shut the doors. *What's the matter with that garret*, Simon, do you suppose?" said she.

"None of your business!" said Legree.

"Oh, it an't? Well," said Cassy, "at any rate, I'm glad I don't sleep under it."

Anticipating the rising of the wind that very evening, Cassy had been up and opened the garret window. Of course the moment the doors were opened, the wind had drafted down, and extinguished the light.

This may serve as a specimen of the game that Cassy played with Legree, until he would have sooner put his head into a lion's mouth than have explored that garret. Meanwhile, in the night, when everybody else was asleep, Cassy slowly and carefully accumulated there a stock of provisions sufficient to afford subsistence for some time; she transferred, article by article, a greater part of her wardrobe and that of the young girl Emmeline, whom she had befriended. All things being arranged, they only waited a fitting opportunity to put their plan in execution.

By cajoling Legree, and taking advantage of a good-natured interval, Cassy had got him to take her with him to the neighbouring town, which was situated directly on the Red River. With a memory sharpened to almost preternatural clearness, she remarked every turn in the road, and formed a mental estimate of the time to be occupied in traversing it.

At the time when all was matured for action, our readers may, perhaps, like to look behind the scenes, and see the final *coup d'etat*.

It was now near evening. Legree had been absent, on a ride to a neighbouring farm. For many days Cassy had been unusually gracious and accommodating in her humours; and Legree and she had been, apparently, on the best of terms. At present, we may behold her and Emmeline in the room of the latter, busy in sorting and arranging two small bundles.

"There, these will be large enough," said Cassy. "Now, put on your bonnet, and let's start: it's just about the right time."

"Why, they can see us yet," said Emmeline.

"I mean they shall," said Cassy coolly. "Don't you know that they must have their chase after us, at any rate? The way of the thing is to be just this. We will steal out of the back door, and run down by the quarters. Sambo or Quimbo will be sure to see us. They will give chase, and we will get into the swamp; then, they can't follow us any farther till they go up and give the alarm, and turn out the dogs, and so on; and, while they are blundering round, and tumbling over each other, as they always do, you and I will just slip along to the creek that runs back of the house, and wade along in it, till we get opposite the back door. That will put the dogs all at fault; for scent won't lie in the water. Everyone will run out of the house to look after us, and then we'll whip in at the back door, and up into the garret, where I've got a nice bed made up in one of the great boxes. We must stay in that garret a good while; for, I tell you, he will raise heaven and earth after us. He'll muster some of these old overseers on the other plantations, and have a great hunt, and they'll go over every inch of ground in that swamp. He makes it his boast that nobody ever got away from him. So let him hunt at his leisure."

"Cassy, how well you have planned it!" said Emmeline. "Who ever would have thought of it but you?"

There was neither pleasure nor exultation in Cassy's eyes— only a despairing firmness.

"Come," she said, reaching her hand to Emmeline.

The two fugitives glided noiselessly from the house, and flitted, through the gathering shadows of evening, along by the quarters. The crescent moon, set like a silver signet in the western sky, delayed a little the approach of night. As Cassy expected, when quite near the verge of the swamps that encircled the plantation, they heard a voice calling to them to stop. It was not Sambo, however, but Legree, who was pursuing them with violent curses.

"Well," said he, chuckling brutally; "at any rate, they've got themselves into a trap now—the beggars. "They're safe enough. They shall sweat for it!"

"Hollo, there! Sambo! Quimbo! All hands! called Legree, coming to the quarters when the men and women were just returning from work. "There's two runaways in the swamps. I'll give five dollars to any nigger as catches 'em. Turn out the dogs! Turn out Tiger, and Fury, and the rest!"

The sensation produced by this news was immediate. Many of the men sprang forward officiously to offer their services, either from the hope of the reward, or from that cringing subserviency which is one of the most baleful effects of slavery. Some ran one way, and some another. Some were for getting flambeaux of pine-knots. Some were uncoupling the dogs, whose hoarse, savage bay added not a little to the animation of the scene.

"Mas'r, shall we shoot 'em if we can't cotch 'em?" said Sambo, to whom his master brought out a rifle.

"You may fire on Cass, if you like; it's time she was gone to the devil, where she belongs; but the gal, not," said Legree. "And now, boys, be spry and smart, five dollars for him that gets 'em; and a glass of spirits to every one of you, anyhow."

The whole band, with the glare of blazing torches, and whoop, and shout, and savage yell, of man and beast, proceeded down to the swamp, followed at some distance by every servant in the house. The establishment was, of a consequence, wholly deserted when Cassy and Emmeline glided into it the back way. The whooping and shouts of their pursuers were still filling the air; and, looking from the sitting-room windows, Cassy and Emmeline could see the troop with their flambeaux, just dispersing themselves along the edge of the swamp.

"See there!" said Emmeline, pointing to Cassy; "the hunt is begun! Look how those lights dance about! Hark! the dogs! Don't you hear? If we were only *there*, our chance wouldn't be worth a picayune. Oh, for pity's sake, do let's hide ourselves. Quick!"

"There's no occasion for hurry," said Cassy coolly; "they are all out after the hunt—that's the amusement of the evening! We'll go upstairs by and by. Meanwhile," said she, deliberately taking a key from the pocket of a coat that Legree had thrown down in his hurry—"meanwhile I shall take something to pay our passage."

She unlocked the desk, took from it a roll of bills, which she counted over rapidly.

When Emmeline reached the garret, she found an immense box, in which some heavy pieces of furniture had once been brought, turned on its side, so that the opening faced the wall, or rather the eaves. Cassy lit a small lamp, and, creeping round under the eaves, they established themselves in it. It was spread with a couple of small mattresses and some pillows; a box near by was plentifully stored with candles, provisions, and all the clothing necessary to their journey, which Cassy had arranged into bundles of an astonishingly small compass.

"There," said Cassy, as she fixed the lamp into a small hook, which she had driven into the side of the box for that purpose; "this is to be our home for the present. How do you like it?"

"Are you sure they won't come and search the garret?"

"I'd like to see Simon Legree doing that," said Cassy. "No, indeed; he will be too glad to keep away. As to the servants, they would any of them stand and be shot, sooner than show their faces here."

The two remained some time in silence. Emmeline, overcome with the exhaustion, fell into a doze and slept some time. She was awakened by loud shouts and outcries, the tramp of horses' feet and the baying of dogs. She started up with a faint shriek.

"Only the hunt coming back," said Cassy coolly; "never fear. Look out of this knot-hole. Don't you see 'em all down there? Simon has to give it up for this night. Look, how muddy his horse is, flouncing about in the swamp; the dogs, too, look rather crestfallen.—Ah, my good sir, you'll have to try the race again and again—the game isn't there."

"Oh, don't speak a word!" said Emmeline; "what if they should hear you?"

"If they do hear anything, it will make them very particular to keep away," said Cassy. "No danger; we may make any noise we please, and it will only add to the effect."

At length the stillness of midnight settled down over the house. Legree, cursing his ill-luck, and vowing dire vengeance on the morrow, went to bed.

29

Uncle Tom's Last Prayer

THE ESCAPE of Cassy and Emmeline irritated the before surly temper of Legree to the last degree; and his fury, as was to be expected, fell upon the defenceless head of Tom. When he hurriedly announced the tidings among his hands, there was a sudden light in Tom's eye, a sudden upraising of his hands, that did not escape him. He saw that he did not join the muster of the pursuers. Tom had remained behind, with a few who had learned of him to pray, and offered up prayers for the escape of the fugitives.

When Legree returned, baffled and disappointed, all the long-working hatred of his soul towards his slave began to gather in a deadly and desperate form. Had not this man braved him—steadily, powerfully, resistlessly ever since he bought him? Was there not a spirit in him which, silent as it was, burned on him like the fires of perdition?

"I *hate* him!" said Legree that night, as he sat up in his bed; "I *hate* him! And isn't he MINE? Can't I do what I like with him? Who's to hinder, I wonder?"

But then Tom was a faithful, valuable servant; and although Legree hated him the more for that, yet the consideration was still somewhat of a restraint to him.

The next morning he determined to say nothing, as yet; to assemble a party from some neighbouring plantations, with dogs and guns; to surround the swamp, and go about the hunt systematically. If it succeeded, well and good; if not, he would summon Tom before him, and—his teeth clenched and his blood boiled—*then* he would break that fellow down.

"Well," said Cassy, the next day, from the garret, as she reconnoitred through the knot-hole, "the hunt's going to begin again today!"

Three or four mounted horsemen were curveting about on the space in front of the house; and one or two leashes of strange dogs were struggling with the negroes who held them, baying and barking at each other.

The men were, two of them, overseers of plantations in the vicinity; and others were some of Legree's associates at the tavern-bar of a neighbouring city, who had come for the interest of the sport. A more hard-favoured set, perhaps, could not be imagined. Legree was serving brandy profusely round among them, as also among the negroes who had been detailed from the various plantations for this service.

Cassy placed her ear at the knot-hole; and, as the morning air blew directly towards the house, she could overhear a good deal of the conversation. A grave sneer overcast the dark, severe gravity of her face, as she listened, and heard them divide out the ground, discuss the rival merits of the dogs, give orders about firing, and the treatment of each, in case of capture.

*　　*　　*　　*　　*　　*　　*　　*　　*

THE HUNT was long, animated, and thorough, but unsuccessful; and, with grave, ironic exultation, Cassy looked down on Legree, as, weary and dispirited, he alighted from his horse.

"Now, Quimbo," said Legree, as he stretched himself down in the sitting-room, "you jest go and walk that Tom up here, right away! The old cuss is at the bottom of this yer whole matter; and I'll have it out of his old black hide, or I'll know the reason why!"

Sambo and Quimbo both, though hating each other, were joined in one mind by a no less cordial hatred of Tom. Legree had told them, at first, that he had bought him for a general overseer in his absence; and this had begun an ill-will on their part, which had increased, in their debased and servile natures, as they saw him becoming obnoxious to their master. Quimbo, therefore, departed with a will to execute his orders.

Tom heard the message with a forewarning heart; for he knew all the plan of the fugitives' escape, and the place of their present concealment; he knew the deadly character of the man he had to deal with, and his despotic power. But he felt strong in God to meet death, rather than betray the helpless.

He set his basket down by the row, and, looking up, said, "Into Thy hands I commend my spirit! Thou hast redeemed me, O Lord God of truth!" and then quietly yielded himself to the rough, brutal grasp with which Quimbo seized him.

"Ay, ay!" said the giant, as he dragged him along; "ye'll cotch it now! I'll be boun' mas'r's back's up *high*! No sneaking out, now! Tell ye, ye'll get it, and no mistake! See how ye'll look, now, helpin' mas'r's niggers to run away! See what ye'll get!"

The savage words none of them reached that ear—a higher voice there was saying, "Fear not them that kill the body, and after that have no more that they can do". Nerve and bone of that poor man's body vibrated to those words, as if touched by the finger of God; and he felt the strength of a thousand souls in one. His soul throbbed—his home was in sight—and the hour of release seemed at hand.

"Well, Tom!" said Legree, walking up, and seizing him grimly by the collar of his coat, and speaking through his teeth, in a paroxysm of determined rage, "do you know I've made up my mind to KILL you?"

"It's very likely, mas'r," said Tom calmly.

"I *have*," said Legree, with grim, terrible calmness, "*done—just—that—thing*, Tom, unless you'll tell me what you know about these yer gals!"

Tom stood silent.

"D'ye hear?" said Legree, stamping, with a roar like that of an incensed lion. "Speak!"

"*I han't got nothing to tell, mas'r*," said Tom, with a slow, firm, deliberate utterance.

"Do you dare to tell me, ye old black Christian, ye don't *know*?" said Legree.

Tom was silent.

"Speak!" thundered Legree, striking him furiously. "Do you know anything?"

"I know, mas'r; but I can't tell anything. *I can die!*"

Legree drew in a long breath; and, suppressing his rage, took Tom by the arm, and, approaching his face almost to his, said, in a terrible voice: "Hark'e, Tom!—ye think, 'cause I've let you off before, I don't mean what I say; but, this time, I've *made up my mind*, and counted the cost. You've always stood it out again me: now, I'll *conquer ye or kill ye*!—one or t'other. I'll count every drop of blood there is in you, and take 'em one by one, till ye give up!"

Tom looked up to his master, and answered, "Mas'r, if you was sick, or in trouble, or dying, and I could save ye, I'd *give* ye my heart's blood; and, if taking every drop of blood in this poor old body would save your precious soul, I'd give 'em freely, as the Lord gave His for me. Oh, mas'r! don't bring this great sin on your soul! It will hurt you more than 'twill me! Do the worst you can, my troubles'll be over soon; but, if ye don't repent, yours won't *never* end!"

Lilce a strange snatch of heavenly music, heard in the lull of a tempest, this burst of feeling made a moment's blank pause. Legree stood aghast, and looked at Tom; and there was such a silence that the tick of the old clock could be heard, measuring, with silent touch, the last moments of mercy and probation to that hardened heart.

It was but a moment. There was one hesitating pause—one irresolute, relenting thrill—and the spirit of evil came back, with sevenfold vehemence; and Legree, foaming with rage, smote his victim to the ground.

"He's most gone, mas'r," said Sambo, touched, in spite of himself, by the patience of his victim.

"Pay away, till he gives up! Give it to him!—give it to him!" shouted Legree. "I'll take every drop of blood he has, unless he confesses!"

Tom opened his eyes, and looked upon his master. "Ye poor miserable crittur!" he said, "there an't no more ye can do! I forgive ye, with all my soul!" and he fainted entirely away.

"I b'lieve, my soul, he's done for, finally," said Legree, stepping forward to look at him. "Yes, he is! Well, his mouth's shut up at last—that's one comfort!"

Yes, Legree; but who shall shut up that voice in thy soul?— that soul, past repentance, past prayer, past hope, in whom the fire that never shall be quenched is already burning!

Yet Tom was not quite gone. His wondrous words and pious

prayers had struck upon the hearts of the imbruted blacks who had been the instruments of cruelty upon him; and, the instant Legree withdrew, they sought to call him back to life—as if *that* were any favour to him.

"Sartin, we's been doin' a dre'ful, wicked thing!" said Sambo; "hopes mas'r'll have to 'count for it, and not we."

They washed his wounds—they provided a rude bed, of some refuse cotton, for him to lie down on; and one of them, stealing up to the house, begged a drink of brandy of Legree, pretending that he was tired, and wanted it for himself. He brought it back, and poured it down Tom's throat.

"Oh, Tom!" said Quimbo, "we's been awful wicked to ye!"

"I forgive ye, with all my heart!" said Tom faintly.

"Oh, Tom! do tell us who is *Jesus*, anyhow?" said Sambo— "Jesus that's been a-standin' by you so, all this night!—Who is he?"

The word roused the failing, fainting spirit. He poured forth a few energetic sentences of that wondrous One—his life, his death, his everlasting presence, and power to save.

They wept—both the two savage men.

"Why didn't I never hear this before?" said Sambo; "but I do believe!—I can't help it!—Lord Jesus, have mercy on us!"

"Poor critturs!" said Tom, "I'd be willing to bar all I have, if it'll only bring ye to Christ! O Lord! give me these two more souls, I pray!"

That prayer was answered!

30

George Shelby Finds Uncle Tom

TWO days after, a young man drove a light wagon up through the avenue of Chinz trees, and, throwing the reins hastily on the horses' neck, sprang out and inquired for the owner of the place.

It was George Shelby; and, to show how he came to be there, we must go back in our story.

The letter of Miss Ophelia to Mrs Shelby had, by some unfortunate accident, been detained for a month or two at some remote post-office, before it reached its destination; and, of course, before it was received, Tom was already lost to view among the distant swamps of the Red River.

Mrs Shelby read the intelligence with the deepest concern; but any immediate action upon it was an impossibility. She was then in attendance on the sick-bed of her husband, who lay delirious in the crisis of a fever. Master George Shelby, who, in the interval, had changed from a boy to a tall young man, was her constant and faithful assistant, and her only reliance in superintending his father's affairs. Miss Ophelia had taken the precaution to send them the name of the lawyer who did business for the St. Clares; and the most that, in the emergency, could be done, was to address a letter of inquiry to him. The sudden death of Mr Shelby a few days after, brought, of course, an absorbing pressure of other interests for a season.

Mr Shelby showed his confidence in his wife's ability by appointing her sole executrix upon his estates; and thus immediately a large and complicated amount of business was brought upon her hands.

Mrs Shelby, with characteristic energy, applied herself to the work of straightening the entangled web of affairs; and she and George were for some time occupied with collecting and examining accounts, selling property, and settling debts; for Mrs Shelby was determined that everything should be brought into tangible and recognizable shape, let the consequences to her prove what they might. In the meantime, they received a letter from the lawyer to whom Miss Ophelia had referred them, saying that he knew nothing of the matter; that the man was sold at a public auction, and that, beyond receiving the money, he knew nothing of the affair.

Neither George nor Mrs Shelby could be easy at this result; and, accordingly, some six months after, the former, having business for his mother down the river, resolved to visit New Orleans in person, and push his inquiries, in hopes of discovering Tom's whereabouts and restoring him.

After some months of unsuccessful search, by the merest accident George fell in with a man in New Orleans, who happened to be possessed of the desired information; and with his money in his pocket, our hero took steamboat for Red River, resolving to find out and repurchase his old friend.

He was soon introduced into the house, where he found Legree in the sitting-room. The latter received the stranger with a kind of surly hospitality.

"I understand," said the young man, "that you bought, in New Orleans, a boy named Tom. He used to be on my father's place, and I came to see if I couldn't buy him back."

Legree's brow grew dark, and he broke out passionately: "Yes, I did buy such a fellow—and a h—l of a bargain I had of it, too! The most rebellious, saucy, impudent dog! Set up my niggers to run away; got off two gals, worth eight hundred or a thousand dollars apiece. He owned to that, and, when I bid him tell me where they was, he up and said he knew, but he wouldn't tell; and stood to it, though I gave him the cussedest flogging I ever gave nigger yet. I believe he's trying to die; but I don't know as he'll make it out."

"Where is he?" said George impetuously. "Let me see him." The cheeks of the young man were crimson, and his eyes flashed fire; but he prudently said nothing, as yet.

"He's in dat ar shed," said a little fellow, who stood holding George's horse.

Legree kicked the boy, and swore at him; but George, without saying another word, turned and strode to the spot.

Tom had been lying two days since the fatal night; not suffering, for every nerve of suffering was blunted and destroyed. He lay, for the most part, in a quiet stupor; for the laws of a powerful and well-knit frame would not at once release the imprisoned spirit. By stealth, there had been there, in the darkness of the night, poor desolated creatures, who stole from their scanty hours' rest that they might repay to him some of those ministrations of love in which he had always been so abundant. Truly, those poor disciples had little to give—only the cup of cold water; but it was given with full hearts.

Tears had fallen on that honest, insensible face—tears of late repentance in the poor, ignorant heathen, whom his dying love and patience had awakened to repentance, and bitter prayers breathed over him to a late-found Saviour, of whom they scarce knew more than the name, but whom the yearning ignorant heart of man never implores in vain.

Cassy, who had glided out of her place of concealment, and, by overhearing, learned the sacrifice that had been made for her and Emmeline, had been there, the night before, defying the danger of detection; and, moved by the few last words which the affectionate soul had yet strength to breathe, the long winter of despair, the ice of years, had given way, and the dark, despairing woman had wept and prayed.

When George entered the shed, he felt his head giddy and his heart sick.

"Is it possible—is it possible!" said he, kneeling down by him. "Uncle Tom, my poor, poor old friend!"

Something in the voice penetrated to the ear of the dying. He moved his head gently, smiled, and said:

> "Jesus can make a dying bed
> Feel soft as downy pillows are".

Tears which did honour to his manly heart fell from the young man's eyes, as he bent over his poor friend.

"Oh, dear Uncle Tom! do wake—do speak once more! Look up! Here's Mas'r George—your own little Mas'r George. Don't you know me?"

"Mas'r George!" said Tom, opening his eyes, and speaking in a feeble voice; "Mas'r George!" He looked bewildered.

Slowly the idea seemed to fill his soul, and the vacant eye

became fixed and brightened, the whole face lighted up, the hard hands clasped, and tears ran down the cheeks.

"Bless the Lord! it is—it is—it's all I wanted! They haven't forgot me. It warms my soul: it does my old heart good! Now I shall die content! Bless the Lord, O my soul!"

"You shan't die! you *mustn't* die, nor think of it! I've come to buy you, and take you home," said George, with impetuous vehemence.

"Oh, Mas'r George, ye're too late. The Lord's bought me, and is going to take me home—and I long to go. Heaven is better than Kintuck."

"Oh, don't die! It'll kill me!—it'll break my heart to think what you've suffered—and lying in this old shed, here! Poor, poor fellow!"

"Don't call me poor fellow!" said Tom solemnly. "I have been poor fellow; but that's all past and gone, now. I'm right in the door, going into glory. Oh, Mas'r George! *Heaven has come*! I've got the victory!—the Lord Jesus has given it to me! Glory be to His name!"

George was awe-struck at the force, the vehemence, the power, with which these broken sentences were uttered. He sat gazing in silence.

Tom grasped his hand, and continued: "Ye mustn't, now, tell Chloe, poor soul! how ye found me!—'twould be so dre'ful to her. Only tell her ye found me going into glory; and that I couldn't stay for no one. And tell her the Lord's stood by me everywhere and al'ays, and made everything light and easy. And oh, the poor chil'en, and the baby!— my old heart's been 'most broke for 'em, time and ag'in! Tell 'em all to follow me—follow me! Give my love to mas'r, and dear good missis, and everybody in the place! Ye don't know! 'Pears like I loves 'em all! I loves every creatur', everywhar!—it's nothing but love! Oh, Mas'r George, what a thing 'tis to be a Christian!"

At this moment Legree sauntered up to the door of the shed, looked in with a dogged air of affected carelessness, and turned away.

"The old Satan!" said George, in his indignation. "It's a comfort to think the devil will pay *him* for this, some of these days!"

"Oh, don't!—oh, ye mustn't!" said Tom, grasping his hand; "he's a poor mis'able crittur! it's awful to think on't! Oh, if he only could repent, the Lord would forgive him now; but I'm 'feared he never will."

"I hope he won't!" said George; "I never want to see *him* in heaven."

"Hush, Mas'r George!—it worries me. Don't feel so. He an't done me no real harm—only opened the gate of the kingdom for me; that's all!"

At this moment, the sudden flush of strength which the joy of meeting his young master had infused into the dying man gave way. A sudden sinking fell upon him; he closed his eyes; and that mysterious and sublime change passed over his face that told the approach of other worlds.

He began to draw his breath with long, deep inspirations; and his broad chest rose and fell heavily. The expression of his face was that of a conqueror.

"Who—who—who shall separate us from the love of Christ?" he said, in a voice that contended with mortal weakness; and with a smile he fell asleep.

George sat fixed with solemn awe. It seemed to him that the place was holy; and as he closed the lifeless eyes, and rose up from the dead, only one thought possessed him—that expressed by his simple old friend—"What a thing it is to be a Christian!"

He turned. Legree was standing sullenly behind him.

Something in that dying scene had checked the natural fierceness of youthful passion. The presence of the man was simply loathsome to George; and he felt only an impulse to get away from him, with as few words as possible.

Fixing his keen, dark eyes on Legree, he simply said, pointing to the dead: "You have got all you ever can of him. What shall I pay you for the body? I will take it away, and bury it decently."

"I don't sell dead niggers," said Legree doggedly. "You are welcome to bury him where and when you like."

"Boys," said George, in an authoritative tone, to two or three negroes who were looking at the body, "help me lift him up, and carry him to my wagon; and get me a spade."

One of them ran for a spade; the other two assisted George to carry the body to the wagon.

George neither spoke to nor looked at Legree, who did not countermand his orders, but stood whistling, with an air of forced unconcern. He sulkily followed them to where the wagon stood at the door.

George spread his cloak in the wagon, and had the body carefully disposed of in it, moving the seat so as to give it room. Then he turned, fixed his eyes on Legree, and said, with forced composure;

"I have not, as yet, said to you what I think of this most atrocious affair; this is not the time and place. But, sir, this innocent blood shall have justice. I will proclaim this murder. I will go to the very first magistrate, and expose you."

"Do!" said Legree, snapping his fingers scornfully. "I'd like to see you doing it. Where you going to get witnesses?—how you going to prove it?—Come, now!"

George saw at once the force of this defiance. There was not a white person on the place; and, in all Southern courts, the testimony of coloured blood is nothing. He felt at that moment as if he could have rent the heavens with his heart's indignant cry for justice, but in vain.

"After all, what a fuss for a dead nigger!" said Legree.

The word was as a spark to a powder-magazine. Prudence was never a cardinal virtue of the Kentucky boy. George turned, and, with one indignant blow, knocked Legree flat upon his face; and as he stood over him, blazing with wrath and defiance, he would have formed no bad personification of his great namesake triumphing over the dragon.

Some men, however, are decidedly bettered by being knocked down. If a man lays them fairly flat in the dust, they seem immediately to conceive a respect for him; and Legree was one of this sort. As he rose, therefore, and brushed the dust from his clothes, he eyed the slowly-retreating wagon with some evident consideration; nor did he open his mouth till it was out of sight.

Beyond the boundaries of the plantation, George had noticed a dry, sandy knoll, shaded by a few trees: there they made the grave.

"Shall we take off the cloak, mas'r?" said the negroes, when the grave was ready.

"No, no—bury it with him.—It's all I can give you now, poor Tom, and you shall have it."

They laid him in; and the men shovelled away silently. They banked it up, and laid green turf over it.

"Witness, eternal God!" said George, kneeling on the grave of his poor friend, "oh, witness that, from this hour, I will do *what one man can* to drive out this curse of slavery from my land!"

31

Family Affairs

FOR SOME remarkable reason, ghostly legends were uncommonly rife about this time among the servants on Legree's place.

It was whisperingly asserted that footsteps, in the dead of night, had been heard descending the garret stairs, and patrolling the house. In vain the doors of the upper entry had been locked; the ghost either carried a duplicate key in its pocket, or availed itself of a ghost's immemorial privilege of coming through the keyhole, and promenaded as before, with a freedom that was alarming.

Authorities were somewhat divided as to the outward form of the spirit, but we have private reasons for knowing that a tall figure in a white sheet did walk, at the most approved ghostly hours, around the Legree premises—pass out the doors, glide about the house—disappear at intervals, and, reappearing, pass up the silent stairway into that fatal garret; and that, in the morning, the entry doors were all found shut and locked as firm as ever.

Legree could not help overhearing this whispering; and it was all the more exciting to him from the pains that were taken to conceal it from him. He drank more brandy than usual; held up his head briskly, and swore louder than ever in the day-time; but he had bad dreams, and the visions of his head on his bed were anything but agreeable. The night after Tom's body had been carried away, he rode to the next town for a carouse, and had a high one. He got home late and set a chair against the door; he set a night-lamp at the head of his bed; and he put his pistols there. He examined the catches and fastenings of the windows, and then swore he "didn't care for the devil and all his angels", and went to sleep.

Well, he slept, for he was tired—slept soundly. But finally there came over his sleep a shadow, a horror, an apprehension of something dreadful hanging over him. It was his mother's shroud, he thought; but Cassy had it, holding it up, and showing it to him. He had heard a confused noise of screams and groanings; and, with it all, he knew he was asleep, and he struggled to wake himself. He was half awake. He was sure something was coming into his room. He knew the door was opening, but he could not stir hand or foot. At last he turned, with a start; the door *was* open, and he saw a hand putting out his light.

It was a cloudy, misty moonlight, and there he saw it!— something white, gliding in! He heard the still rustle of its ghostly garments. It stood still by his bed; a cold hand touched his; a voice said, three times, in a low, fearful whisper, "Come! come! come!" And, while he lay sweating with terror, he knew not when or how, the thing was gone. He sprang out of bed, and pulled at the door. It was shut and locked, and the man fell down in a swoon.

After this, Legree became a harder drinker than ever before. He no longer drank cautiously, prudently, but imprudently and recklessly.

There were reports around the country, soon after, that he was sick and dying. Excess had brought on that frightful disease that seems to throw the lurid shadows of a coming retribution back into the present life. None could bear the horrors of that sick room, when he raved and screamed, and spoke of sights which almost stopped the blood of those who heard him; and, at his dying bed, stood a stern, white, inexorable figure, saying, "Come! come! come!"

By a singular coincidence, on the very night that this vision appeared to Legree, the house-door was found open in the morning, and some of the negroes had seen two white figures gliding down the avenue towards the high-road.

It was near sunrise when Cassy and Emmeline paused for a moment in a little knot of trees near the town.

Cassy was dressed after the manner of the Creole Spanish ladies—wholly in black. A small black bonnet on her head, covered by a veil thick with embroidery, concealed her face. It had been agreed that, in their escape, she was to personate the character of a Creole lady, and Emmeline that of her servant.

Brought up from early life in connection with the highest

society, the language, movements, and air of Cassy were all in agreement with this idea; and she had still enough remaining with her of a once splendid wardrobe, and sets of jewels, to enable her to personate the thing to advantage.

She stopped in the outskirts of the town, where she had noticed trunks for sale, and purchased a handsome one. This she requested the man to send along with her. And accordingly, thus escorted by a boy wheeling her trunk, and Emmeline behind her, carrying her carpet-bag and sundry bundles, she made her appearance at the small tavern, like a lady of consideration.

The first person that struck her, after her arrival, was George Shelby, who was staying there, awaiting the next boat.

Cassy had remarked the young man from her loophole in the garret, and seen him bear away the body of Tom, and observed with secret exultation his rencontre with Legree. Subsequently she had gathered, from the conversation she had overheard among the negroes, as she glided about in her ghostly disguise after nightfall, who he was, and in what relation he stood to Tom. She therefore felt an immediate accession of confidence when she found that he was, like herself, awaiting the next boat.

Cassy's air, manner, address, and evident command of money, prevented any rising disposition to suspicion in the hotel. People never inquire too closely into those who are fair on the main point, of paying well—a thing which Cassy had foreseen when she provided herself with money.

In the edge of the evening, a boat was heard coming along, and George Shelby handed Cassy aboard, with the politeness which comes naturally to every Kentuckian, and exerted himself to provide her with a good state-room.

Cassy kept her room and bed, on pretext of illness, during the whole time they were on Red River; and was waited on with obsequious devotion by her attendant.

When they arrived at the Mississippi River, George, having learned that the course of the strange lady was upward, like his own, proposed to take a state-room for her on the same boat with himself—good-naturedly compassionating her feeble health, and desirous to do what he could to assist her.

Behold, therefore, the whole party safely transferred to the good steamer *Cincinnati*, and sweeping up the river under a powerful head of steam.

Cassy's health was much better. She sat upon the guards, came to the table, and was remarked upon the boat as a lady that must have been very handsome.

From the moment that George got the first glimpse of her face, he was troubled with one of those fleeting and indefinite likenesses which almost everybody can remember, and has been, at times, perplexed with. He could not keep himself from looking at her, and watching her perpetually. At table, or sitting at her state-room door, still she would encounter the young man's eyes fixed on her, and politely withdrawn when she showed by her countenance that she was sensible of the observation.

Cassy became uneasy. She began to think that he suspected something; and finally resolved to throw herself entirely on his generosity, and entrusted him with her whole history.

George was heartily disposed to sympathize with anyone who had escaped from Legree's plantation—a place that he could not remember or speak of with patience; and, with the courageous disregard of consequences which is characteristic of his age and state, he assured her that he would do all in his power to protect and bring them through.

The next state-room to Cassy's was occupied by a French lady, named De Thoux, who was accompanied by a fine little daughter, a child of some twelve summers.

This lady, having gathered from George's conversation that he was from Kentucky, seemed evidently disposed to cultivate his acquaintance, in which design she was seconded by the graces of her little girl, who was about as pretty a plaything as ever diverted the weariness of a fortnight's trip on a steamboat.

George's chair was often placed at her state-room door; and Cassy, as she sat upon the guards, could hear their conversation.

Madame de Thoux was very minute in her inquiries as to Kentucky, where she said she had resided in a former period of her life. George discovered, to his surprise, that her former residence must have been in his own vicinity; and her inquiries showed a knowledge of people and things in his region that was perfectly surprising to him.

"Do you know," said Madame de Thoux to him one day, "of any man in your neighbourhood of the name of Harris?"

"There is an old fellow of that name lives not far from my father's place," said George. "We never have had much intercourse with him, though."

"He is a large slave-owner, I believe," said Madame de Thoux, with a manner which seemed to betray more interest than she was exactly willing to show.

"He is," said George, looking rather surprised at her manner.

"Did you ever know of his having—perhaps you may have heard of his having a mulatto boy, named George?"

"Oh, certainly—George Harris—I know him well; he married a servant of my mother's, but has escaped now to Canada."

"He has?" said Madame de Thoux quickly. "Thank God!"

George looked a surprised inquiry, but said nothing.

Madame de Thoux leaned her head on her hand, and burst into tears. "He is my brother," she said.

"Madame!" said George, with a strong accent of surprise.

"Yes," said Madame de Thoux, lifting her head proudly, and wiping her tears, "Mr Shelby, George Harris is my brother!"

"I am perfectly astonished," said George, pushing back his chair a pace or two, and looking at Madame de Thoux.

"I was sold to the South when he was a boy," said she. "I was bought by a good and generous man. He took me with him to the West Indies, set me free, and married me. It is but lately that he died, and I was coming up to Kentucky to see if I could find and redeem my brother."

"I have heard him speak of a sister Emily, that was sold South," said George.

"Yes, indeed! I am the one," said Madame de Thoux; "tell me whlat sort of a—"

"A very fine young man," said George, "notwithstanding the curse of slavery that lay on him. He sustained a first-rate character, both for intelligence and principle. I know, you see," he said, "because he married in our family."

"What sort of a girl?" said Madame de Thoux eagerly.

"A treasure," said George; "a beautiful, intelligent, amiable girl. Very pious. My mother had brought her up, and trained her as carefully, almost, as a daughter. She could read and write, embroider and sew, beautifully; and she was a beautiful singer."

"Was she born in your house?" said Madame de Thoux. "No. Father bought her once, in one of his trips to New Orleans, and brought her up as a present to mother. She was about eight or nine years old then. Father would never tell mother what he gave for her; but, the other day, in looking over his old papers, we came across the bill of sale. He paid an extravagant sum for her, to be sure—I suppose, on account of her extraordinary beauty."

George sat with his back to Cassy, and did not see the absorbed expression of her countenance as he was giving these details.

At this point in the story she touched his arm, and, with a face perfectly white with interest, said, "Do you know the name of the people he bought her of?"

"A man of the name of Simmons, I think, was the principal in the transaction. At least, I think that was the name on the bill of sale."

"Oh, my God!" said Cassy, and fell insensible on the floor of the cabin.

Poor Cassy, when she recovered, turned her face to the wall, and wept and sobbed like a child—perhaps, mother, you can tell what she was thinking of! Perhaps you cannot, but she felt as sure, in that hour, that God had had mercy on her, and that she should see her daughter—as she did, months afterwards, when— but we anticipate.

32

Not in Vain

THE REST of our story is soon told. George Shelby, interested, as any other young man might be, by the romance of the incident, no less than by feelings of humanity, was at the pains to send to Cassy the bill of sale of Eliza, whose date and name all corresponded with her own knowledge of facts, and left no doubt upon her mind as to the identity of her child. It remained now only for her to trace out the path of the fugitives.

Madame de Thoux and she, thus drawn together by the singular coincidence of their fortunes, proceeded immediately to Canada, and began a tour of inquiry among the stations where the numerous fugitives from slavery are located. At Amherstberg they found the missionary with whom George and Eliza had taken shelter on their first arrival in Canada, and through him were enabled to trace the family to Montreal.

George and Eliza had now been five years free. George had found constant occupation in the shop of a worthy machinist, where he had been earning a competent support for his family, which, in the meantime, had been increased by the addition of another daughter.

Little Harry, a fine, bright boy, had been put to a good school, and was making rapid proficiency in knowledge.

The worthy pastor of the station in Amherstberg, where George had first landed, was so much interested in the statements of Madame de Thoux and Cassy, that he yielded to the solicitations of the former to accompany them to Montreal in their search—the former bearing all the expense of the expedition.

The scene now changes to a small, neat tenement in the outskirts of Montreal; the time, evening. A cheerful fire blazes on the hearth; a tea-table, covered with a snowy cloth, stands prepared for the evening meal. In one corner of the room was a table covered with a green cloth, where was an open writing-desk, pens, paper, and over it a shelf of well-selected books.

This was George's study. The same zeal for self-improvement which led him to steal the much-coveted arts of reading and writing, amid all the toils and discouragements of his early life, still led him to devote all his leisure time to self-cultivation.

At this present time he is seated at the table, making notes from a volume of the Family Library he has been reading.

"Come, George," says Eliza, "you've been gone all day. Do put down that book, and let's talk, while I'm getting tea—do."

And little Eliza seconds the effort by toddling up to her father, and trying to pull the book out of his hand, and install herself on his knee as a substitute.

"Oh, you little witch!" says George, yielding, as, in such circumstances, man always must.

"That's right," says Eliza, as she begins to cut a loaf of bread. A little older she looks; her form a little fuller; her air more matronly than of yore; but evidently contented and happy as woman need be.

"Harry, my boy, how did you come on in that sum today?" says George, as he laid his hand on his son's head.

Harry has lost his long curls; but he can never lose those eyes and eyelashes, and that fine, bold brow, that flushes with triumph as he answers, "I did it, every bit of it, *myself*, father; and *nobody* helped me!"

"That's right," says his father; "depend on yourself, my son. You have a better chance than ever your poor father had."

At this moment there is a rap at the door; and Eliza goes and opens it. The delighted—"Why!—this you?"—calls up her husband; and the good pastor of Amherstberg is welcomed. There are two more women with him, and Eliza asks them to sit down.

Now, if the truth must be told, the honest pastor had arranged a little programme, according to which this affair was to develop itself; and, on the way up, all had very cautiously and prudently exhorted each other not to let things out, except according to previous arrangement.

What was the good man's consternation, therefore, just as he had motioned to the ladies to be seated, and was taking out his pocket-handkerchief to wipe his mouth, so as to proceed to his introductory speech in good order, when Madame de Thoux upset the whole plan by throwing her arms around George's neck, and letting all out at once, by saying: "Oh, George! don't you know me? I'm your sister Emily."

Cassy had seated herself more composedly, and would have carried on her part very well, had not little Eliza suddenly appeared before her in exact shape and form, every outline and curl, just as her daughter was when she saw her last. The little thing peered up in her face; and Cassy caught her up in her arms, pressed her to her bosom, saying, what at the moment she really believed, "Darling, I'm your mother!"

In fact, it was a troublesome matter to do up exactly in proper order; but the good pastor at last succeeded in getting everybody quiet, and delivering the speech with which he had intended to open the exercises; and in which, at last, he succeeded so well, that his whole audience were sobbing about him in a manner that ought to satisfy any orator, ancient or modern.

They knelt together, and the good man prayed—for there are some feelings so agitated and tumultuous, that they can find rest only by being poured into the bosom of Almighty love—and then, rising up, the new-found family embraced each other, with a holy trust in Him, who from such peril and dangers, and by such unknown ways, had brought them together.

In two or three days, such a change has passed over Cassy that our readers would scarcely know her. The despairing, haggard expression of her face has given way to one of gentle trust. She seemed to sink at once into the bosom of the family, and take the little ones into her heart, as something for which it long had waited. Indeed, her love seemed to flow more naturally to the little Eliza than to her own daughter; for she was the exact image and body of the child whom she had lost. The little one was a flowery bond between mother and daughter, through whom grew up acquaintanceship and affection. Eliza's steady, consistent piety, regulated by the constant reading of the sacred word, made her a proper guide for the shattered and wearied mind of her mother.

Cassy yielded at once, and with her whole soul, to every good influence, and became a devout and tender Christian.

After a day or two, Madame de Thoux told her brother more particularly of her affairs. The death of her husband had left her an ample fortune, which she generously offered to share with the family. When she asked George what way she could best apply it for him, he answered: "Give me an education, Emily; that has always been my heart's desire. Then I can do all the rest."

On mature deliberation it was decided that the whole family should go for some years to France; whither they sailed, carrying Emmeline with them.

The good looks of the latter won the affection of the first mate of the vessel; and, shortly after entering the port, she became his wife.

George remained four years at a French university, and, applying himself with an unintermitted zeal, obtained a very thorough education.

Political troubles in France at last led the family again to seek an asylum in this country.

George's feelings and views, as an educated man, may be best expressed in a letter to one of his friends:

"I feel somewhat at a loss as to my future course. True, as you have said to me, I might mingle in the circles of the whites in this country, my shade of colour is so slight, and that of my wife and family scarce perceptible. Well, perhaps, on sufferance, I might. But, to tell you the truth, I have no wish to.

"My sympathies are not for my father's race, but for my mother's. To him I was no more than a fine dog or horse: to my poor heartbroken mother I was a *child*; and though I never saw her after the cruel sale that separated us till she died, yet I *know* she always loved me deary. I know it by my own heart. When I think of all she suffered, of my own early sufferings, of the distresses and struggles of my heroic wife, of my sister, sold in the New Orleans slavemarket—though I hope to have no unchristian sentiments, yet I may be excused for saying I have no wish to pass for an American, or to identify myself with them.

"It is with the oppressed, enslaved African race that I cast in my lot; and, if I wished anything, I would wish myself two shades darker, rather than one lighter."

Of our other characters we have nothing very particular to write, except a word relating to Miss Ophelia and Topsy, and a farewell chapter which we shall dedicate to George Shelby.

Miss Ophelia took Topsy home to Vermont with her, much to the surprise of that grave, deliberative body whom a New Englander recognizes under the term "*Our folks*". "Our folks", at first, thought it an odd and unnecessary addition to their well-trained domestic establishment; but so thoroughly efficient was Miss Ophelia in her conscientious endeavour to do her duty by her *élève*, that the child rapidly grew in grace and in favour with the family and neighbourhood. At the age of womanhood she was, by her own request, baptized, and became a member of the Christian church in the place; and showed so much intelligence, activity and zeal, and desire to do good in the world, that she was at last recommended and approved as a missionary to one of the stations in Africa; and we have heard that the same activity and ingenuity which, when a child, made her so multiform and restless in her development, is now employed, in a safer and whole-somer manner, in teaching the children of her own country.

P.S.—It will be a satisfaction to some mother also to state that some inquiries which were set on foot by Madame de Thoux have resulted recently in the discovery of Cassy's son. Being a young man of energy, he had escaped some years before his mother, and been received and educated by friends of the oppressed in the North.

33

Liberty at Kentuck

GEORGE Shelby had written to his mother merely a line, stating the day that she might expect him home. Of the deathscene of his old friend he had not the heart to write. He had tried several times, and only succeeded in half choking himself; and invariably finished by tearing up the paper, wiping his eyes, and rushing somewhere to get quiet.

There was a pleased bustle all through the Shelby mansion that day, in expectation of the arrival of young Mas'r George. Mrs Shelby was seated in her comfortable parlour. A supper-table, glittering with plate and cut glass, was set out, on whose arrangements our former friend, old Chloe, was presiding.

Arrayed in a new calico dress, with clean, white apron, and high, well-starched turban, her black polished face glowing with satisfaction, she lingered, with needless punctiliousness, around the arrangements of the table, merely as an excuse for talking a little to her mistress.

"And missis has heard from Mas'r George?" she said inquiringly.

"Yes, Chloe; but only a line, just to say he would be home tonight, if he could—that's all."

"Didn't say nothin' 'bout my old man, s'pose?" said Chloe, still fidgeting with the tea-cups.

"No, he didn't. He did not speak of anything, Chloe. He said he would tell all when he got home."

"I'm a-thinkin' my old man won't know de boys and de baby. Lor'! she's de biggest gal, now—good she is, too, and peart, Polly is. She's out to the house, now, watchin' de hoe-cake. I's got just de very pattern my old man liked so much, a-bakin'. Jist sich as I gin him the mornin' he was took off. Lord bless us! how I felt, dat ar morning!"

Mrs Shelby sighed, and felt a heavy weight on her heart at this allusion. She had felt uneasy, ever since she received her son's

letter, lest something should prove to be hidden behind the veil
of silence which he had drawn.

"Missis had got dem bills?" said Chloe anxiously.

"Yes, Chloe."

"'Cause I wants to show my old man dem very bills de
perfectioner gave me. "And," says he, "Chloe, I wish you'd stay
longer." "Thank you, mas'r," says I, "I would, only my old man's
coming home, and missis—she can't do without me no longer."
There's jist what I told him. Berry nice man, dat Mas'r Jones
was."

Chloe had pertinaciously insisted that the very bills in which
her wages had been paid should be preserved to show to her
husband, in memorial of her capability. And Mrs Shelby had
readily consented to humour her in the request.

The rattling of wheels now was heard.

"Mas'r George!" said Aunt Chloe, starting to the window.

Mrs Shelby ran to the entry-door, and was folded in the arms
of her son. Aunt Chloe stood anxiously straining her eyes out
into the darkness.

"Oh, *poor* Aunt Chloe!" said George, stopping compassionately,
and taking her hard, black hand between both his; "I'd have given
all my fortune to have brought him with me, but he's gone to a
better country."

There was a passionate exclamation from Mrs Shelby, but Aunt
Chloe said nothing.

The party entered the supper-room. The money, of which
Chloe was so proud, was still lying on the table.

"Thar," said she, gathering it up, and holding it with a
trembling hand to her mistress, "don't never want to see nor
hear on't again. Jist as I knew 'twould be—sold, and murdered
on dem ar' old plantations!"

Chloe turned, and was walking proudly out of the room. Mrs
Shelby followed her softly, and took one of her hands, drew her
down into a chair, and sat down by her.

"My poor, good Chloe!" said she.

Chloe leaned her head on her mistress's shoulder, and sobbed
out, "Oh, missis! 'scuse me, my heart's broke—dat's all!"

"I know it is," said Mrs Shelby, as her tears fell fast; "and I cannot heal it, but Jesus can. He healeth the broken-hearted, and bindeth up their wounds."

There was a silence for some time, and all wept together. At last, George, sitting down beside the mourner, took her hand, and with simple pathos repeated the triumphant scene of her husband's death, and his last messages of love.

*   *   *   *   *   *   *   *   *

ABOUT a month after this, one morning, all the servants of the Shelby estate were convened together in the great hall that ran through the house, to hear a few words from their young master.

To the surprise of all, he appeared among them with a bundle of papers in his hand, containing a certificate of freedom to every one on the place, which he read successively, and presented, amid the sobs and tears and shouts of all present.

Many, however, pressed around him, earnestly begging him not to send them away; and, with anxious faces, tendering back their free papers.

"We don't want to be no freer than we are. We's allers had all we wanted. We don't want to leave de ole place, and mas'r and missis, and de rest!"

"My good friends," said George, as soon as he could get a silence, "there'll be no need for you to leave me. The place wants as many hands to work as it did before. We need the same about the house that we did before. But, you are now free men and free women. I shall pay you wages for your work, such as we shall agree on. The advantage is that in case of my getting in debt, or dying—things that might happen—you cannot now be taken up and sold. I expect to carry on the estate, and to teach you what, perhaps, it will take some time to learn—how to use the rights I give you as free men and women. I expect you to be good, and willing to learn; and I trust in God that I shall be faithful, and willing to teach. And now, my friends, look up, and thank God for the blessing of freedom."

An aged, patriarchal negro, who had grown grey and blind on the estate, now rose, and, lifting his trembling hand, said, "Let us give thanks unto the Lord!" As all kneeled by one consent, a more touching and hearty Te Deum never ascended to heaven, though borne on the peal of organ, bell, and cannon, than came from that honest old heart.

"One thing more," said George, as he stopped the congratulations of the throng; "you all remember our good old Uncle Tom?"

George here gave a short narration of the scene of his death, and of his loving farewell to all on the place, and added:

"It was on his grave, my friends, that I resolved, before God, that I would never own another slave while it was possible to free him; that nobody, through me, should ever run the risk of being parted from home and friends, and dying on a lonely plantation, as he died. So, when you rejoice in your freedom, think that you owe it to that good old soul, and pay it back in kindness to his wife and children. Think of your freedom every time you see UNCLE TOM'S CABIN; and let it be a memorial to put you all in mind to follow in his steps, and be as honest and faithful and Christian as he was."